PENGUIN BOOKS

LANDSCAPE WITH DEAD DONS

Robert Robinson is well known as a broadcaster on radio and television. *Landscape with Dead Dons* was his first book, published by Gollancz shortly after he came down from Oxford. He is the author of a novel, *The Conspiracy*, and a collection of articles, *Inside Robert Robinson*. In 1982 Allen Lane brought out a further selection of his pieces under the title *The Dog Chairman*. Robert Robinson is married, has one son and two daughters, and lives in Chelsea.

ROBERT ROBINSON

LANDSCAPE WITH
DEAD DONS

PENGUIN BOOKS

Penguin Books Ltd, Harmondsworth, Middlesex, England
Penguin Books, 625 Madison Avenue, New York, New York 10022, U.S.A.
Penguin Books Australia Ltd, Ringwood, Victoria, Australia
Penguin Books Canada Ltd, 2801 John Street, Markham, Ontario, Canada L3R 1B4
Penguin Books (N.Z.) Ltd, 182–190 Wairau Road, Auckland 10, New Zealand

—

First published in Great Britain by Victor Gollancz Ltd 1956
First published in the United States of America by Rinehart & Company, Inc., 1956
Published in Penguin Books in the United States of America by arrangement with Holt, Rinehart
and Winston
Published in Penguin Books 1963
Reprinted 1983

—

—

Made and printed in Great Britain
by Hazell Watson & Viney Ltd,
Aylesbury, Bucks
Set in Monotype Baskerville

—

NOTE

*My description of the subterranean economy
of the Bodleian Library is entirely fanciful.*

R. R.

To my Mother and Father

Caste now your royal eie on everich hond,
How pleyn disordinaunce is in your lond;
Rancour and Ryot now are sovereyn,
In oon accord to wierken aller peyn;
Swich traytours mote be shent and that anon –
To-hanged on a galwes, everich-on.
Els is the king namore a king, I rede –
Lost is his croun, his pouer and his drede.

Oft lurketh Deeth wythyn the greene shawe,
Whan foul rebelling trampleth on the lawe...

CHAUCER: *The Boke of the Leoun*

Chapter 1

NICHOLAS FLOWER whistled lightly as he turned into the High Street, dodging the shopping baskets and the pavement traffic. It was a sunny Saturday morning in Eights Week and Oxford was full. Commercial travellers strode into Balliol trying to book rooms, and Cambridge scientists, relaxing after a week of alkali reactions, zoomed over Magdalen Bridge in fast cars.

Flower experienced a certain priggish satisfaction as he picked his way between men in scarves from the University of North Staffordshire; everyone was on holiday except him. He made his way along the pavement, deftly avoiding the lecturers from European foundations who were peeping out of hotels uncertain of their expenses, and continued to enjoy his own urbanity. But as he turned into the Cornmarket it occurred to him that if he was going to the Bodleian he was going a very long way round. His whistling slid sadly off key and he blushed.

All right, thought Flower as if he were countering a derisive attack from the morning-coated, white-spatted man with the sandwich-board who was walking briskly along the gutter – all right, tell yourself the truth! You came the long way round because you thought it gave you a better chance of running into *her*.

Flower's whistling grew louder and more truculent. Well, he said to himself, you do have to go to Bodley. You do have to read that Milton. Or is it all just an excuse to hang round Oxford on a Saturday in the hope of –

The day before Nicholas Flower had gone into the Radcliffe Camera to read *Paradise Lost*, but the only copy he could lay his hands on was in double-columns and small print. He sat and stared at it, smelling the floor-polish and the radiators. Next to him there was a girl who was also reading *Paradise Lost*. She underlined every Homeric simile she came to like a runner tipping hurdles over. Flower stuck it for half an hour, then gave up. He decided he would order a real Milton for tomorrow, he would order the Bodley *Paradise Lost*, the showpiece, the original. He'd do the work – and make an aesthetic occasion of it into the bargain.

And an excuse, Flower now admitted, as he turned into the Broad past the little dark green churchyard on the corner. Dear me, thought Flower, it shouldn't happen to a dog. I could have understood it if it had been Egg – Egg was just the type to go into solution over a girl like Balboa Tomlin. Sentimental like all hearties. *Normal chaps*. Nicholas Flower sighed again, and thought how terribly easy it was to fit something foolish into the pattern of character you had predetermined for someone else. It wasn't his room-mate, poor old Egg – it was himself, poor old Flower!

The sun was shining on the New Bodleian, turning the stone a dark yellow so that the building looked like a cardboard box. Flower went through the arch of the Clarendon Building, and into a sandy courtyard where the breeze sent the dust against the railings.

There was absolutely no doubt in the world that the girl was a cow. She was vain and stupid and arrogant. She had a wonderful pair of legs and a bosom like – like – Really stupid – the sort of stupid cow who never would get over the novelty of being able to call a don by his first name.

And what a name! Fairlight. *Dimoke Fairlight*. Flower shuddered theatrically and entered the Old Schools Quadrangle.

He read out the titles over the doorways as he walked across: SCHOLA NATURALIS PHILOSOPHIAE, SCHOLA MUSICAE. They had been painted up in the nineteenth century in an access of olde tea shopperie, but Flower rather liked them. They suggested musty, far-off, scholarly things – tattered gowns and snuff and anecdotes. Flower slipped into his donnish *persona* and developed a slight stoop, mumbling absentmindedly and wiping his nose on the back of his hand for the benefit of three schoolgirls who were looking at the statue of Sir Thomas Bodley.

But he couldn't keep Balboa and Fairlight out of his mind. What a rampart of idle egotism the man was! A real live Third-programme don – just Balboa's infantile cup of tea.

I wonder what they do, thought Flower. I wonder if they do. I wonder if she would . . .

She won't for me.

Flower walked into Bodley and inhaled deeply. The smell was like a cupboardful of old boots, but today Flower decided it was the odour of wisdom. He climbed the wooden staircase to Duke Humphrey (as the most ancient section of the Library is called) and came out into a dark gallery with high windows.

There were shelves of brown books across the walls, glass cases containing memorabilia down the centre of the room, and at one end an old wooden throne. Another gallery went away at right angles, and in alcoves leading off the second gallery dons and undergraduates sat reading. The ceiling was dark with blazon, and above the level of the book-shelves thin white faces gazed rheumily out of their ancient varnish.

Flower stopped at a small lattice-work booth that stood at the intersection of the two galleries and handed his order-slip to a nice-looking girl in a woolly. The floor of Duke Humphrey creaked pleasantly as the girl walked to the rear of her stall, and Nicholas watched her legs, for they reminded him of Balboa.

The girl returned with the book and Flower gave her a fragrantly academic look. The *Paradise Lost* was a thin quarto in musty reversed leather, scored over with indented rules, and with a title tooled about in gold leaf. Flower took it gingerly and tiptoed down the second gallery. He spotted a seat by a window overlooking Exeter Garden and edged past a venerable and groaning palaeographer to sit on it.

Nicholas Flower was constitutionally unable to begin to read a book straight away. Sitting in College with a book newly open on his knees, he would find himself spelling out words in the newspaper which lay upside down on a chair at the other end of the room. Sometimes he would wind his watch. He would very often walk round the room, then stand on one leg and look out of the window. Sometimes he would even begin to read another book. After a bit he would generate enough guilt to launch himself fairly on the first chapter.

He picked up *Paradise Lost* and looked slyly about him to see if anyone had appreciated the prize he carried. But no one had noticed. His neighbour, the palaeographer, had propped his chin on the lower rung of his reading-stand and groaned stertorously as he slept. Flower laid down *Paradise Lost* and gazed out of the window.

He watched a gardener in Exeter clip the verge of a bed of roses and envied him his satisfaction when he had finished. Then he had a look at the pictures. *Narcissus Marsh, Archiep. Armach. olim Coll. Exon.* . . . . What jolly foxy faces those Bishops had, he thought. I wonder did they actually pose with their fingers stuck up like that? No – paint the face first then shove the accessories in wholesale afterwards.

Flower craned his neck round hard so that he could see the gargoyle which jutted out beneath his window. Didn't the medieval masons use to caricature people in gargoyles? Yes – it was probably the Master of Balliol or someone, *circa* 1500. Flower took a good look at the tongue and the stone teeth. Would it do as a take-off of any of the dons today? Flower struggled to extract from the gargoyle an actual likeness.

Bloody hell, Fairlight! The lips. And that long, weak chin.

Flower sighed and rested his head on his hand and thought about Balboa's legs. By God, there wasn't another pair of legs like 'em in Oxford. That girl in the green cardigan in the booth had a nice pair, but Balboa's were really something.

Flower's chin sank more heavily on his hand. The rest of her was really something too – if ever I get a chance to find out for sure with bloody Fairlight filling his bloody boots. . . .

There was a sharp crack as the chin of the sleeping palaeographer slid off his reading-stand and struck the table-top. Flower roused himself from his lethargy and stretched out a hand to the *Paradise Lost*. Milton, he thought: my essay. He had drummed up enough *angst* to be able to put off his study no longer. He concentrated his attention, turned his gaze to the book and opened it.

For some seconds the low snoring of the palaeographer who had contrived to get his chin on to the reading-stand again was the only sound to be heard. Then Nicholas Flower said 'Good God!' out loud.

He said it in that abrupt uncontexted irrelevant-sounding way that people who like to think they are blasé have when they are really surprised.

Flower looked at the book again, then he looked up. Then he looked at it once more. Then he said 'Good God!' again, out loud, and this time quite tonelessly.

At the first sharp cry from Flower the ancient palaeographer had sat up, and he was now actually staring at the undergraduate, the expression on his face signifying an emotion as near to curiosity as he was still capable of experiencing.

For the third time Flower looked down at the book open in front of him, and as he looked his heart began to thump like a trip-hammer. He had a sensation of sudden and complete insecurity.

The sheets of blank paper that had been stuffed between the leather boards to keep them apart lay on his lap where they had fallen; and of the brown priceless script – the very record and insignia of Milton's own voice – there remained only tufted slivers of parchment left by the unknown hand which had ripped and torn and wrenched the pages out.

Chapter 2

In the mid morning when the sun is shining and people with suit cases are throwing sharp shadows across the platforms, there is a peace to be had in an empty first-class carriage which can be had nowhere else. Autumn, relaxing in his corner, deliberately postponed the lighting of his pipe in order not to mix the two pleasures; and as the train pulled out, considered again the conversation he had had earlier that day with the Commissioner.

'We've been expecting it,' said the Commissioner. He put his hands carefully together in front of his lips.

'You read the papers? Of course you do, and you read them carefully.'

Autumn never read the papers because he thought they told lies.

'So you will have noticed' – Autumn nodded – 'the number of reports there have been over the last eighteen months or so of destruction – vandalism – in libraries. Libraries all over the place – in Europe and America. I've got the clippings somewhere' – he fiddled with the papers in a drawer – 'doesn't matter, I remember most of the details. The most recent was the – er – the – er' – he snapped his fingers and Autumn wriggled uncomfortably – 'yes, you remember – those papers and books, theological stuff, taken from the Vatican Library. They turned up some days afterwards in the middle of St Peter's Square' – the Commissioner paused again, and Autumn nodded – 'burnt to ashes.'

Autumn did remember this. 'Wasn't – ?'

'*The Times*,' went on the Commissioner, who wasn't letting Autumn in as cheaply as that, 'had a leader. A very good leader. But were they' – he stared intently at Autumn – 'were they on the right track?'

Autumn blushed. He didn't even know how much *The Times* cost.

'Because that's rather the point. The significance of the

burning. In such a public place. But consider – let us con-
sider – the other instances. Leyden. The destruction at
Leyden. Mathematical treatises and some alchemical
papers. Chopped up – *minced* – and the bits stuck up on
the doors of the University with drawing-pins.'

'Drawing-pins,' said Autumn.

'I see you relish the touch. Then there was the fire – oh,
not a very big fire, you recollect – in the rare manuscript
section at Johns Hopkins. And another at Yale. The Yale
one was bigger. They both got into the papers. And there
have been – you may not have seen all of them – there
have been other instances in at least a dozen other similar
institutions. All over the place.

'And now here. It has started here. In Oxford. I repeat,
we expected it.'

As the Commissioner walked round his desk, Autumn
wondered if his hair was going to be pulled, and if he was
going to be asked to repeat what had been said so far. The
Commissioner, who had been a tutor in political science
at the London School of Economics, perched in the corner
among the inkwells.

'And those are the facts. What of their significance? A
very high incidence – well, we know that. And the books
have been destroyed *in public*. Suggestive, that.'

All of a sudden, the Commissioner's eyes started to
twinkle.

'What would you' – and the eyes twinkled away –
'what would *you* do, my dear Autumn, if you wanted to
stimulate national insecurity, if you really wanted to
worry people?'

It was the Commissioner's lecture-room manner: a
game of billiards with a Home Secretary at a house party
had been the Yard's gain, the London School's loss.

'Close the pubs,' said Autumn.

The Commissioner laughed.

'Most apropos. But seriously. Just how would you make
people *unsteady*, make the whole country feel that life itself
was coming loose at the roots?'

'Oh, I suppose I might sprinkle a few atom-bombs
about.'

'Of course you would,' grinned the Commissioner rudely, 'and it wouldn't do any good at all. Bombs only break up the surface of things, they don't disrupt people *inside*.'

'Oh, I don't know.'

'Not at all, no, no. You can raze cities to the ground and you won't unbalance people inside. The material landmarks disappear but they still know where *they* are. Why? Because there is a Magnetic North which keeps the individual orientated in the midst of even the most devastating holocaust.'

Autumn wondered if the Commissioner had got religion.

'A Magnetic North called "tradition". Not the one with the capital "T", the one that gets flags waved at it. I mean the "tradition" that is a sense of the past, the sense of the past which gives each of us' – the Commissioner fumbled for his image – 'gives each of us our personal map-reference in Time. Our personal map-reference in Time.'

The Commissioner held up one finger.

'A sense of the past is the basis for every kind of security. Every kind of *political* security, that is. In order to make people feel life's coming away in their hands, so to speak, you've got to impair tradition. Bombs would help,' said the Commissioner cautiously, 'but there are subtler ways.'

'I don't want to make anyone feel insecure, Commissioner – '

'Aha,' exclaimed the Commissioner joyously, as he saw his discourse winding a classic way before him, 'of course you don't, my dear man, but there are lots of chaps who do. Chaps who don't like governments. Revolutionaries. A sense of security is the revolutionary's worst enemy, his *basic* obstacle. He's got to make people flounder before they'll listen. A man floundering grasps at anything. Cut the ground from under their feet – that's the revolutionary's first job. Destroy – impair – the sense of *belonging*. In short, the target is tradition.'

The Commissioner, who had been leaning forward eagerly, sat back.

'Forgive me,' he said, 'for making a complex thing sound impossibly glib.'

I underrated him, thought Autumn.

The Commissioner said: 'Now you see why they destroyed the books in public? There wouldn't have been much point in having a go at tradition – in one of its particular and concrete aspects – if people couldn't *see* it under destruction, would there? It would only get into the papers if it was done flamboyantly. You see that?'

'Always old books?'

'Very old, very priceless. Unique. "Our heritage."' The Commissioner grinned at the inverted commas. 'Heritage, you see. That's what they're getting at.'

The Commissioner was silent. Then he said:

'One must keep the thing in its right proportion. A specialised attack such as this is only one small element in the preparation of a *climate*, a climate of unrest. You follow up your specific attack with propaganda, strikes, delayed trains, shortages – the homelier inconveniences. And of course it's a slow business. How long was it, I wonder, before the publicity gentlemen could be sure young women would swoon when Mr Crosby sang?'

'But do people really care about – '

'Tradition? Can't help it, my dear man. It's an instinct. You wait,' said the Commissioner, 'you wait till they start on the art galleries. Chap who reads in his Sunday paper about the horrifying destruction of the *Mona Lisa*, the abominable burning of *The Laughing Cavalier*, or the shredding into thin strips of *The Last Supper* – well, he may never have been in the Tate in his life but I bet you anything you like he goes off his food that Sunday. Oh, yes,' said the Commissioner, 'it's a reflex – like feeling dizzy when you've been spun round. You can't avoid it.'

'They'll start on art galleries?'

'Sure of it. I'm rather surprised they didn't kick off with galleries. People feel more about pictures than books. But then libraries are ramparts of security, aren't they? Something solid, something *always there* about them. Sacrosanct. Upsetting when they turn out not to be . . .

'Oh, yes,' said the Commissioner, 'libraries, art galleries

then they might have a crack at architecture. Tougher proposition, architecture, but very rewarding if you can pull it off. Imagine the destruction of Buckingham Palace. That's why I said bombs might help – '

'Guy Fawkes,' said Autumn.

'Oh, precisely.' The Commissioner beamed. 'They had immediate ends in view, of course, but the whole conception of blowing up Parliament went a great deal deeper.

'And then' – the Commissioner actually licked his lips – 'there's civil war. An attack on tradition at its most traditional – *order*. Oh, tremendously rewarding.'

He rattled the pennies in his pockets, and swung his legs, sitting on the corner of the desk.

'Johnson said that no public disaster ever made a man miss his dinner. But he really meant other people's disasters. We've all a vested interest in tradition: to take tradition away is to uproot all the signposts. People start to run in a world where direction has lost its meaning. *That's* when the questions come tumbling out, the questions no one had time to ask before: *what is this life* . . .; and of course the answers (as the revolutionaries know) command their own price. Independence . . .'

The sound of horns and motors in Whitehall chimed through the room as the Commissioner fell silent.

'Well, well,' he said briskly, 'there have been two lots of book destruction at Oxford. One lot was discovered by a young man who opened an autograph edition of *Paradise Lost* and found all the pages had been torn out. When the Bodley people checked they found a lot more in the same condition. Then there was a second outbreak last night. A lady – a rather odd lady, I gather, who is given to looking out of her window at night through a telescope – saw a sort of glow behind St Mary's Church which turned out to be a smaller edition of the kind of bonfire they had in St Peter's Square.'

'I go down, then.'

'You go *up*, my dear fellow. Of course, the two occurrences may have no connexion with the things that have been happening over the last eighteen months. You'll have to find that out for yourself. But with the situation as it is we're not leaving it to the local people. Apart from any-thing else, there's that Chaucer thing. Whoever's destroy-ing these books is going to have a go at that if he can.'

Autumn had heard of the Chaucer thing.

'What's the name of it again?'

'*Book of the Lion*. All the papers had it. The poem they found at Ewelme. The biggest literary find since – since – ' It was not the Commissioner's subject. 'Even the *Worker* had a piece on it – "Courtly Love, Bah!", and the tele-vision. Vast public interest – which is what makes it so vulnerable if the Oxford business is tied in with the other – '

Autumn said: 'Where is the Chaucer thing now?'

'With the man who found it. Oh, safe enough. I know these academics' – the Commissioner's smile was very worldly – 'he'll cherish that book like an ailing child.'

'Well, I'll go then.'

'Don't worry about hotels – the Vice-Chancellor's putting you up at his own College. I think he wants to keep an eye on us. Rather a bad-tempered old person. Still, Bodley's librarian is at the same place – Warlock – which may be handy.'

They walked to the door.

'It'll be an experience,' said the Commissioner. 'Ox-ford. Why,' he added humorously, 'they'll probably pinch your helmet.'

Autumn lit his pipe after the train left Reading and congratulated himself afresh on the lower-middle-class upbringing which still allowed him, in middle life, to enjoy a simple pleasure like first-class travel at his em-ployers' expense.

He had enjoyed the Commissioner's theory. It had been very high-class and interesting. They had had a very cultural chat. But it had left him somewhat restless.

It was an extraordinarily convincing theory. And yet – criminals engaged in vast philosophical crimes: *creating a climate* – imagine that! Fascinating –

The thing is, I'm not used to it, Autumn said to himself. The crimes I'm used to are ordinary. Chaps killing their wives because they've been carrying on with the wireless-man. . . .

But good lord where's your imagination? These things happen. God, how it narrows a man, a daily round of theft, murder, and rape. That's the real occupational hazard for chaps like us – we frequent the criminal class and we get to partaking in the criminal mentality. 'Motive' to us means money or sex . . .

In spite of his attempts to unleash his imagination, Autumn continued to feel restless. With a sigh, he succumbed to the shabby vice he had many years ago abandoned all hope of curing, and put his feet up on the seat opposite.

No – that wasn't true about the money and sex, he thought. What I really mean is that, by common experience, most crime has a personal rather than an impersonal motive. If the Commissioner is right, the chaps doing this are acting very impersonally indeed. I'm not saying, Autumn said to himself, that I should reject the Commissioner's idea. I'm just saying what it is that makes me a bit restless about it.

And having analysed his own motives, Autumn sucked his pipe contentedly, and thought about Oxford.

His experience of universities had been confined to the Boat Race, and the extra-mural activities of London University on Guy Fawkes night. As a bobby, it had been his business to see that the lads maintained a favourable balance between outrage and the Comedy Element. He had displayed a massive indifference to the rollicking scientists who would strike up *Lloyd George Knew My Father* in a spirit of abandoned wickedness.

Dons he knew nothing whatever about. As the train shuttled through the small stations between Didcot and Oxford, Autumn tried to visualize them. But he got no further than the features of an elderly pimp of his acquaintance, who bore a striking resemblance to the Proctor in *A Yank at Oxford*.

What sort of personal motives were dons moved by? Hmmmm. Autumn looked out of the window as the train ran in. He was hoping for the dreaming spires, but saw only gasometers. He descended in company with some baggy-eyed young men, and several elderly persons in bow ties who were returning to postponed tutorials after a hard week-end in the television panel programmes.

Autumn gave in his ticket, and walked out into the road to get himself a taxi.

'Bum, old boy,' someone shouted.

Autumn glanced round. A man in a camel hair coat advanced upon him.

'Bum, old boy,' the man said.

A taxi drew up, and Autumn paused, one hand upon the door.

'Bum, old boy,' said the man in the camel hair coat again, and shook his hand, adding: 'Of the *Knell*.'

Chapter 3

'Iт's not my regular beat at all, old boy,' said Mr Bum, climbing into the taxi with Autumn, 'only our crime man's doing eighteen months.'

Autumn said to the driver: 'The police station.'

'And as I was down here already, they told me to stay when they heard about the bonfire last night.'

'You were here already?'

'Yes, old boy, came down to get a profeel of the bloke who dug up the Chaucer. I think the bastard's been trying to avoid me. Astonishing,' Mr Bum shook his head like a horse troubled with flies, 'astonishing how out of touch some of these fellows are.'

'Nailed him yet?'

'He's invited me to dinner at Warlock College this evening, but I don't know if he'll play. I stuck to him for three days – even sat through a lecture on a tour round the Hebrides, and geography isn't my first love.'

Autumn looked out of the window: the streets teemed with bicycles and coloured shirts and pretty frocks, and the sun shone.

'I don't like these cultural barneys, old boy,' said Mr Bum, 'they don't suit me at all. I usually cover the South Coast resorts this time of year, but the Editor's mother's just moved to Margate and he's doing them himself – '

Mr Bum glanced out of the window gloomily.

'They're a very odd lot,' he said, 'very odd indeed . . .'

Mr Bum continued to look out of the window as if he were observing a primitive tree-dwelling society, to whom he would have to apply in pidgin English if his metropolitan habits were to be comprehended. The taxi drew up at the traffic lights by Carfax.

'Still,' said Mr Bum, 'I hear the food's all right.'

The taxi turned right.

'Chucking those old books about, and burning them. Nasty bit of vandalism, old boy. Though why' – he looked curiously at Autumn – 'they called in the Yard. If you ask me I should say it was drunken students with too much time on their hands . . .'

They were passing Christ Church, and Autumn's wandering attention was suddenly held. Not by the words of Mr Bum, but by a fat man in a brown suit. The man was bustling out of Christ Church – he may have been using Tom Quad as a short cut from the river – and his waistcoat was undone all the way down.

'If there's anything you can tell me, old boy – I've done them a background piece, the dreaming spires, titled undergrads – '

The fat man stopped at the kerb. There was a heterogeneous quality about his get-up – the brim of his hat undulated wildly – but the most noticeable thing about him was his air of purposeful occasion. It stuck out because it was laid on so thick: as if he found himself out of his element, but was determined not to notice.

'But they're pestering me for something hard – '

Autumn glanced back through the rear window of the taxi, and saw the fat man walking across the road with one eye on his feet and one on his nose. Where on earth had he seen him before? . . .

'Oh,' said Autumn, as Bum persisted, 'Oh, yes. Trouble is, you know as much as I do. I'm going to have a word with the local man: if there's anything doing, I'll let you know.'

A few seconds later, the taxi drew up in front of the police station. As Autumn stepped out he was still trying to remember where he had seen the fat man before.

The sun came down through the gargoyles and battlements, and the close-cropped grass of the Summerhouse Quad lay dappled in strange shadows. Long shafts of light set the assorted colours of the stone aflame, and Autumn, entering Warlock for the first time, was presented with an architecture, miscellaneous to the point of delirium.

Aubrey is succinct about William Warlock, founder and benefactor of the College: 'Hee was short, I think under five feete. He sayd he would strike more coin, but it solved nought. Hee wore a red wigge. Sir John Coventry sayd he

23

had been much troubled with the *boyls*. His Coll. in Oxford exotick; he would have all in the building, *viz.* pagodies, etc. "They should give the exhibition, and there an end" – A. Wood (*Quare* there was Madness in it.)'

Noddy Warlock had been Chancellor of the Exchequer during the Restoration, and his tenure of the office was marked by a series of entirely novel and entirely disastrous financial manoeuvres; very soon after attempting to balance the economy of the country by the simple expedient of minting lead halfpence, Noddy retired to Dorking and devoted himself to occasional verse.

But verse (only one poem – 'Prescript for a Rural Oeconomy, Inspired in a Distant Prospect of Box Hill' – is to be found in the contemporary anthologies) was not enough, and Noddy, who was a wealthy man, decided to leave his mark in a more lasting fashion. He founded Warlock, and directed the building himself.

'La, sir,' pouts a censorious vizard, in Shadwell's *Serviceable Virtue, or The Maid In The Cupboard*, 'thy verse is more benoduled and beparapeted and beturreted in a melancholy combination of erratick styles than is the new College in Oxford. . . .'

Her comparison was good. Warlock is a standing monument to the entire history of architecture. What Noddy forgot, later generations added. For every Saxon doorway there is a Norman tower, for every Doric column, there is a Corinthian, an Ionian, a Composite, and a Tuscan. Pediments and cornices peep out round flying-buttresses, and are lost amid the roundheaded arches, the quoins, the baroque jambs, the voussoirs, and the Mohammedan domes. Battlements are flung about the roofs like confetti, and in the Summerhouse Quad there is a pagoda.

For cloisters, Warlock is the first in the world; Mrs Radcliffe (who was once up for the weekend) is said to have seen the Summerhouse Cloisters and to have started on *Udolpho* the same afternoon. Frescoes and statuary jostle for place among the eaves and gables, and gargoyles grimace from architrave and entablature. The stylistic assortment had become so various by the nineteenth century that Sir George Gilbert Scott chucked in the towel, and went away to build the Albert Memorial.

Apart from the Fellows who drew their stipend from the College endowment, nobody seemed very keen about Warlock when it was finished, and it remained a graduate society much the same as All Souls. From time to time, undergraduates who had failed to get into other Colleges came to Warlock, but there were never more than half a dozen in residence at any one time.

For several minutes Autumn stood in the quadrangle, and tried very hard to digest the building. Then he followed the porter across Summerhouse to the guest-room.

It was seven o'clock and the scouts were riding in from Cowley and Folly Bridge. Rugger men bellowed mono-syllabic songs as they climbed out of their baths, and far out in North Oxford, dons, monstrously dissembling a mounting elation, commended their families to tinned salmon, and piled cheerfully on to No 4 buses. It was dinner-time.

How different, Autumn reflected comfortably, from the police canteen. Dinner was over, and the dons of Warlock sat in their Senior Common Room and took dessert. Autumn received the nutcrackers from the don on his left, and cracked a nut.

'I must again apologize for the absence of the Master,' said the don, whose name was Undigo, and who had presided at dinner, 'but as I hinted previously, it is not an unusual thing.'

Manchip, Master of Warlock and Vice-Chancellor of the University, was a man of impulse. He very often invited guests to dine, and failed to arrive himself. It was symptomatic (Common Room opinion was agreed) both of his cussedness and of his devotion to brass-rubbing. His hobby took him to outlying village churches on his bicycle, without warning and for days at a time.

'His interests are four,' quavered a very old man called Falal, 'Gynander, brasses, crosswords, and malice. Ha, ha, ha.'

25

'Pass the port, Humphrey,' admonished Undigo. 'Your capacity is diminished.'

'And,' continued the old man, 'he is the unhappy victim of an obsessive mania.' He glanced rheumily round the table. 'He wishes,' Falal turned to Autumn, 'to admit women to this University as undergraduates. Undergraduates, upon my soul, yes, that is his idea. It is an idea which must horrify us all. The admission of women to this University would be a catastrophe comparable in effect to the fall of Troy.'

'What a shockin' thing to say,' a loud deep voice bassooned. 'Talkin' about women as if they didn't exist. Shockin'.'

It was Pearl Corker – the manly Corker of Walpurgis Hall. Beneath the table her knees were spread wide apart, and the elastic end of one woollen knicker-leg obtruded. She was Undigo's guest.

'My dear Humphrey,' broke in a strong-faced, silver-haired don called Christelow, who was the man who had found the Chaucer poem, 'you know very well women are as much a part of the University as you are yourself. Manchip simply wishes more women to come here.'

'Ah, indeed. Entirely plausible, I don't doubt.' Falal was ironic. 'Were Manchip to succeed in contaminating Oxford in the fashion he proposes I would *shoot* him. Indeed, I would. With my bare hands,' he added.

Christelow laughed.

'Your refusal to face facts reminds me of the two Christ Church men. One bet the other five pounds there was no such College as Wadham.'

'Who won?' asked Undigo, solemnly.

Autumn smiled.

Christelow said: 'I must tell you how I played golf with Manchip once. I thought I'd take the opportunity of learning something about his favourite poet, so I said to him as he teed off: "Tell me, Master, what sort of a poet is Gynander?" "Oh," he said in that deep voice of his, "a very interesting poet indeed." "Yes," I said, "I should have thought he was. But," I said, "what sort of a poet is he?" "Why," said Manchip, chipping away with his

26

iron, "do you realize, Christelow, there are only six fragments of Gynander still extant?" "Really, Master?" I said. "But what sort of a poet is he?" "And," he went on, cutting the turf about, "there is one construction that appears no less than twice in each, which is seen nowhere else in Greek literature. Now, what do you think of that, hey?" "Very interesting," I said. "But, Master, what sort of a poet is Gynander?" "Surprisingly careless about genders," he said, getting himself on the green, and rolling off the other side. "Yes," said I. "But what sort of a poet is he?" "Ah," he said as I bunkered myself, "you mean the *gush* side of criticism. . . .'"

'He's a fool.'

The words came from a gingery-haired scientist, who wore round wire-rimmed spectacles.

'He's ashamed of his College because it's small, he is arrogant and unmannerly, and I do not see, I never have seen, why we put up with it – '

Undigo's eye snapped.

'You speak like a tradesman who has been snubbed by a Duchess, Rankine. If Manchip is unpleasant at times, he is at least distinguishedly so. Warlock would be the duller without him.'

They rose from the table, and walked across the room to the armchairs. They all sat down.

Autumn was well at ease. He was passing through the hallucinatory after-dinner phase which attacks most visitors to Senior Common Rooms, in which the victim sees the life of a don as the only ultimate earthly good.

They had been a large party to dinner, and there remained, in addition to Christelow, Rankine, Undigo, Falal, and Miss Corker – Bum (who had declined all drink save whisky); McCann, a tall grey-faced dark-eyed Scotsman, who was librarian of Bodley, and who had sat all through dinner listening to Pearl Corker as if absorbing material for a new and sensational edition of *The Monstrous Regiment*; Fairlight, the New Critic; and Clapp, lecturer in Military History. All, save Miss Corker, were of in Warlock.

Fairlight said: 'Wouldn't it be fun if Manchip turned

out to be the Inspector's quarry? Nipping into Bodley and setting fire to the fiction shelf.'

'Wouldn't be surprised,' said Clapp, sitting bolt upright in his soft chair. 'Man who throws the College open to Russians, capable of anything. Fellow from Russia, the undergraduate who came up this term. All Manchip's doing. Hijus prospect, fillin' the place with Russians. Manchip's idea from start to finish.'

Clapp drank a glass of port. He was a short man, and wore a double-breasted suit of narrow military cut.

'Oh, come now, Clapp, you call him a Russian. He's only Russian-born, you know.'

Undigo said: 'I suspect the idea of having any kind of Russian here appealed to Manchip. Would you say so? I relished it myself. Though Archangel has probably never been nearer Russia than Highgate Pond. We might make a regular thing of it – Rhodes Scholars from Russia, eh? Excellent. A liberal atmosphere has always suited the Slavonic temperament: I should make them all feel quite at home by telling them how my father poulticed those carbuncles on Marx's bottom which make *Das Kapital* such bitter reading. And we should insist on Rankine controlling his prejudices. He thinks' – Undigo grinned at the ginger-haired scientist – 'that Archangel is a spy.'

'Not at all,' snapped Rankine. 'I told you before, Undigo, I consider it a foolish precedent. With English lads up and down the country waiting to get in here, it's a crying shame to hand out places to foreigners – especially foreigners who may be undesirable.'

'Hear, hear,' murmured Clapp.

'Oho,' shouted Undigo exultingly, '*your* liberal education is bearing fruit. Are not *all* foreigners undesirable? Rankine, Rankine, you have plainly been attending meetings.'

Rankine said: 'There's a difference between bad manners and humorous remarks. At your age, you should know it. Good night.'

He got up and walked out.

'Humorous remarks! God bless my soul. Is that really what I make? Would you say so?'

Fairlight, the New Critic, had moved over to the wireless set in the corner to hear the recording of his talk – 'Nonce Words in Akenside' – on the Third. He returned.

'Deary me, Manchip *does* upset people, doesn't he? Poor old Rankine – he can't bear to think that Manchip has turned Lord Pinner down.'

Fairlight sat on the floor, fair-haired and fortyish. His hairy suit looked like a long woollen sock.

'Well, but we are not all favourite Uncles on the Don's Hour, Fairlight,' said Undigo. 'We must make our way as best we can. If Rankine's Lord Pinner founds his College, I see no reason why Rankine should not hope for the Mastership. Patronage. Is it so disgraceful?'

'But how impossibly *moche* to accept the Mastership of a College founded upon the perdition of millions of immortal souls. Lord Pinner made his money out of rubber goods.'

'Let contraception thrive,' boomed Pearl Corker.

'*Dreadful* trade,' capped Fairlight. 'But Manchip's almost an R.C. about that sort of thing. Pinner's College won't come to anything while Manchip wields the veto.'

Miss Corker said: 'Gimme a cigar, Henry, and get the Inspector to tell us about the Cleft Chin case.'

The butler came in with a fresh decanter, set it down, and walked over to Undigo.

Bum opened his mouth to say something. He had spent most part of the evening trying to pick from his mind the splinters left there by the coarse-grained generalizations required of him by his newspaper. He had put himself at what seemed to be gaps in the conversation, only to have them turn, half way through his leap, into five-barred gates.

Before he could try again, Undigo said to the butler: 'Won't it wait?'

'I don't think so, sir.'

Undigo followed the butler out of the room and returned a few minutes later looking bewildered.

'Dimbleby,' he said to the butler, 'get the opera-glasses from my bureau and bring them to me in the quad. This is very odd,' he continued to the others, 'a curious thing indeed. Undergraduates, perhaps. . . . Would you care to come and – ah – have a look? It won't take a moment – '

In the quad it was twilight. The porter stood beside Undigo, staring at the murky bulk of the Chapel. The details of the architecture were obscured in the dusk, but the statuary which marched round the periphery of the roof – Regency charmers in uncontrollable garments, Hanoverian senators with scrolls – sailed erect across the darkening sky.

'Well, Henry, where's the damned eclipse?' asked Miss Corker.

'Undergraduates . . . I wonder. . . . Christelow, just count those figures on the near side.'

'One, two – but surely – '

'Perhaps you'd care to take an observation through your lenses, sir,' said the butler.

Undigo took the binoculars, and looked through them at the roof of the Chapel. He focused them on one statue, then the next. He reached the corner of the parapet, then returned to the beginning.

He handed the glasses to Autumn.

'Look.'

'A jape, a wheeze, a romantic revival. Sentimental verses in the *Isis*, poems on spires – ' trilled Fairlight.

The glasses showed up with tolerable clarity the dimples on the charmers. Autumn re-focused them, and considered each statue in turn. At number three, he paused.

It was no charmer, nor ever had been. The face was male, and to the congenitally disagreeable expression on it, had been superimposed another, that of surprise.

It was Manchip, but there would be no embarrassment. He was quite dead.

Chapter 4

THEY lowered Manchip down the side of the Chapel in the glare of a searchlight. The frowns and dimples of the carven statuary frosted wanly in the white beam, as their latest recruit swung down, rotating gently, past plinth and parapet, to the grass below. He was as stiff as a post.

Two sweating constables ran the winch slowly round, and Manchip's gown snapped about him like a flag round a flagpole, the two white fingers of his Vice-Chancellorian cravat tapping his chin like a pale chuck from the hand of Death itself.

Things had happened too swiftly, and maladjustment was rife among the spectators. The responses of the dons, as they huddled behind the searchlight, had become fundamental: and a certain amount of timorous facetiousness emphasized rather than disguised the fact. Even Autumn, professionally inured to sensational events, found himself not immune to the suddenness of the thing.

He had climbed up the tortuous little stair which led to the roof of the Chapel, and, edging out on to the narrow duckboard track which ran round the edge of the tiles, had reached the dead man. Manchip had a dessert-knife in his back – one of his own – and he was propped upright against two spars of wood. His eyebrows were raised, and his mouth open. Surprised.

He had been killed on the roof: Autumn decided this as he came down. If he had been killed elsewhere and lugged up, there would have been marks on the walls or the stairway.

'It was a *thing*,' said Fairlight, 'a thing he had about the roof. He believed it gave the only comprehensive view of Oxford. He was always pestering people to go up with him and see – '

'But he was pleased that they didn't.' Undigo shivered in the night air. 'It was part of his singularity. He liked being the only one. It's a stiff climb.'

Manchip lay on his belly on the grass, the haft of the

knife sticking out of his back, glinting dully in the beam.

Autumn said: 'He persuaded someone in the end. . . .'

Police doctors were a sophistication that had not caught on at the local police station. Dorcas, the local Inspector, a somewhat harassed officer, had called up the Regius Professor of Medicine. The Professor's subject was trauma, but he was doing very well, considering.

'He died last night, or early this morning. He was stabbed to the heart from beneath the left shoulder blade.'

The Professor looked again at the body.

'Tch, tch,' he murmured, shaking his head as though one of his pupils had split the formalin, 'poor Manchip. Such a disagreeable person. An inadequacy complex, promiscuously transferred. Ah, death – the Great Psychiatrist, Inspector, one visit – '

He shook hands, and flapped off, terrified, to Norham Gardens.

'But fancy no one noticing,' said Rankine the scientist, who had been awakened by the lights, and was wearing a dressing-gown. 'Stuck up there all the time in broad daylight – '

'Ah, that's the cunning of it, sir,' said the porter. 'Who's expectin' to see anything stuck up there? Dart a 'asty glance, and all you sees is statues. You sees them statues every day of your life. You gets used to 'em. One more ain't goin' to notice. It was accident I spotted it at all – '

'Right enough,' said Christelow. 'And I don't suppose there'd be much room to stow a body out of sight between the parapet and the duckboards. Propping him up was clever – '

'And whoever it is has got a day's start, if the doctor's right,' Autumn said. 'But there's nothing more we can do at the moment, and I'd be glad if you'd all go to bed.'

The quad cleared.

Inspector Dorcas went back to the station in an ambulance with the body of Manchip, the two constables turned out the searchlight, and Autumn, having told the porter to warn everyone for interview at eleven the next day, made his way to the guest-room, swallowed three aspirins, and went to sleep.

Autumn's first emotion on waking was unbelief. He sat up in bed, and looked out of the window: the gargoyles and turrets of Warlock crumbled in the watery sun like cheese; a man in a cap and gown walked slowly across the green grass; in the distance, there was the drone of a lawn-mower; a clock struck.

His unbelief was abolished, and in its place there came a sensation of panic, the sort of panic that descends on a candidate for an examination who has read the paper through and is dizzy with the conviction that he can answer nothing. Autumn had known this momentary wild helplessness before. And then the feeling went out of him.

By the time he was walking across Summerhouse on his way to the lodge wonder had dwindled into whimsical speculation. A Vice-Chancellor! One might have supposed so exalted an office carried immunity to the extraordinary casualties. Autumn grinned, and repeated the sentence. But all the time he was thinking: Do the books come into it?

The porter's name was Tantalum.

'The only College in the University as no one can climb into, and they've tried 'ard enough, I'll lay. Ladders and scalin' irons, and that kind, but it's no go. Even the windows 'as got bars to 'em. And only one door. This one 'ere. What you'd *need*,' he leant towards the Inspector, heavy with humour, 'what you'd *need* is a 'elicopter.' He said: 'What I mean, of course none of the dons'd want to climb in. But we've got four men' – Autumn was unfamiliar with the idiom, but knew instinctively he meant undergraduates – 'who might. ' *Ere!* '

The last was an ear-shattering bellow, a summons to someone invisible.

'They knock on the gate after twelve, and then I fines 'em. After twelve-fifteen, they sees the Master. ' *Ere!* ' He bellowed again.

'All of 'em,' said Tantalum, answering Autumn's next question.

'All of 'em were in the night the doctor says he was killed. All the dons, the four undergraduates, one guest –

33

Lord Pinner – and Mr Diamantis, the late Vice-Chancellor's secretary. '*Ere!*'

An undernourished youth with red knuckles emerged from the lodge.

'The Boy from Botley' – Tantalum jerked his head towards the youth – 'had gone orff. My assistant.'

Tantalum named the inmates of Warlock on the evening of the incident, and Autumn scribbled them down on a piece of paper.

'Dr Undigo, the Senior Fellow – he'll likely be the Master now. The Reverend Bow-Parley – he's got rooms in College, but he lives out down the Woodstock Road with his wife ordinarily. Mr Rankine and 'is guest, Lord Pinner, Dr McCann, the Librarian of Bodley, Mr Christelow, Mr Shipton, Professor Falal – he isn't a proper Professor, having retired, what they call Emer-eetus – Colonel Clapp, the Bursar, then there's the four men – Mr Flower, Mr Dogg, Mr Egg, and Mr Archangel. Not counten Mr Diamantis previously mentioned. All in College. The Boy' – he jerked his head again – 'don't count cause he'd gone orff with the rest of the servants.'

Upon one point Mr Tantalum was immovable.

'But surely,' Autumn persisted, 'you can't pretend to know that everyone who has come into the College during the day has in fact gone out again.'

'I see them come and I see them go. Everyone who came in that day went out again.'

'How can you be so sure?'

'What,' said Tantalum, setting the ultimate conundrum, 'do you suppose I'm put 'ere for, sir?'

''E' put 'ere to watch that door,' said the Boy from Botley.

''E's right,' said Tantalum, amazed at the lad's acumen, ''e's right.'

Tantalum continued: 'Perhaps you don't understand about porters in Oxford, sir. We know everyone, and we see everything. That's what we're here for. No one comes in through that door but I sees 'em, no one goes out but I sees 'em. It's like a law of nature, as it might be put.'

'An' if 'e misses 'em, *I* sees 'em,' said the Boy from Botley.

'But he's never called on to see 'em, because I don't miss 'em.'

Autumn decided to accept it. So whoever did it must have been in College, one of the inhabitants –

'Inspecto-o-oor!'

Someone hallooed from the other side of the quad. It was Christelow. He ran across.

'Whoof! There you are. Do I interrupt? Good. A small thing, but it's on my mind rather – '

They moved out of the lodge.

'If we could just have a look, I should be able to reassure myself. The *Book* – my *Book of the Lion* – I may have mentioned it last night? Yes,' Christelow nodded quickly, 'the Chaucer MS. My "discovery" – not properly mine, I only recognized it for what it was' – he laughed, pleased, but on edge – 'Manchip borrowed it. I hadn't had it back from him. It occurred to me – you spoke of your Commissioner's theory – revolutionaries – '

Oh, God, groaned Autumn inwardly, as they walked round the cloisters, why the hell didn't he say so before –

Bow-Parley, the Chaplain, was sunning himself gravely in the Master's Garden, as Christelow and Autumn entered through a narrow archway. Christelow introduced the Inspector. Bow-Parley had not been at dinner the previous night.

'I am distressed not to have been on hand for your arrival but you have no time for my apologies. How should the forms concern any of us at this melancholy juncture? The word, the sad word, has gone about, is known – '

In conversation it always seemed as if the Rev. Cyprian Bow-Parley were using his hands as antennae, as sensitive apparatus whereby he might put himself in touch with corporeality. He would clamp his hand on the arm of the person he addressed as if apprehensive that the slightest break in contact might involve instant sublimation of Bow-Parley-on-Earth, and a reappearance (crystalline and ethereal) somewhere in the region of the ceiling.

'You are on your way – But of course, a sombre necessity, the diligence of law requires, demands it. A crumb of evidence, eyes all for detail – '

He had a repetitious, thesaurian way with him.

'I left the *Book* with Manchip, and after this awful thing I'm somewhat anxious – '

'A prudent consideration. There should be no further delay. Why not,' the Chaplain continued, 'follow Shipton? He passed me by not two minutes ago, and I am fairly, yes, I think, fairly sure he too was bound for Manchip's rooms. I could hazard no guess as to his purpose.' He blinked, charmingly myopic. 'Perhaps he has – um – *information*?'

'Shipton?' queried Autumn.

Christelow barely heard. His mind stumbled over the new topic like a wheel over a stone. He was too much occupied with his own affair.

'What? Oh – geographer.'

Shipton was on the threshold when they reached Manchip's rooms. He was a dark young man.

'Hullo.' He was abrupt. 'You coming in, Christelow? Came to get some essays he borrowed from me.' He knew who Autumn was.

'We've come for the Chaucer.'

'I'd be glad,' said Autumn evenly, 'if you'd tell me exactly what it is you've removed?'

'My own property.' Shipton's black hair hung in a dry hank over his forehead. He held out the papers. 'Essays, mine. He was all for reading other people's stuff – "the curse of specialization".'

Shipton paused.

'A nasty nosey old person,' he said.

'Should we not allow the iniquity of oblivion blindly to scatter her poppy?' asked the Chaplain, as if the notion had just struck him.

Autumn coughed, and moved past the dark young man into the room. As he went, he saw Shipton's eye meet the Chaplain's. For an instant there was communion. Then the young man walked away into the garden. Autumn thought: Who hates who?

36

Christelow roamed Manchip's sitting-room like a man who has lost his back-stud, bending down to look under sofas, lifting up books, opening drawers, and then going into the bedroom and dining-room beyond, and exploring them in the same way. Autumn followed, occasionally picking out a book, and once or twice bending down to examine things close to the floor.

Christelow came back into the larger room, where the bookcases swarmed like creeper over the walls. He had glanced down them hurriedly on entering, and now scanned them again, more closely.

'Oh, by George, here it is.'

Christelow almost shouted.

'He'd wrapped a dust jacket round it. How thoughtful of Manchip, how very thoughtful of Manchip.'

'That's it?' asked Autumn.

'Here.'

Autumn took the thin brown quarto from Christelow, who was grinning like a happy child. Autumn opened it; it seemed quite intact.

'*Caste now your royal eie on everich hond,*' he read,
'*How pleyn disordinaunce is in your lond . . .*'

Autumn glanced at the gap made in the shelf by the withdrawal of the book. He pulled two or three neighbouring volumes out, rubbed his finger idly in the dust lying in ridges between them.

'Someone's been looking for something. See the dust?'

'Samples for analysis, a tell-tale particle,' whinnied Bow-Parley.

Autumn said abstractedly: 'The edges of the books overlap the ridges in the dust.'

'Significant detail! The gift was Chaucer's,' Bow-Parley exclaimed, 'but might not Manchip himself – '

Autumn said sourly: 'If he did, he moved a lot of other things as well. Chairs, tables, the sideboard, the bed in there. Someone looking for something, carefully putting everything back in its right place – but not quite. After the Chaucer, perhaps. A good thing the scouts don't have

37

Chaucer's eye for significant detail, or they might have dusted the room.'

'Good Lord,' murmured Christelow, leafing through the thin little book, 'supposing we'd lost it again – '

'It does not bear thinking of,' said the Chaplain. 'I should, by the by, be glad to read it through myself. As I glanced at it the other evening, I suspected the poet's imagination was straitened rather than liberated by the allegory – '

'Certainly you must have it. In my own mind, I put it before the *Duchess* and after the *Romaunt*. There is a clarity of *line*. I should be glad to hear what you think – '

The Chaplain wandered about the room.

'I wonder,' he said, 'why the room was searched so *neatly*? Intruders are seldom scrupulous. Is it not so? One reads of upturned drawers, the contents scattered – '

'It's plain enough. If the man who searched the room was the man who killed Manchip, it was in his interest to conceal the crime as long as he could. If the room was seen to be wrecked, the alarm would have been raised at once.'

'The trained mind! Of course, of course.'

Bow-Parley, handling the dead man's Greek lexicon, sighed.

'Well, well,' said Autumn, 'we must get on.'

'A man of breadth,' crooned Bow-Parley, 'a man of parts. Had we not known, we might have wondered that he should have been interested in the geographical essays of Shipton. We might have pondered, excogitated: *why* geographical essays? But as things stand we may say, why *not* geographical essays, why not,' he laughed merrily, 'Shipton's essays?'

Autumn looked at Bow-Parley, but the eyes behind the rimless spectacles distributed nothing more specific than Anglican goodwill.

'I think, and I don't want to be irreverent, that it was more nosiness than breadth,' said Christelow mildly.

There was a loud groaning sound outside. It was Iscariot, the great clock of Warlock, trying to strike eleven. The three men walked back through the garden, into the

Cloisters. The rest of the College was trailing across Summerhouse towards the Hall. Autumn and the other two followed them.

'The complete isolation of the College at the time of the incident carries an obvious inference.'

Autumn's voice echoed and re-echoed in the high Hall.

'The guilty person was within these walls, was one of the known inmates on that evening. I want anyone who believes he can help in any way – especially anyone who thinks he saw or heard anything on the night in question – to come forward at once. Inspector Dorcas of the Oxford City police will interview each one of you during the course of the day. I have no doubt that with your co-operation, the situation will be resolved in a very short time.'

Or, he added to himself, as the College filed self-consciously out, a very long time. I want a drink.

Dons die and not a dog barks at their going. The rest of the world carries on. Christelow worries about his Chaucer, the Chaplain has time to be nosey, Shipton thinks about geographical essays. Autumn was cynical as he walked to the Randolph.

Nosey. Had there been an edge on what the Chaplain had said, an edge to cut someone? He had harped on those essays. Shipton . . .

The rooms. They'd been searched all right. For the Chaucer? And then Autumn thought; perhaps that's what someone wanted to suggest, to draw off speculation in another quarter.

Autumn crossed the Cornmarket as if he were dancing a minuet, advancing as the traffic permitted, retiring as it bore down. Dodging the motor-scooters, he wondered whether Vice-Chancellors could be considered under the category of repositories of tradition? They do not usually get murdered. Shop-girls in Wimbledon got murdered: or salesmen, or housewives, or policemen. The immortal, insignificant souls. Not Vice-Chancellors. You very seldom run up against murdered Vice-Chancellors, seldomer still on Chapel roofs. As he pushed open the swing doors of the Randolph, Autumn was almost indignant. Why, it was usually just a matter of circulating a description or taking a confession.

Bum saw him before he could dodge out again.

'Sher-her-lock himself! A large gin for my legal friend, miss. Sit down, old boy, sit down.'

The man of letters was in high good humour.

'A scoop. "Dessert Knife Spells Finals for M.A.Oxon." The rest of the Street nowhere.' Bum chuckled, then hiccoughed.

'Congratulations.'

Bum waved his glass.

'Wouldn't believe me, old boy. I phoned them. Put the thing over. "Effigy," they said, "how do you spell effigy?" When I got to the pay-off about it being a body, they thought I was pissed. Told me to take an aspirin and get back to the Flower Show. Telephone-reporters, you see. Not very well educated.'

Autumn received his gin, and drank half of it.

'Well,' he said, 'what next?'

'You tell me that, old boy. Jackie Sharpshoot wants some human stuff out of you for page four tomorrow – '

'I'm not feeling very human.'

'It's all a matter of imagination – '

'Go on.'

'About the case, I mean. Let your mind relax and consider the possibilities. Was the murderer a member of a vice-ring anxious to corrupt the morals of students? Was the Vice-Chancellor fiddling the examinations, and being blackmailed?'

'Oh, dear.'

'Well – you've got to use a bit of imagination, haven't you, old boy? It's the same in my line – '

'Nates, old boy – '

'Bum, old boy – '

'Bum, old boy, you're absolutely right. It's my belief,' Autumn lowered his voice, 'my firm belief that Manchip was in fact Festus Hooley, powerful leader of an Oriental tong. Yes, it all begins to fall into place – the Chinese junk moored on the Isis – the Manchurian sailors calling for rice-spirit in the corner of the bar – '

'I think they're coloured students – '

'Disguises, fiendishly clever. An ugly business, Carruthers.'

'Bum, old – '

But Autumn was gone.

Chapter 5

MRS SPECTRE was a lady immemorial and stupendous, and she lived in a very tall house in the High just opposite St Mary the Virgin. She was the owner of a bugle and a telescope, two very necessary things: for Mrs Spectre's house was a garrison, and her own quarters on the top floor, an Observation Post. There she was on watch hourly, waiting for the little men. No one – not even her lodger, Mr Singh, an Indian gentleman who spent his day wrestling with the Jewels of Literature course which reached him in weekly instalments from a correspondence college in Tring, not even her middle-aged daughter – had ever seen the little men: but this gave rise to envy rather than doubt.

It was Mrs Spectre who had spotted the fire in Radcliffe Square, and remembering this, Autumn had deserted Bum, and was now ringing Mrs Spectre's doorbell.

As he lowered his arm, a bus pulled in to the kerb, and as the brakes squealed, a voice shouted: 'Two minds with but a single!' Mr Bum was not to be shaken off.

'I hear she's a very colourful old party,' said Bum, ringing the bell again. 'You might have told me you were going to come here. Filling me up with all that stuff about junks. Those coloured chaps turned out to be medical students.'

They waited.

It was Miss Spectre who opened the door.

'Won't you come in?'

Half Miss Spectre's hair was in curlers: indeed, it was very seldom that half Miss Spectre's hair was not in curlers. Her toilette seemed to be in a constant state of preparation for some gay event which never came. Some people said it was her mother's funeral.

Autumn and Bum sat down on the horse-hair in the front room. Bum whistled through his teeth. Suddenly Miss Spectre's curlers reappeared round the door.

'The password's "pukka",' she said, and disappeared again. Bum's eyes widened.

'Nuts?'

'The place is under siege – at least, her mother thinks it is.'

'Junks again, eh?' Mr Bum winked uncertainly.

The floor shook as someone came down the stairs outside. Then the door of the room in which they were sitting opened. Mrs Spectre stood on the threshold.

'Pukka,' she announced.

'Pukka,' said Autumn.

'Pukka,' mumbled Bum.

'Excellent,' boomed the lady.

She walked over to a high-backed chair, followed by her daughter.

She sat down, and said 'At ease, Lola.'

There was a slight pause.

'Gun-cleaning,' said Mrs Spectre. 'I am in my working gear. My Number Twos.'

Autumn stole a glance at the lady's voluminously decent attire. It was faintly reminiscent of a Dickensian nurse.

'My Number Twos,' the lady said more loudly.

Bum burst out: 'How very roomy,' then went as red as fire. Mrs Spectre ignored him.

'So. You are from the *police*. The civil power are to reinforce me. It is not before time.'

Autumn coloured slightly.

'As soon as we know the situation a little more clearly, ma'am.' He coughed.

'The situation is manifestly simple. The little *men*.' Mrs Spectre stopped.

'We should be more private if your batman withdrew,' she said.

Bum's mouth was open.

'An honest enough fellow, ma'am,' said Autumn, not daring to look at him.

'*Continual* siege. A war of attrition. But they will not attack while I am on watch. My telescope.' She patted it. 'I rely upon it, absolutely. And a few sandbags. Of course,'

43

Mrs Spectre assumed the sardonic tone reserved by house-wives for defaulting shopkeepers, 'we know where they *come* from.'

A bundle of nerves, Bum dropped his pencil.

'From the *television*, in their van.'

One night, a philosophy student who had at the time been staying in the house had returned from the home of his tutor in North Oxford, where he had spent his tutorial hour watching (philosophically enough) a television parlour game based on hopscotch, in which, for an enormous fee, his tutor acted as referee. Mrs Spectre had asked him where he'd been. 'Watching the television,' he replied. 'And what is the television?' she asked. The philosophy student, a clumsy-tongued person, had begun: 'Well, it's a box, do you see, Mrs Spectre, and it's got a little square hole in it, and in the hole you see a lot of little men – ' 'So *that's* where they come from,' she had said.

Mrs Spectre now stared hard at Mr Bum.

'Are *you* from the television?'

'I'm from the *Knell*,' said Bum, knocking his pencil into the air.

'A public house?'

Autumn cleared his throat.

'I understand that things flared up the other evening, ma'am.'

'Literally. Some sort of divisionary movement. I thought for a minute they were putting down smoke.'

'Did you, um, see the little men on this occasion, ma'am?'

'One doesn't *see* them, my dear Commissioner. Their camouflage is excellent. One can only' – she dilated her eyes – 'keep one's eyes open.'

'You saw none at all.'

'None. I sounded the alarm, and was down the stairs myself in a trice. But they had taken cover and left the fire to burn out. I judged it to be a warning beacon. There were no casualties.'

Everyone fell silent.

'Of course,' Mrs Spectre said, 'we know what they *look* like.'

44

She paused impressively, then, lowering her voice to a vibrant bass, she said: 'Fat bottoms, bald heads and blazers.'

Miss Spectre patted her curlers.

'One came up to Mother in the street and interviewed her once. They had the cameras and everything. When he'd finished, he said, "On behalf of myself and the viewers I would like to say thanks most awf'ly," and Mother caught him with her bugle just underneath his ear. He wasn't expecting it, was he, Mother?'

Bum stuck his pencil in his eye.

'I *understand*,' said Mrs Spectre, 'that if one owns a conveyance there is a device one may have fitted which will permanently *put down* the television. I would not myself consider it a fair weapon. I prefer the gun, but Lola, silly girl, buys only blank cartridges.'

Autumn bit his lip.

'The reinforcements, then. You will do what you can. I have written several letters.'

She rose, and tucked the telescope briskly under her arm.

'Back to my post. We don't,' she looked without appetite at her daughter, 'want Lola *raped*.'

When they went to go out into the hall Bum and Autumn jammed each other in the door.

'Pukka,' observed Mrs Spectre, dismissively.

'Pukka weather, indeed,' chimed in her Indian lodger, who was letting himself in at the front door. 'The English climate offers a pleasing diwarsity at all seasons.'

'Pukka,' said Autumn.

'Pukka,' said Bum.

They went out.

'Cor stone me standing load,' said Bum when they stood on the pavement again. 'It is a thousand pities the public houses are shut, because I shall probably be driven to drinking lighter-fuel.'

Bum climbed on to a bus, and hung on to the rail with his forehead pressed against the cool glass. Autumn hesitated at the kerb.

He was about to cross the road, when a young man in a

commoner's gown crammed his bicycle against the kerb, and said:

'You're the policeman.'

'I am.'

'Yes, you were looking so damned bewildered.'

'I was seriously considering asking you to see me across the road.'

'They told me at the Lodge you were looking for me.'

'You're Flower. Yes. Just routine.'

'God, how marvellous. "Just routine" – they *do* say it. Well, for Christ's sake don't go into your routine here; save it for my rooms.' Flower climbed on to his bike again, and coasted along beside the Inspector, one foot against the kerb.

'I can't think why it hasn't happened before. All the intelligences in this place, crammed tight together. They get on each other's nerves. Terribly civilized, hold themselves in – but *occasionally*. The rows they have in Convocation. Symptomatic.'

'Everyone has rows.'

'Yes. But here. Just people sitting on their behinds cultivating their intelligences. They can't use up their by-products in activity like other professional people in offices and places. They don't have *things* to do.'

Flower balanced precariously.

'And vanity. This kind of closeness produces a lot of that. Megalomania, I shouldn't wonder, now and again. All the donnishness, the singularity. *You* know. Why, it might be some poor little man they won't make a lecturer – sees himself as an outcast. Slips out and does in the Vice-Chancellor as a sort of symbolic what's-it – '

'It's a question of looking into things,' said Autumn.

Flower lifted his bike through the lodge gate, and they walked round the quad towards his rooms.

'I share with Egg. Egg is continually oiling his rugger boots.'

At the foot of the staircase, Flower halted, fished in his pocket and brought out a long sickly ear-ring of purple glass which he proceeded to attach to his ear.

'Objective correlative for Egg's stiff upper lip,' he said. They went up the stairs.

He opened a door, and Autumn found himself in a room similar to a hundred other such rooms in the University. The wallpaper was yellow, there were two old-fashioned armchairs which had been reupholstered in a rather stern shade of maroon, and a sofa the same. There were a dark brown sideboard, two stained tables (one round, one square), and a huge deal bookcase not quite full of books. Dirty teacups from the previous day were crowded into the fireplace, and on a plate sat the remains of several Eccles cakes. Membership cards of various University clubs stood on the mantlepiece, and disposed amongst them were a quart pot, a photograph of a girl, some pipes, a small plaque which read DÉFENSE DE SE PENCHER AU DEHORS, and a piece of eighteenth-century porcelain. On the walls there were three or four pictures, and if Autumn had not known that the room was shared by two people – Egg, the other tenant, had scrambled up from the sofa where he had been reading *Bulldog Drummond*, as they entered – the pictures would have suggested it.

There was one above the fireplace, a monochrome mass of shapes – rhomboids, octagons, circles – on a dark ground. Adjacent to it, on the wall by the window, hung a colourful scene cut from a Christmas issue of *Brogue*, inscribed in bold letters at the bottom, 'A Stirrup Cup'. In much the same vein, a brownish study of a recluse toasting a kipper before a dying fire under the scrutiny of an Alsatian dog, hung on the middle wall. It was flanked by a Salvador Dali. Antagonism was at its most acute on the wall across the room from the window, where a Spy cartoon of Sir William Joynson-Hicks hung directly above a graphite head representing *Anathema*.

'Well,' said Flower, 'this is Egg. My chum Egg. Very fashionable chap, Egg. He wanted to cover the furniture in black calico – '

'You're a bloody liar,' said Egg.

' – whereas my own simple tastes warm to the tear-starting depiction of the Alsatian yonder – '

'That's my bloody picture,' said Egg.

47

'Egg, I want you to meet Inspector Autumn. Mr Egg possesses the oiliest pair of rugger boots in the world, Inspector.'

Egg shook hands with Autumn. They were big red hands, and he was wearing a check suit with narrow trousers and a heavily slitted jacket.

'With half an eye,' continued Flower in the manner of a guide at the National Gallery, 'a man on a galloping horse could see that Egg is from the Shires. Most of the people Egg knows *are* men on galloping horses.'

'They ride a bit, you bloody fool,' said Egg. Egg's face hung down on either side of his chin as if he were sucking boiled sweets.

'Well, Inspector, ask away. Don't mind my chum – we shall be perfectly incomprehensible if we stick to the polysyllables.'

Autumn sat down.

'No,' he said, 'you tell me things. I've nothing specific to ask.'

'You saw Mrs Spectre? I was wondering whether she might have spotted the bloke as well as the bonfire that night –'

'No.'

'He must have been quick, then. She's got a bright red glittering eye, and a telescope, and she doesn't miss much. Of course, you know all about my thing, finding the book –'

'That was a shock for you, wasn't it?'

'I went cold all over.'

'Of course,' said Autumn, 'we don't know how the book stuff mixes in with the killing –'

'They *feel* connected. Going round knocking off Vice-Chancellors, burning books –'

'He was a bit of an odd sort, wasn't he, Manchip?'

'Oh, lord, yes. What they call a character.'

'Bolshie,' said Egg.

'Oh, Christ, *no*,' shouted Flower, ecstatically, 'do they still use that word?'

'Mr – whatsisname – Undigo seemed to like him.'

'Oh, sure. He's a – yes, that incredible word – bolshie,

too,' said Flower. 'He got Stanley Matthews his honorary D. Phil., didn't he, Egg?'

'Did he?' asked Egg, surprised. 'Bloody good man him.'

Flower bellowed with laughter.

'And his pa poulticed those boils –'

'On Marx's bottom,' Autumn nodded. 'Yes, he mentioned it last night. The young Marx carbuncular,' he added, wondering if he was striking the undergraduate note. 'Yes, he stuck up for Manchip.'

'I bet the others were running him down, weren't they?' said Flower. 'Except Fairlight, of course!'

For the first time in their short acquaintanceship, Autumn saw that Mr Flower was put out. He had grabbed Egg's football boots from the graphite *Anathema* on which they stood, and hurled them into the fireplace and the Eccles cakes.

'You young swine,' shouted Egg, 'I'd just oiled those.'

'Fairlight, oh no, not Fairlight. He wouldn't run Manchip down, not on your life. Most of them disliked Manchip – he *was* dislikeable – but Fairlight would have kissed his bottom and thanked him for the opportunity. You see, Manchip had a casting vote in the election of a new English professor to the Rockinge Chair – and he'd told Fairlight he'd give it to him. That jolly old general practitioner Bow-Parley was the only other nomination, and Manchip couldn't stand the sight of him. There was a dead heat when they had the election, and Manchip was supposed to be making up his mind this week about where his casting vote should go. Oh no, you wouldn't get Fairlight to run *him* down. Such a pity, though, because it lets him out of the list of suspects –'

'Oh, we can't be sure of that,' murmured Autumn. 'But how is it you know so much about the internal politics of professorial appointments? It's not usual with undergraduates, is it?'

Autumn was surprised to see Flower blush.

'We – Fairlight and I – have a friend in common. A lady. He tells her and she tells me – in order to impress me. A dizzy schoolgirl, Inspector' – Flower's enunciation became artificial as his embarrassment increased – 'one Balboa Tomlin.'

'Hot-bottomed little mare,' said Egg.

The Inspector said tactfully: 'I've never come across a body on a Chapel roof before.'

'I dare say that's how you'll catch him,' said Flower. He sat back in his chair, pausing as a young person will pause while he ponders the quality of some older man's mind, arrogantly uncertain that what he has to say will be received in its proper terms.

'What I mean is, it's a link with a certain kind of mind, isn't it? To make *use* of such a circumstance – that's the clue. It's not just oddity lets a man do a thing like that on a chapel roof. It's more likely to be enormous presence of mind – and presence of mind in *that* degree, well it's going to show –'

'It might.'

'I don't say it'll show so obviously that if you line us all up you'll spot him first go. After all, detection is a specialist's job' – Flower conceded it – 'but I bet it'll be there in *detectable* quantity.'

When Autumn was standing at the door again, Flower said: 'And there's another thing I want to say. I'm frightened. When I found that book and all the pages gone, I was scared. I felt as if someone had been swinging me round by the ankle and had suddenly let me go. A sort of feeling of everything spinning off – And then Manchip on top of it. Honestly, it makes my scalp creep.'

'Bloody queer myself,' said Egg.

'Good bye,' said the Inspector.

There were a couple of letters in the lodge for Autumn, which he picked up and took with him into the nearest tea-shop.

While he waited for the tea to come, he read one of them. It was from his wife. Already the news from Ruislip had an outer-space flavour. That his wife had pruned the rambler-roses was of the order of things; but that there *were* rambler-roses, and that pruning went on, sounded a key that was momentarily unfamiliar. Autumn read on hastily until, at the end of the catalogue of talks over the fence with the man next door whose wireless made the dog bark, a detente with the painter whose bill had exceeded his firm estimate, and sundry good wishes of a personal and affectionate nature, Autumn felt a little less like a man suddenly lost to the world in exotic savannah.

He took a bite of toast, and ripped open the other envelope, pulling out a single sheet of paper. And then he groaned, dropping the sheet on to the tablecloth. It was unsigned, and bore a single sentence pasted up in letters cut from a newspaper. It said: ASK DIM ABOUT THE NOTE.

'Something else?' asked the waitress.

'I shouldn't be surprised,' Autumn said rudely.

Chapter 6

Autumn came out of the shop pushing the sheet of paper into his pocket. As he turned into the street, he met Dorcas, the local Inspector.

'You've got jam round your mouth – no, there,' said Dorcas. Autumn wiped his lip.

Dorcas was a little round man with a worried face and a small tuft of moustache like a damp toothbrush. He was carrying a cardboard file under one arm, and a brown paper parcel under the other. His fingers were stained with Biro.

'I've checked on them,' said Dorcas, as they strolled in the direction of Warlock. 'I've got their answers here' – he twitched his elbow – 'hopeless, of course. Keeping your mind clear and getting them to stick to the essentials, very difficult. I don't like it a bit. The case, you know. Not a bit. Mixed up, all mixed up. Nasty. You know the only way is to ask questions, we always ask questions, but you don't feel it gets you very far, do you? I must say' – and he agitated his little moustache until it seemed to revolve – 'I've never been on a job as |out of the way as this. I have not. You've got a wasp round you – no, there,' he said.

'They are all in their rooms, they say. Well, I dare say, quite likely, but how do *we* know? . . . Rankine says Lord Pinner was drinking whisky with him, but how –?'

'Seen them all?' asked Autumn.

'I haven't got round to Fairlight, yet.' Dorcas revolved his moustache, and picked a hair off Autumn's shoulder. 'I actually went to dinner there, once. I wonder who the hell *did* it?'

Inside the lodge, Autumn took the file from his colleague and read all the statements rapidly through. Dorcas watched him.

'Well? Any ideas? I didn't care for that bloody Russian. He was extraordinarily truculent when I asked him the questions. He wouldn't have got off so light with the

Ogpu.' Dorcas was irritable. 'But take a look at this – I'd like to know where he got hold of that.'

Inspector Dorcas turned slightly pink as he handed over the brown paper parcel to Autumn.

'Dirt. He didn't get that out of the Bodleian Library, I'll be bound.'

Autumn unwrapped the book. It was in mint condition.

'Well, well,' he exclaimed, '*The Memoirs of Fanny Hill*. Have you read it, Inspector?'

Dorcas's moustache revolved.

'I've looked at it. It's worse than the postcards at Brighton. I told him I'd have to take it. He's not in bloody Russia now.'

Dorcas shot a glance at Autumn, and his moustache ticked over like a combustion engine. 'Who d'you think writes 'em?' But Autumn did not seem to hear.

'No,' said Autumn, 'don't destroy it. Just hang on to it for a bit.'

Dorcas jigged about on one foot.

'What do you want me to do with it, then? I've got a lot of young constables down at the Station. I can't take it *home* –'

'We'll give it to Tantalum to keep for us.'

Autumn put his head through the lodge window, and handed the parcel to the porter.

'Now,' said Autumn to Dorcas, 'who's Dim?'

'How d'you mean?'

Tantalum came out to pin up a notice advertising the time of the funeral service for Manchip which was to be held in the Chapel the following day. He said: 'That'll be Mr Fairlight, sir. 'E's Mr Dimoke Fairlight, so he's Dim for short with 'is friends.'

'Is he? Well, since we want a word with him, perhaps you'll tell us where his rooms are?'

'I'll do better than that, sir. I'll tell you where you can *find* him.'

Tantalum looked from one Inspector to the other with that air of suppressed climax seldom disdained, even in homely matters, by members of the simple classes.

'His rooms is across the quad, but he won't be there.

53

He'll be down at Walpurgis. He usually takes 'is tea down there with a Miss Tomlin, a very nice young lady indeed.'

They set off for Walpurgis Hall, largest and most fashionable of the women's Colleges. Reaching Carfax, the centre of the town, where the High runs off into the mercantile fastness of St Ebbe's (a waste land of shoe shops, small pubs, and Americans), they turned left into St Aldate's, and came down that delicate slope where Christ Church turns its great white nose aristocratically skywards and Pembroke affects not to notice.

'Look out – there's a pram wants to get by,' said Dorcas, scampering along beside Autumn. 'Whoops. You got anything on this Fairlight? We ought to cooperate.'

Autumn showed him the letter. Dorcas handed it back hurriedly.

'Dim, yes, that'll be him, I suppose. But I leave it entirely to you, old friend. You can handle that one. I don't know when I've been mixed up in anything like this before, s'elp me God, I don't.'

They entered Walpurgis through a red-tiled lodge, and Autumn rather shyly pushed open a glass-paned door which gave access to the porteress's office. Dorcas stood half in and half out of the doorway, not knowing what to do with his hands, and pursing his lips as if about to whistle. The territory was terrifyingly female.

As soon as he was inside the office, Autumn knew he had been precipitate. The porteress still held the electric shaver with which she had been scything her chin. There was more than coolness in the directions she gave Autumn, and they were barely three yards from her door before the razor was buzzing contemptuously.

The policemen walked through the huge single quadrangle of Walpurgis, by lawns and gravelled walks, populous with litter-bins and tennis-courts. There was nothing here of the quaint, the cramped or the medieval: Walpurgis was large and airy and modern, and had been designed exclusively for big, normal, strenuous, red-legged young women with glasses.

54

These were the daughters of BBC comedians and rural deans, London editors and Inspectors of taxes, novelists and policemen (the Commissioner's daughter was at Walpurgis), commission agents and superannuated rajahs. They spent three years at Walpurgis, prodding the cruxes out of Beowulf and the dates out of Fisher, rowing in the Ladies' Eight, playing Cleopatra for the OUDS, and being taken to nine or ten Commemoration Balls in succession, returning themselves on each of the nine or ten mornings severely intact.

Many of them were now recreating themselves in a cheerful and ladylike fashion, romping about after tennis-balls. Others were taking tea on the grass, grouping themselves round divers slim young men; in relation to these slim young men, the ladies wore so much the air of cannibals that it was surprising that the young men were not scattering for their lives.

As the Inspectors traversed the vast quadrangle, passing along the broad asphalt of Pankhurst Way, Dorcas said: 'Ever noticed the way they never have outside conveniences in ladies' institutions?'

Autumn shook his head.

'They never do, though.'

They walked on in silence.

'Funny –'

Square casement on square casement, frilled with flowered curtaining, punctured the pink brick of Walpurgis. In every window the back of a postcard reproduction of Van Gogh's *Sunflowers* was clearly distinguishable. From time to time, windows were thrown up, and damp undergarments manifested themselves on ledges. The silence of Autumn and Dorcas deepened, and became a rampart.

Dorcas suddenly started to edge Autumn to the grass verge, as an oddly dressed figure approached on a bicycle. It wore the brief variety of knicker favoured by rowing men, a hairy pullover, a scarf wrapped many times round its neck after the fashion of the giraffe-necked women of Borneo, an eton crop, and pince-nez. In one hand it held a megaphone.

'What-ho, the coppers!' it boomed, nearly falling off

55

the bike as it waved the megaphone. 'Any of my gels in trouble?'

Autumn bit back the courteous 'sir'.

'No, ma'am, we're just looking for a gentleman.'

'Don't tell me – Fairlight. I know. The girl Tomlin's rooms are over there.' She pointed. 'Bloody fool that man. He'll be putting her in pod one of these days; then there'll be a stink. Why doesn't he *row*?'

She clambered on to her bike again, and darted a sharp look at Dorcas.

'You suffer from stomach trouble, don't you? Try a twenty-mile walk and a couple of bottles of beer.'

Dorcas stared after her.

'An educated woman. Thank God my girl's going in to be a stenographer.' Their shoes echoed on the polished parquet as they entered the building. Young women darted in and out of doors with boiling kettles in their hands: the corridors swam in a strange effluvia compounded in equal parts of floor-polish, cosmetics, and cosy secrets.

When they came to Balboa's door, they heard singing.

'We'd better knock loud,' said Dorcas uncomfortably, 'and then wait a bit.'

Autumn rapped on the door.

'Enter,' shouted a male voice, and they went in. They found Fairlight staring hard at a mirror, examining his teeth. Behind a further door the singing continued, and the sound of splashing from the same quarter suggested that Balboa was bathing.

'I saw you talking to Corker,' grinned Fairlight, turning from the mirror. 'Isn't she *exactly* like Boris Karloff – a sort of *rowing* Boris Karloff? I have a plan for rendering her down and distributing her in capsule form to debilitated gym mistresses.'

'Who is it?' screamed Balboa from the bathroom.

'The police,' bellowed Fairlight, then roared with laughter at the words.

'Tell them not to arrest you till I come and watch,' shouted Balboa, and went on singing.

'Tirra lirra,' sang Balboa, 'tirra lirra lirra,' and she

56

soaped one olive breast with a will, transforming it into the agreeable likeness of a coffee ice-cream with a cherry on top.

Balboa sang very flat like a small child, in a piping treble, and huskily. She shrilled and twittered as she rubbed away at her body – a body that was about as yellow as old parchment, but certainly no yellower.

She had tied up her blonde hair like the tail of a horse, so that it titupped as she piped, shook as she plunged the violet soap into the depths of her armpits, lay down along the sallow nape of her neck as she leant forward and picked at her toenails.

It was an odd thing, the effect of that blonde hair. On its own it might have passed for a very decent sort of straw colour: cut short, you might have played tennis in it. But taken in conjunction with the olive skin – well, there could be no thought of tennis with the olive skin, for the olive skin would certainly not know the rules. Set as it was over the dun-coloured body, the hair was whiter – like sand or faded lemonade-powder. And the skin too benefited from the contrast: on its umbery own it might have taken you no further than Hampstead, but with the hair, your destination grew remote.

This couldn't have been better, for international parentage has been the basis of all true social success at Oxford these many years. Balboa, therefore, had never even had to try.

Her father was Balboa Jack Tomlin, as notable a procurer in the Barcelona of his day as ever had his shoes cleaned on the Ramblas. Some of the oldest-established houses in Southern Europe had relied on Jack. His deliverly way with yearning daughters of small-town manufacturers had permitted them to accept their destination as a sort of accolade.

Yet he had barely found time to set a tooth-pick to the gold-filled smile he had flashed Balboa's mother before she, Cretan prestidigitatrice that she was, had procured *him*.

The couple stayed on in Barcelona for a while, but Jack's touch had gone. His Cretan bride had crumpled

57

his conceit as easily as she crumpled a handkerchief in her golden hand, and without it he was as helpless as a tight-rope walker suddenly fearful of heights. The Madames along the Spanish coast, and as far north as Marseille, no longer smiled as the boatloads from Barcelona snugged in-to the wharfs: *por Dios!*, they complained, the goods were not worth the freight charges, let alone the percentage.

A procurer's career is highly remunerative, fanciful and short. With an effort of self-contemplation that transcend-ed vanity, Jack realized that his career was over. His assets, he decided, must now be ploughed back into digni-fied and (if possible) lucrative retirement.

It had to be a restaurant, and Jack had suggested the Left, but his wife said no, the South Bank, because there would surely be a market for *tortillas* and *abondigas* among the hard-up half-educated who queued for the gallery at the Old Vic.

But – as it turned out – the customers never really cared for the oil, preferring (as, in a moment of environmental insight that was to make him a fortune, Jack realized) grease.

Out of the decision taken that moment there rose an empire. The aroma of the Tomlin Chip Emporia spread waxily from Tooting into Streatham, from Collier's Wood into Clapham, covering at last, as chip-shop followed chip-shop in adipose succession, the entire face of South London.

To Jack it must sometimes have seemed that fish and chips were South London's safety valve against immoral-ity: the great natural yearning for the commodity matched in primitive voracity that entertained by the matelots of the *vieux Port* for Neapolitan virgins.

Soon the Tomlin Hygienic Crisp ('Have a Tomlin – they're *pure*'), now so much a feature of our smart bars, had taken the imagination of the whole country, and Jack, a little to his surprise, found himself golfing at Sun-ningdale.

Balboa had been born at the Tomlins' Chertsey place the week following Jack's Viscountcy, and she had been brought up to a code of such staggering inhibition that (as

Jack's wife was fond of saying) it could only have been devised by a pimp. After Chertsey and a Belgian convent, it was small wonder that Balboa thought of Oxford – as she thought of it now, lying in her bath – as a soft candle flame, warming and liberating her enormously amalgamated blood.

Dorcas said: 'We have to do this, ask the questions. Though I don't suppose,' he said to Fairlight, 'if you'd killed the Vice-Chancellor you'd tell us.'

Dorcas had completed a rather rabbity questionnaire. Fairlight's account of himself and his actions at the relevant times had been no more and no less illuminating than the others.

Balboa came out of the bathroom wearing black trousers and a waistcoat, and Fairlight introduced the policemen.

Autumn said to Fairlight: 'Manchip dying was rough luck on you, wasn't it? Didn't he back you for the Professorship?'

A fragment of Fairlight's self-possession fell out, like a badly glazed pane in a highly coloured window.

'Why, yes,' said Fairlight, slowly, 'yes, he did.'

'He had the casting vote, if I understand it –'

'He did, he did.'

'Which he wasn't going to give to the other nominee, the Chaplain?' Dim seemed curiously disconcerted. Apart from the occasions when he suspected someone was laughing at the diminutive form of his own first name, he seldom looked like that. That Autumn knew about Manchip's preference should hardly have surprised him – since Fairlight himself had never ceased to proclaim it in the Warlock Senior Common Room.

'No, he wasn't,' he said shortly.

'Well,' and Autumn was smiling politely, 'you had a plain motive for keeping him alive. Always supposing,' he added pleasantly, 'that circumstances were as you say they were –'

'Why should they change?'

Autumn raised his eyebrows.

59

'Change?'

'No change. I was his man.' Fairlight seemed annoyed, and it made him pale. 'Manchip wanted me to have the Chair. Now he's dead.'

Fairlight spread his hands in a gesture of resignation. He really meant it. And yet a second later he was registering a more deliberate variety of unconcern: the sort of unconcern with which he sometimes accompanied little jokes he made about "Dim".

Balboa spoke. Her voice had a timbre and a pitch – high and decisive and clear, but by no means loud – which made people look round.

'Perhaps the policemen have finished, and we can have tea somewhere.'

Dorcas accepted the inflection which so unerringly cast himself and his colleague below stairs.

'It has to be done, you see, Miss. The darta. Certain amount of inconvenience, but the situation –'

'Miss Tomlin is an intelligent young lady, and understands very well,' smiled Autumn. 'We shall walk with you as far as the gate.'

'Escorted,' murmured Miss Tomlin.

They all walked out of the building into the quadrangle.

'You'd think,' said Fairlight, as the heads of the girls sitting on the grass turned towards them, 'that dons were film-stars. It's always the same, Inspector – at lectures one almost expects warm autograph books to be produced from navy-blue knicker legs. I am told by my pupils that certain ladies sit in the front row when McCann is denouncing Restoration morality *simply* so they shall be spat on.'

As they approached the lodge, Autumn was reflecting how to put the question. If it misfired, he wanted to be able to retreat in good order.

'It's the painstaking search for detail, the patient sifting of seemingly unrelated fact, that counts in police-work,' Dorcas said rather mournfully.

'How wretched for you,' Balboa murmured.

The direct approach, thought Autumn, that's the ticket. Get *some* reaction – and don't press it.

The large white face of the porteress hovered in the porch. She disappeared into her office, banging the door, and the air was pungent with after-shave lotion.

Autumn said casually: 'Can I see that note?'

Fairlight turned his head so quickly that he twisted his neck, and put a hand up to the pain. His face turned very red.

Dorcas scanned the horizon for a bus: 'Where they all get to, I don't know —'

Balboa said quickly: 'Notes? Banknotes?' She looked from Fairlight to Autumn, a soldier appraising situations in the field.

The colour in Fairlight's face was normal again. He began quietly: 'Note? Do you mean did Manchip ever send me a note? It was only a verbal —'

But Autumn, after the one quick look he had given Fairlight as he asked the question, had also become preoccupied with buses.

'There's one —' he said, and started moving into the road.

'Quick!' The policemen ran.

'Thanks,' Autumn shouted over his shoulder, 'for helping us. Much appreciated.' He waved hastily, and climbed on to the already moving vehicle.

As the bus reached the shallow brow of Folly Bridge, Autumn, hanging on to the rail beside his colleague, looked back. Fairlight and Balboa still stood where they had been deserted so precipitately. As Autumn watched, they turned and walked slowly away.

Yes, thought Autumn, *yes*.

Chapter 7

'What was that you asked him?'

Dorcas made a feint of trying to pay the conductor as they stood on the platform. The bus stopped outside the Town Hall, and Dorcas scrambled after Autumn with the fourpence still in his hand.

'Just about the letter I got.'

The eye of the bus-conductor dwindled, swallowed up in the massive detail of the Cornmarket traffic. Dorcas looked at his watch.

'Cell inspection in ten minutes.' He pushed the file firmly into the crook of Autumn's arm. 'You'd better have these. We'll meet tomorrow, eh? And, um, check.' His evenings were spent profitably, for his wife organised whist-drives, and he was a champion. 'Slow business. Well, ta-ta. See you in the "nick".' And with this grave-yard attempt at professional pleasantry, departed.

Autumn now looked at his own watch. Five-thirty. He remembered a lecture-list he had seen in Warlock. Mc-Cann – denouncing Restoration morality – he'd be doing it now. He'd be finished inside twenty minutes, and they could both go and have a look at Bodley.

Autumn turned into the High Street, and set off briskly towards the Schools, where lectures took place.

Had Fairlight reacted? Undoubtedly. Was he conceal-ing something? It looked like it.

A newsvendor outside a bank wailed passionately 'Death, destruction, divorce and mur – *ur* – ur – der!' as if they had all happened to him. Autumn almost jumped.

Always the same on the first day, he thought, as he crossed Alfred Street – too tense. He gazed at the tall pin-nacles of St Mary the Virgin, and crossed to the other side of the High, intent on seeing where the bonfire had taken place.

When he entered Radcliffe Square the sun was stream-ing across the grey cobbles, so that each cobble threw a shadow, and the whole square looked like a scale model of some anonymous countryside. Autumn walked across the thin green grass round the Radcliffe Camera, and came to a place under one of the windows, where the flagstones were stained brown.

He scuffed his toe moodily on the blackened surface, and he thought of murders – on the South Downs, where the wind blows through the gorse bushes, in Welsh villages beneath slagheaps, at the sea-side (so often at the sea-side), at Maidenhead, at Coventry. There is a flavour, a common flavour, he thought, and one looks for the same things – self-seeking and fear.

Inspector Autumn sighed as he strolled back towards the High Street. To look for such things in Oxford – it was not good. But perhaps the Commissioner is right, and the destruction and even the murder is the work of altruistic if misguided men.

I wish I could believe it, thought the Inspector.

'Gown, sir,' said a stocky, wire-haired terrier of a man, as Autumn walked into the vestibule of the Schools.

'No gown,' said the Inspector, 'police.' The terrier looked doubtful. 'I am meeting Dr McCann.' Autumn dug into his pocket and brought out an old season-ticket. 'Scotland Yard, Scotland Yard.'

'Ah, yes, sir,' said the terrier. 'You'll find him in the North Hall.'

Autumn's feet echoed like a company of soldiers, and he thought that the marble corridors of the Schools looked like nothing so much as a well scrubbed jakes. He found the North Hall, pushed open the double doors, and made his way to an empty seat at the back of the room.

The voice of McCann rolled across a black sea of gowns. Most of the female students seemed to be towards the front, but the Inspector was too far away to see clearly whether McCann was spitting.

'It was indeed, then, a comedy of manners, a comedy – if you will allow it – of bad-manners. The dramatists mirrored and re-rendered the hedonism of the times. We do not condemn them for that – how should we? – for a dramatist, no less than anyone else, belongs to his own age.

No, if we condemn, we must condemn the things mirror-
ed, the punks and the pox, the keepers and the roaring-
boys. . . .'

McCann had an Inverness-shire accent, and it seemed
to give his words a relish. A man in a scholar's gown near
Autumn wriggled appreciatively.

'A handful of leisured, educated people, intent upon
diversion. That was England. While the rest of the coun-
try, the millions, were thankful simply to exist –'

Progressive, thought Autumn.

To left and right of the Inspector it was all going down.
'Condemn punks . . . handful of educ. people . . . rest of
country . . .' Scribble, scribble, scribble.

Six struck, and the Pierian spring was turned off. The
male undergraduates strolled through the open doors with
their hands in their pockets, yawning; the ladies engaged
each other in earnest conversation. Autumn continued to
sit, waiting for McCann, who was at the far end of the room.

'Please!'

Autumn looked round. Behind him stood a young man
with a square head, prominent ears, and rimless spec-
tacles.

'Please!' said the young man again, very abruptly.
'You are the Police?'

'Certainly,' Autumn replied good humouredly.

'You not only respect property – it is orthodox in your
country – but you do not condone corruption?'

'I must attend,' said Autumn, 'your next lecture.'

'Please!' continued the young man peremptorily, hold-
ing up one finger. 'Having established this, I now ask you
to report your colleague, or make it a matter of your per-
sonal intervention to recover from him a book of which I
am the owner.'

The Russian laddy, thought the Inspector.

'Liberality,' said Autumn, entering into the rather
didactic spirit of the conversation, 'should not be confused
with licence.'

'You generalize. The book is mine.'

Archangel had no accent to speak of, apart from his
preciseness.

'It might be of interest to me to know where and how you came by this book.'

'Its provenance would not arouse your interest at all. Death,' said the Russian from Highgate, 'is your territory.'

'Whose territory,' responded Autumn, who had read parodies of the Russian drama at the back of the *New Statesman*, 'is it not?'

'You will die,' promised the Russian without malice. 'I, too. It is not worthy of remark. Meanwhile, there is my book.'

'It has been confiscated.' Autumn recalled films. 'In the best interests of the community. The – um – Central Office will examine it. There will be interrogations –'

'Can I have a receipt?'

'You can have a thick ear,' said Autumn. 'Now clear off.'

McCann approached, and Archangel, after hovering a few seconds, departed.

'Is there further news?' McCann enquired.

How his gown and black cap suited him, the Inspector thought. McCann's was the kind of face that never looks well-shaven; it was pale, and over all the hair-bearing quarters of the face it seemed as if, not a razor, but a brush loaded with midnight blue, had passed. McCann had left the small patches of hair on each cheekbone uncropped; above these, his eyes sank backwards. It was a long cold face, and looked like a Dalmatian's – without the spots, but with that animal's undeniable air of hungry premonition.

'Yes. Yes,' said McCann. 'Certainly you should have a look at the Stack. I do not think, however, that you will find much of direct assistance there, because it is obvious, as you will see, that anyone with a little circumspection, could have got *at* it.'

'The Stack?'

'You will not be familiar with the terminology. The Stack is the major corpus of books in the Bodleian, and is contained in the area beneath Radcliffe Square. It would be impossible, as you will readily appreciate, to display so great a number of books on the open shelves. Even if it were desirable. Yes. Anyone could have got *at* the Stack – the assumption has always been that no one would want to. One cannot, after all, steal a First Folio and hope to sell it.'

'One can burn it,' Autumn murmured.

'There is an ordinary deal door across the stairway leading down into the Stack from the Old Library, and that was open all day to allow my staff to get the books as they were required. And to be perfectly' – he said 'pairfectly' – 'truthful, I do not suppose it was ever locked at night either. Though now, of course, it is locked all the time.

'Of course, if anyone was seen walking out of Bodley with books that obviously belonged to the Library he would be stopped. But this is a town where everyone has an armful of books, and again the assumption has been that no one will want to walk out with books that do not belong to him.

'I can well understand – *well* understand – that someone from outside the University might regard the absence of invigilation in these matters as somewhat lax. But you must remember that availability of books is one of the fundamental requirements of this society. No one even thinks about it. . . .'

They had come out into the High Street.

'We have not bargained for irrational behaviour. I find that not unreasonable. Now, of course, anyone bringing books with him *into* the Library must deposit them with the doorkeeper and collect them as he goes out. I recognize the necessity.'

McCann loped laboriously along, as if the High were a steep hill. Even as he stooped, he was taller than Autumn.

He smiled bleakly when the Inspector, exploring other avenues, referred to the Rockinge Chair.

'Manchip preferred Fairlight. He did not care for Bow-Parley, possibly because Bow-Parley is a Baconian, the sort of person' – McCann turned towards the Inspector as if to note whether he was up to such academic distinctions – 'who always *is* a Baconian. Manchip was a High Churchman and took his religion seriously. I have heard him say more than once – for he was a malicious man – that the difference between Bow-Parley's membership of the Church of England and his membership of Brooks' was the subscription. That may have been another cause of disaffection. Even I as a Presbyterian had more in common with Manchip. Thoroughpacedness, perhaps.'

What a far-away sort of chap you are, thought Autumn. McCann was extremely informative and talked fluently without prompting – but there was no core to his conversation. Like a gramophone record, the *person* was absent. What really engaged him, the Inspector wondered. Progressive morality?

'But now, with Manchip dead' – they entered the quadrangle by the Divinity Schools – 'it will be difficult to say. Fairlight is left rather in the air. Poor Fairlight,' McCann continued, smiling faintly, 'is the only man in Warlock who has not congratulated Christelow on the literary discovery of the century. Fairlight does not care much for Chaucer, or, indeed, for anyone writing prior to the nativity of Mr T.S. Eliot. An irrational position' – McCann almost began to inhabit his own conversation – 'which he is never called upon to defend since he has never openly admitted adopting it.'

Manchip wasn't the only malicious one, Autumn thought.

McCann led the way through a room where visitors were examining missals and autographs. In one corner stood a small counter, where postcard reproductions of pictures in the Ashmolean and views of Oxford were displayed on a revolving stand. McCann loped on into a panelled passageway. Set into the panelling was a small door which he unlocked and pushed open.

'Down here' – he pointed to a narrow staircase which dropped down below floor level – 'is the Stack. It expands in a system of galleries beneath Radcliffe Square.'

'Right. Let's get down and have a look.'

There are many silences in the Bodleian Library, from the impure quiet of the Camera, where crepe soles squeak and lawyers breathe heavily, to the analeptic calm of Duke Humphrey. But no silence compares with the silence of the Stack. As Autumn and McCann went down, it crept into the Inspector's ears like cotton-wool; it was so tangible that he felt it clip his body like a quicksand.

The smell was indescribable – the stink of books pressed together in uninterrupted embraces for centuries, headier than bergamot or balm, and rank as death. As the two men filed through the leaning walls of calf, the smell and the silence lay about them like a thick, invisible fog.

In a few moments McCann said: 'We are at the centre of the system now. From this point lanes radiate to the circumference where a single circular gallery circum-navigates the whole. In plan, it is something like the spokes and rim of a cartwheel. . .'

The words expired as they were spoken, so absorbent was the air. As if, Autumn reflected, the books were jealous of any sound save the inaudible clamour of their own pages.

'Not very cheerful.'

He peered about him in the yellow light which came from single naked bulbs.

'Oh, one cultivates a taste for it, no doubt.'

They moved along the lane.

'But it is a strange place,' said McCann meditatively. 'One seldom comes down oneself. Books, books, books. . . .'

A mouse ran across the dusty gallery in front of them, squeezing its fat small body underneath the lowest shelf.

They came to the end of the lane, where it joined the outer gallery. Either side of them rack upon rack of books curved away into the yellow darkness.

'Yes, the door above is now locked, and I hold the key. A pity, but the exigencies –'

Autumn suddenly turned his head sideways; as abrupt-ly, McCann had at the same instant stopped talking. They stood immobile. After a few seconds, McCann turned to the Inspector. Then, very quietly, he said: 'Did I –'

He broke off, turning his head again to listen.

The silence rolled round them, pillowing their ears like velvet, soft and deep. Neither man stirred.

There was a creak. The kind of anonymous creak that is heard in the night. Then the silence was deeper than ever.

Autumn turned, and walked swiftly back to the centre of the Stack. He stood there for a few moments, then, very slowly, put his head round the wall of books. The gallery he stared down was empty.

He looked back to where McCann was still standing, his head cocked birdlike to one side, listening. Autumn started to walk back. As he reached McCann, the Librarian put his finger to his lips.

Something moved, halted, moved again. The silence ached.

'The outer gallery,' suddenly shouted McCann, and started to run. As McCann moved, there was a scurry further away in the Stack, but the close air sucked all direction from it.

Autumn dived back to the centre, ran down one of the lanes, came into the outer gallery, and raced into McCann running in the opposite direction.

'The other way, the other way –' shouted the Librarian.

'*Damn*,' said Autumn, and turned about.

They ran together round the outer gallery. Autumn's elbow caught the spine of a jutting book, and it fell to the floor like a cannon ball.

They stopped. No sound.

Autumn darted back to the staircase, and bounded up the steps to the doorway. He halted precipitately at the top, looking left and right. McCann scrambled up the stairs behind him, pushed past, and ran into the room where the exhibits stood.

'Not here –' he shouted to Autumn.

A woman and a little girl stood in front of the revolving stand. People stood browsing over the glass cases.

'Outside –' said McCann.

Autumn followed him to the door. In the quadrangle there were half a dozen saunterers. Autumn turned and went slowly back into the lower room. McCann followed.

'*Clean* away,' said McCann, panting between his teeth.

The Inspector went over to the counter and questioned

the attendant. No, he had seen nothing. A janitor was sent for, and he and the counter-attendant went down into the Stack, while Autumn and McCann waited at the head of the stairs.

'I'll have this Library closed, I'll have it – I'll have it –' McCann could barely speak for anger, and Autumn felt a twinge of surprise. He had been so controlled.

The counter-man and the janitor came up the stairs. They had found nothing.

'Confounded behaviour,' McCann said, and his face was cold again, his eyes submerged. 'If more books are gone –'

As they walked back to Warlock, McCann said nothing.

Autumn could not sleep. In the small hours he rolled about in bed, and his eyes ached. He cursed the moonlight which struck through the small monkish window, and he felt more and more like a novice who has been bedevilled, in the course of his translations, by inscrutable runes.

The events of the day occurred and recurred to him, over and over again, and when he slept at last, his dreams were gigantic.

Once, he seemed to be looking at a vast television screen on which Balboa in a hip bath was having her back scrubbed by Dorcas. Behind her the figure of Fairlight, the New Critic, rose up to a terrifying height, and he was shouting through a megaphone, 'In the circumstances, in the changed circumstances, in the *very* changed circumstances –' And then suddenly McCann the Librarian was dancing a stately gavotte with Mrs Spectre, and the head of Mrs Spectre leaning over his shoulder seemed to be nodding at Autumn as it had nodded to him during his interview that afternoon. She said something, whispering at first, and finally shouting in a voice that cracked and rolled like thunder. She said it over and over again, something she had said to Autumn that very day, something he had forgotten.

'Yes,' said Autumn in his dream. 'Yes, that was it, that was what you said this afternoon. I will remember, I will, I will.'

'Nine o'clock sir,' he heard the scout saying, and with a start the Inspector sat up. He was awake, and it was daylight, and of the dream of Mrs Spectre he remembered not a word.

Chapter 8

THE tall black doors stood open, and the organ's ruminative soft requiem stole out over the mourners as they filed into the quadrangle. Penguins and flamingoes and kingfishers, they seemed, for every variety of academic dress had its representative, every colour of gown and hood. Robes of rich scarlet hung from the stoop shoulders of the Doctors of Letters, and the dark blue hoods of the Philosophers, the brocaded silk of the Musicians, amplified, deepened, the mood of ritual black. The Chancellor himself was there, the Earl of Blamis; he had cancelled his after-lunch bridge at Tight's, thrown his golf-clubs into the Daimler, and driven down that morning. The Fellows of the College and the dead man's secretary stood together, and close to them clustered the four undergraduates, poor relations in their bottom-starving Commoners' gowns.

'In Russia,' whispered Archangel, 'we burn them. It is considered hygienic. The notion of the cleansing quality of the fire is particularly acceptable to those with the religious taste. There is dancing.'

'Dancin' at a funeral?' Egg queried. 'Sort of mournful dances, eh? Sort of Russian dances?'

'Superbly immodest dances,' whispered Flower, centring his made-up white bow. 'The women disrobe in frenzied abandon and are lashed with raffia torn from old vodka bottles.'

'There is no raffia on vodka bottles,' said Archangel.

Bum, the metropolitan journalist, approached, fingering his notebook. 'In the midst of life,' he said reverently. 'You young fellows must have known the deceased very well.'

'He was like an elder brother to us all,' said Flower, 'always ready to throw off his cravat and join us in a frolic – whether it was the merry siege of some lady's lavatory or a simple game of pontoon.'

'He'd been young himself,' nodded Bum, scribbling.

Mr Bum was preparing a 'colour piece' for the readers

72

of the *Knell*. The readers of the *Knell* were composed (so it was said in Fleet Street) of odd-looking ladies in non-smoking carriages.

'A boy at heart,' said Mr Flower. 'A great-hearted boy. Excuse my dashing a suspicious moisture from my eye.'

'He was an elderly gentleman,' said Archangel.

'Why, Flower simply means that Manchip was youthful in a metaphorical sense. I think that was your meaning, Nicholas?' said Orson Dogg, the Rhodes Scholar who was reading psychology.

Egg said: 'Flower's barmy.'

The mourners started to drift into the Chapel.

'Beta,' an anxious classicist was saying of the dead man's intellectuals. 'Beta, or beta plus. Definitely not alpha.'

'He had an extremely annoying habit of doing *The Times* crossword over your shoulder out loud,' Christelow said in a low voice.

There were two things on the Inspector's mind: the length of his collar stud (for beneath his stiff collar the wretched thing was digging into his wind-pipe), and the dream of Mrs Spectre which, try as he might, he could not recollect. Added to which, he found something distinctly unprofessional about attending a man's funeral in the company of the man's murderer. Autumn looked about him. . .

Bow-Parley's wife was directly in front of the Inspector as they moved into the Chapel; Bow-Parley was not with her, he would be conducting the obsequies. Julia Bow-Parley was attractive in a hard, flat-heeled sort of way, and her black coat and skirt set off a mature slimness. The gown she wore was the gown of a Bachelor of Arts, for she was not a don herself and had never taken her M.A. It was said that Bow-Parley had married her as an unpaid 'feed' for his interminable commentary.

The Inspector insinuated himself between the narrow stalls, shifting sideways from foot to foot after Julia Bow-Parley until he reached his place. There was the murmurous rustle of leaves turning, and then the organ went full-steam into the anthem.

Murderers they might be, thought the Inspector, looking over the congregation, but they made an uncommon impressive display. They swelled into the first hymn, and in the soaring fullness of the singing it seemed to Autumn that the Chapel came alive, that the saints in their niches had but newly knelt down.

He raised his eyes again above the level of his hymn book – he was singing without its aid, for he had got the words by heart long since on cold mornings in an elementary-school hall – and watched the sun in the eastern lights rain down in bloody pools across the coffin of Manchip.

The man who did it is here.

Shipton did not sing. He held his book half-heartedly, and his lips did not move. He seemed utterly preoccupied. It occurred to Autumn that church was one of the places where people's faces told explicit stories.

Clapp, as smartly turned out as if he had expected the dead man to inspect him, blinked at his book, constantly losing the place as he darted frostbitten glances about the Chapel. Perhaps he is looking for someone with his buttons undone, thought the Inspector. Undigo sang in an ugly, flat, booming voice, mellowly at ease. He did the singing as the Inspector suspected he did most things – vigorously, with just an ounce of ironic detachment, and enjoying it.

Across the aisle, in the end stall, Falal was so old as to be hardly present. He was not singing, perhaps he had forgotten the words, for how should an old man remember so few out of so many? He was examining the detail in the carving of his stall, and as Autumn watched him, the Professor glanced slyly to right and left, then drew a small silver-framed magnifying glass from his waistcoat pocket to get a better look.

And now Bow-Parley had begun to speak the words, Bow-Parley, cherubically out of the top-drawer. Ladies loved his 'speaking voice', but none loved it better than he. It was a dispensation to be considered, pondered, with satisfaction, that so civilized a voice should have found such selfless, such seemly, employment – Autumn stopped himself; his occasional habit of making up the thoughts of others sometimes ran away with him.

Gently melancholy, the Chaplain announced a psalm. What with psalms not having recognizable tunes, some of those who had been singing the hymn with confidence were disconcerted, Christelow was undeterred, and sang on with gusto, like Undigo, but with none of Undigo's slight irony. Christelow concentrated on the service with the whole-heartedness that some men are able to bring to things that do not intimately concern them. Had he cared more for Manchip (so Autumn reflected) he could not have enjoyed the service half so much.

There was a big man with shiny black hair standing next to Rankine, wearing no gown, who the Inspector supposed was Lord Pinner. Lord Pinner's manner had been badly concocted; he was at pains to combine casual formality with personal importance, but had been unable to find the right place in the book, and was obliged to mouth each word the instant after everybody else had sung it. The effect was inexpressibly imbecile. Lord Pinner did not look over Rankine for Rankine's book was as tightly shut as his lips, and Rankine was practising a comprehensive detachment. Bloody fool, thought the Inspector.

Slowly the four bearers lowered the long brown coffin into the floor where Manchip was to lie with his predecessors, furthest from the altar. A choir of trebles took up the theme, and the sound rose, shivering among the wooden angels. The congregation joined in for the last time and Autumn pushed his finger beneath his collar, easing the stud.

McCann's big white hands were folded placidly in front of him as he stood darkly silent in the chorus about him. Did Presbyterians sing, Autumn wondered. Next to McCann, Fairlight's head quivered as it was thrown back, and his mouth was wide open, for Fairlight believed himself to be the possessor of a light 'baritone' of pleasing quality. He brayed, embarrassingly audible; *he* had been staring at the Inspector.

The four undergraduates stood in a line like a rather

buffo male voice chorus; Egg, with a red sweaty face, doing the musical equivalent of mumbling; Flower starting each verse tenor, and going very creditably bass when it got too high; Archangel wagging his thick finger in time with the music; Dogg peering intently about after traumas.

Next to Dogg, Diamantis stood, who had been Manchip's secretary; he had been pointed out to Autumn earlier in the morning. Diamantis sang very seriously and with great feeling for the occasion, much like the public schoolboy he seemed to be. He was young, his face was round and pink, and his fair hair lay across to his head in tight, wiry curls.

'Sa-a–ave him,' intoned the mellifluous Bow-Parley who had a penchant for putting in colourful bits. 'Sa-a–ave him from the horn of the unicorn and from the mouth of the lion . . .'

They came out into the sunlight, cheerful. The Earl of Blamis nodded his head. In the Chapel he had considered the dead man's approach shots.

'Impeccable,' he now said, 'though I don't say it didn't help him when the wind was with him.'

The congregation was resolving itself into its component parts and going off to lunch. The Earl of Blamis departed to the Mitre in the company, appropriately enough, of a Bishop. When everyone had gone the Fellows were left straggling about the doors like caretakers.

'Did you notice the way the Earl sang? As if the object of his singing were to remove caramel from his incisors.' Undigo smiled.

Bum came down the steps.

'Well, gentlemen, there is nothing like a reminder of the eternal verities. I don't think I've ever heard a more tasteful speaking voice on the BBC itself than the Reverend Parley's. It reminded me very clearly of that commentator they put in the roof on occasions of national grief. Very very nice indeed. If Mr Parley won't think that a little harmless publicity will offend his cloth I should like to mention him by name in my article –'

'I am sure, Mr Bum, you will find the Chaplain's sense of public responsibility in apple-pie order. He is not the man to fail the readers. But what pity now, that you can't mention the other gentleman by name, the gentleman who was in Chapel with us. The *murderer*.' Undigo smiled sourly.

'I dare say Bow-Parley would like to know who it was,' said Shipton, 'if only to thank him for the opportunity of playing to a capacity house.'

'Shipton is too bad, really he is,' said Christelow, as the dark-haired man walked off with his hands in his pockets, whistling. 'Bad manners, bad manners.'

Bow-Parley came out of the vestry and walked with his wife towards the group round the steps.

'I'm off,' Christelow said. 'I don't like funerals, and I should be a hypocrite if I pretended I were grief-stricken. Lunch?' he asked Fairlight.

As the pair strolled away Bum nudged Autumn: 'Still got that bloody profeel to do and the blighter won't play. Doesn't seem to realize what publicity means.'

Bow-Parley came up in off-parade style. In this *persona* he often saw himself giving people tips for the three-thirty or buying them drinks in pubs.

'There you all are,' he said cheerfully, his arm dropping bonhommous round the shoulders of the man nearest. 'The simple business is done, and that's that.' It was spiritual alka-seltzer, absolving everyone from religious hangovers. 'We have not studied Monuments, nor have we studiously declined them. No wahld enormities,' he sketched them, stirring the air, 'of ancient magnanimity—'

'None,' said Undigo.

Autumn became aware that Diamantis wanted something. He hovered from foot to foot, and when the Inspector glanced at him enquiringly, he said: 'I'm Diamantis— I was wondering if — whether I could have a word with you —'

'Yes. In private?'

'Oh, no — no, it's not important, I mean I suppose it's not important. I just thought — well, the fact is, I can't find the Vice-Chancellor's diary.' Diamantis stopped, thinking this might sound foolish. 'Of course, I didn't *want* the diary — what I mean is, he had one, and now it seems to have disappeared. I just thought I'd mention it – '

Autumn said: 'What sort of a diary?'

'Oh, not the ordinary pocket sort of thing, you know – it was a big desk-sized one. That's why I missed it. It was a journal, really. He wrote it up every night –'

'A journal,' murmured the Chaplain, who had been listening, 'a journal. Manchip kept a journal. Men have to die before one knows them at all –'

'He called it his commonplace book,' Diamantis said.

'Crossword puzzles, brasses, essays – other people's essays –' Bow-Parley laughed gently, looking at his wife. 'Oh, the interests of the man, the full, the happy life. And a commonplace book – ah, one ponders, one enquahs – commonplaces, but to whom?'

Autumn said: 'When did you miss it?'

'Well, I didn't start straightening things up till after lunch yesterday. I thought' – Diamantis blushed – 'you might want things left the way they were. So I suppose I noticed it wasn't on his desk about three o'clock, something like that. I didn't like to say anything right away – it might have turned up, you know. But I had a jolly good look round – in drawers and things. So I thought I'd better – this morning –'

'Why, why,' Bow-Parley stuttered sublimely, 'this is legendary, fabulous. Dahries! One has not read widely in the detective authors, occasionally, on trains, the longer journeys, but one is perfectly well aware of the position, the – ah – key position occupied by dahries. Instrumental often, indispensable always. And of course' – he spread his arms in humorous atonement for his lack of faith in light fiction – 'it happens!'

Autumn said to Diamantis: 'You were sharp to spot it.'

Diamantis was horribly uncomfortable in the limelight.

'I just thought I'd mention it. I'll be in my rooms if you need me.' He blushed again – would a Detective Inspector need *him*? – then nodded and walked quickly away.

'A pleasant lad,' said Undigo to the Inspector, 'but I fear he had been patronized out of existence by Manchip. Manchip gave him a job as his secretary after his father –

Manchip had been his father's tutor I think – was hammered on the Stock Exchange a couple of years ago. When he first came I should have said he was a brisk lad enough, certainly he didn't stammer. Six months with Manchip, and he couldn't drink a cup of tea without spilling it. Would you say so, Chaplain?'

'Alahs. Yet it is pleasant to observe that the boy's observation remains unimpaired. Yes, the dahry, Inspector' – Bow-Parley leant forward in one of his characteristic poses, using his arm as a stethoscope, pushing his fist against Autumn's ribs as if he were sounding him for moral palpitations – 'the dahry, one is curious to know, one will not be content until one sees that it has an *organic* bearing on the unhappy situation. So often in the novels it is a mere device. Commonplace book – one wonders, might it not be a delicious misnomer? Perhaps we shall never know, possibly it is already destroyed. But Diamantis is to be congratulated, acute, entahly acute –'

Bow-Parley departed with his wife. Autumn watched them go, and asked himself what the expression on Julia Bow-Parley's face had meant. Not just irritation. If only one could preserve such moments, and play them back, over and over, until one had got their significance.

Lord Pinner addressed the Inspector for the first time.

'This thing lined up?'

He spoke sharply in the way some men try to crush your fingers when you shake hands with them.

'Suicide for my money,' said Lord Pinner. 'Just the type.' And Lord Pinner waved his arm as if it was a magic-wand, reducing life to a size that can be clipped into the inside-pocket.

'Knew him like the backer me own hand.'

'You knew him well.'

'Yes, I knew him well. And what's more, I didn't like what I knew. A daft old schoolmarm,' and Lord Pinner stared hard at the Inspector, expecting (as people who confuse the rude with the forthright always do) to be congratulated.

'Short-sighted, and toffee-nosed into the bargain.'

Lord Pinner sent copies of his small booklet, *Streamlined Families*, to all who announced their engagements in *The Times*. He received many rude answers. He also sold television-sets on hire-purchase to large families in small rooms – an ingenious attempt (as Manchip had once remarked) at demonstrating the practical advantages of streamlining.

Lord Pinner's rule was to have reasons for everything, and he had adduced a dozen to show why Oxford should incorporate a new College, preponderantly scientific in establishment; a foundation which he himself was prepared to undertake, and which would bear his name. Certain academic circles had been for letting him have his way, and at one time it seemed that Lord Pinner – permanently and ubiquitously out of his depth as he at all times was – might be in a fair way to succeed.

It was unfortunate for his lordship that in the middle of the negotiations Manchip had become Vice-Chancellor. It was at this point that his project ceased to exist. Manchip mobilized his forces, and they were impregnable. There was going to be no Pinner Hall, and it was Manchip who was saying no. Pinner tried everything: he hoped, he wheedled, he tried to bully. He dashed up to Town and ate a declamatory lunch with the Earl of Blamis, and came back to shake the news over Manchip's head: Manchip hadn't raised his eyes from his book.

The late Vice-Chancellor was a man to whom singularity, minority, cussedness and opposition were as the breath of life; but in their reference to Lord Pinner these motives were secondary. Quite simply, Manchip detested Lord Pinner and all Lord Pinner's works with a detestation that was entirely instinctive. And that was unalterably that.

Even Pinner had seen it, and had retired into murmurous collusion with Rankine, finding in the ginger-haired scientist that same devotion to short views as he practised himself.

Autumn said: 'Suicide? It could hardly have been that, Lord Pinner. He was stabbed in the back.'

'Let's have a little imagination, officer, shall we? You've read books, haven't you? Easy make suicide look like murder. Fall on his back,' Lord Pinner waved his magic arm again, 'fall on his back, holding the knife behind him. Finnee!'

Lord Pinner tapped his forehead.

'Dead odd that chap was.'

Chapter 9

'Just a few nuts and a glass of port with the others, eh?'

'*Nuts?*'

'With the port.'

'I am not a great nut-eater, Mr Bum. Very few of us in the Common Room are fond of nuts. Falal sometimes –'

Bum sighed.

'What I'm trying to get at, Mr Christelow – you see, these are the things the readers will want to know – is do you fit in with the normal quiet life of the average' – Bum adjusted his specs – 'the average don. Nuts –'

Pity we got off to a duff start, Bum reflected. Back at the office Bum had gone through the cuttings in search of background; unfortunately Mr Sharpshoot had got Christelow's name wrong, and Bum's researches had referred to a Professor of Eastern Dialects. It was hardly surprising that Christelow had been avoiding the journalist, for at their first encounter Bum, having rubbed up a few phrases with the help of a café proprietor in Fetter Lane, had addressed him in Cypriot.

'No nuts, Mr Bum,' said Christelow.

'We'll leave the nuts and try boyhood. You had the bookish turn at an early age, I dare say, Mr Christelow.'

'I fear I was unable to read until I was nine.'

Bum breathed hard.

'Well it's a gimmick, anyway.'

'It must be very difficult, this sort of thing, Mr Bum?'

'You've got to have the knack, getting on with people, knowing the form. I very nearly had to use my last resort with you, Mr Christelow.'

'Your last resort?'

'For getting people to see me who won't.' Bum grew confidential. 'I tell 'em I've come to write their obituary.'

'God bless my soul!'

'In like lightning as soon as they hear that. I've had bestselling novelists laid up with broken legs prancing round the bedroom like two-year-olds. Just to show me.

A very respectable Eastern potentate actually suspended himself from a brass chandelier by his teeth –'

The scout entered with the tea.

'Now then, what about hobbies?' said Bum, warming imperceptibly. 'A nice quiet walk after a day's studying, or a game of darts' – he threw out encouragingly – 'with the other Regius Professors?'

'Do they play, do you think?' asked Christelow, his eyes wide open.

'I hope so, Mr Christelow. It gives the readers a nice warm feeling inside to learn that the intellectual classes relax the same as they do. I *wish*,' said Mr Bum, shaking his head regretfully, 'you did the football pools.'

'I have already told you –'

'Oh, it can't be helped, Mr Christelow; don't worry. Now let's see,' Mr Bum looked up from his notebook. 'Anything extraordinary?'

'You are so oblique –'

'I mean, do you have any tastes that the ordinary person might call extraordinary? There's, now let's see, there's' – Bum tapped his lip with his pencil – 'bull-fighting, yes, or collecting engine-numbers, for instance. Things like that. They've got to be extraordinary, really extraordinary, you see, because if they're just a bit colourful like say going to night-clubs or driving Rolls Royces the readers get envious and resent it. It's the warm off-beat human note I'm after here –'

'No,' said Christelow thoughtfully, 'no, I don't think I strike it.'

'Hmm, funny.' Bum nodded. 'Though you get it very often in the academic world. I once interviewed a teacher at a Technical College in Porthcawl who constructed replicas of Buckingham Palace in tin-foil.'

Christelow buttered a muffin meditatively.

'An exacting business, Mr Bum, writing for the common man.'

'Ah, we call him the man-in-the-street, Mr Christelow. It's got a nice homely community flavour, with none of the class atmosphere of the other. It had the advantage,' Bum lowered his voice, 'of being meaningless.'

There was a knock on the door, and the scout poked his head in:

'The Inspector, sir.'

Autumn had been worrying about the safety of *The Book of the Lion* all afternoon. The Bodley business yesterday evening had reminded him that books were still in jeopardy, and though the Commissioner had been confident that the Chaucer was safe in the possession of the man who had found it, it was Autumn who would carry any cans if the thing were pinched.

He put it to Christelow, and was relieved to encounter no opposition.

'Of course, of course, I quite see it, Inspector. It would be unfair to you to have it otherwise. Bow-Parley has it, there will be no difficulty –'

Christelow was straightening the invitation cards along his mantlepiece. There was an air of constraint about him, as if he wanted to say more. He walked to the window – his rooms were on the ground floor – and pulled the curtains further back.

'Then I can pick it up now.'

'Yes, yes, of course.' He paused. 'Oh, dammit,' Christelow said, 'I suppose I'd better tell you something foolish.'

He stuck his hands in his pockets and blinked, embarrassedly, at both Bum and Autumn.

'I wasn't going to say anything; it was probably all imagination.' He stopped. 'Well, the fact is, I thought I heard someone fiddling with the window last night. I listened for a bit then got up and came in here to have a look. Of course, I saw nothing, and when I had another look this morning there weren't any signs – no footprints, no scratches.' Christelow laughed sheepishly. 'I honestly don't know why I mention it.'

'I'm glad you did.'

Autumn walked over to the window himself, pushed it open, and scrutinized the woodwork.

'No, there are no marks, but that means nothing.' He drew in his head. 'They only leave marks in detective books.'

'Well, you take the *Lion*, Inspector. I don't pretend to be a hero.'

'Oh, lovely,' said Mr Bum, scribbling, 'human and controversial.'

Christelow stirred hot water into a silver teapot.

'Yes, Bow-Parley has it. He is most interested. Sugar? Extremely interested. As indeed are all my colleagues. It is most flattering, I enjoy it very much. Mr Bum and I may differ about what sort of notoriety is desirable, but I am certainly a glutton for my kind.'

He laughed.

Of the dons of Warlock, Christelow and Fairlight were the only ones not yet to have published a book; in the microcosm of College life those who do not produce books are slightly under suspicion. A man's book is his Union card. Fairlight was said – at least, he said it – to be at work upon a critique of metaphysical poetry and its latter-day influences. No one had seen the manuscript, although Fairlight had been observed passing between his rooms and the Radcliffe Camera with files under his arm. The colours of the files varied, but not so much (Falal said) that they ever clashed with his suit.

Christelow, who was considered one of the best brains in the University, wrote essays in the scholarly quarterlies which were intensely stimulating in an impressionistic sort of way; but he had not pretended to a larger work. His commentary on the *Book of the Lion* might repair the deficiency.

'Yes,' said Autumn, 'we'll get it under lock and key. We don't want to lose it again after you've been to the trouble of digging it up for us.'

'Quite. Though to be truthful, I didn't dig it up. I merely had the good fortune to recognize it for what it was. I have an acquaintance who has – or had, I should say, for he has been selling it up – a wonderful library. While he was cataloguing the stuff for the sale – some death duties, I gathered, had to be paid – he came across our *Book of the Lion*. He is no bookman – he kept on his stable, which would have realised far more than his library – but had wit enough to read the inscription which

85

makes a direct reference to the author. He brought it to me. Well, of course, I wanted to say right away that it *was* the authentic article, in my bones I knew it was –'

Mr Bum was making rapid notes.

'Nice personal stuff, this,' he said.

Christelow laughed.

'But detective work was called for. Chaucer had imitators, but the one thing you can't imitate is cast of mind, it's got to be *there* before you begin. And, well, I found that it was Chaucer's cast of mind in *The Book of the Lion* – his attitude to things, the tolerance, the irony, the lack of condemnation –' Christelow sipped his tea.

'Most of the English and transatlantic Chaucerians have seen it now, one or two have been cautious – Coghill found some rather odd dialect forms, and Lewis says the allegory is weak, indeed it *is* weak, no poet is consistent, and it is early stuff – but all are agreed that it is the real thing.'

Christelow was in the full stride of his enthusiasm.

'One little piece of detective work that may tickle your professional fancy, Inspector – the *story* the poem tells provides a most plausible reason why the thing has been lost for so many centuries. We always knew there had *been* a *Book of the Lion* because Chaucer himself refers to it in the Retraction at the end of the *Canterbury Tales*, and we had assumed it was probably a translation of a French poem of the same title by Guillaume de Machault. But you see, it wasn't. *The Book of the Lion* tells how the Lion, king of the beasts, was deposed by the Tiger – the Tiger was treacherous, the Lion was weak. The Lion wanders the forest with his young and lovely queen, bewailing his fate, but making no attempt to rally his people and destroy the traitor. Finally, the Lion is put to death by the Tiger, and the poem ends with the Dove lamenting rebellion, and telling the Tiger that his only hope of grace is to be a better king than the one he deposed, though nothing will excuse his mortal sin.'

'A lesson for the times,' said Bum sanctimoniously.

'Exactly!' cried Christelow. 'You see, the story is allegorical. The Lion was Richard ii, the Tiger was Henry

86

Bolingbroke, and what happened in the poem happened in real life. Now this is an early poem of Chaucer's – and the deposition of Richard didn't take place till towards the end of the poet's career. The poem was an accurate prophesy, for Chaucer must have seen which way the wind was blowing.'

Christelow leaned forward eagerly.

'Now this is where the detective bit comes in. Bolingbroke's father was John of Gaunt – and John of Gaunt was Chaucer's patron. Is it surprising that the poet *himself* hushed the poem up? Why Chaucer wrote the thing in the first place I don't presume to say – perhaps he wanted to show it, perhaps he *did* show it, privately, to the young Richard. A delicate warning, a courtly chastisement? But there you are –'

'Full marks,' said Autumn.

'I thought you'd be interested. My guess is that the poem never went outside the Chaucer family circle – Ewelme it was found, and Ewelme is the burial place of one Thomas Chaucer, said to be a son of Geoffrey Chaucer. Fascinating, isn't it? The manuscript we have isn't the original, its late fifteenth-century – but I'd bet any money the scribe who copied it was a clerk in the family of Chaucer's son. He wasn't going to lose one of his father's poems, but he was keeping it dark, and wisely too –'

Autumn understood a little why Undigo had described Christelow as the most popular tutor in the College. 'He has a trick of intriguing his pupils via himself. I have more Firsts, perhaps, but he was more fun.'

'Dear, oh dear, you come to tea, and I treat you like a couple of pupils!'

'Then you treat your pupils handsomely,' said Autumn, rising. 'I'll slip over to Bow-Parley's.'

'You haven't a picture, have you, Mr Christelow?' asked Bum, rising too. 'One in your mortar-board for preference.'

'Talk, talk, talk,' Bum said, outside. 'Try and get something out of it,' he waved his notes, 'but I can't see it making the paper.'

The air was thick and still as Autumn walked across Summerhouse to the Chaplain's quarters. The afternoon had been close, with a glaring lemony sky and no sun. The thunder, which had been festering all day, was going to break.

No answer. Autumn pushed open the door. No one was in. He saw *The Book of the Lion* on the Chaplain's desk, was about to take it, then hesitated. Better tell the man first. He shut the door.

Back in the quad he met Tantalum.

'He's gorn acrosst over to Burford, sir, to see 'is cousin the Bishop. Won't be back till late. His missis is in London for the day and she's pickin' 'im up here when she gets back.'

Better wait. Autumn went into the Chaplain's rooms again, then came out and handed the porter a key.

'Tell the Chaplain I've locked Mr Christelow's book up in his desk drawer, will you? Give him the key, and ask him to ring me as soon as he comes in.'

The sky was turning blacker, like an ugly spreading bruise, as Autumn went towards the Summer Tower. Any minute now, he thought, turning his face to the clouds. He walked through the baroque portico (it looked as if it had been leant against the wall by an amnesic stage-hand) and climbed to his room.

For seconds the sky was purple, apoplectic. Then pat, pat, like the steps of a tiny giant, the first heavy drops spattered the quadrangle; far into the distance, the clouds heaved, as if the heavens had collapsed under some universal stroke, and faintly, like the rumble of a fall in an upstairs room, the thunder broke.

Chapter 10

MIDNIGHT. Thirteen times Iscariot struck the hour, betraying the College as it had betrayed it for centuries. The rain drove against the clock face, and Iscariot wept.

Autumn slept soundly in a high backed chair. On a small table beside him lay three sheets of the report he had been composing for the Commissioner; the pen had slipped from his fingers an hour before, and he had fallen asleep to the torrid arpeggios of the rain upon the roof.

He was awake suddenly, hearing the thunder crack; but it was the telephone that had roused him, and it rang again. With his mouth sticky from sleeping, Autumn blundered over to the instrument and lifted it from the hook.

'Hullo.'

The rain slattered against the small window, and Autumn put a finger in his ear. No one had answered, but at the other end a man was speaking. It sounded distant, like a crossed line, but the Inspector realized it was the voice of the Chaplain talking to someone in his own rooms.

'. . . not strictly ethical,' Bow-Parley said, far away, and laughed. Then suddenly his voice came louder, as if a volume control had been turned up. He was speaking into the receiver.

'Yes? Inspector? It is you? My apologies, but I had a message of Tantalum – yes, he told me as I came in. I had hoped to be home earlier, but when one is dining with a Bishop . . .' The Chaplain's plump giggle was reduced to a tinny snicker over the wires. 'I would have contacted you anyway, I have something I wish to communicate. Would it be too much to ask you to slip over? Splendid, splendid. I believe – I am certain' – there was a note of complacent triumph in his voice – 'that I have something to show you which will assist the enquahry materially –'

Autumn said, 'Right,' and without waiting to change his slippers, walked out of the room and down the stairs. The rain was sleeting across the quadrangle as he peered out into the darkness. One thing, in this monsoon that pagoda will look intentional.

He slipped out into the cloisters, and his slippers clapped on the flagstones as he made his way towards the Chaplain's rooms. One or two lights still shone from windows, and the rain hung over them like mist. The gutters gurgled, but the Inspector was sheltered by the preposterous arcade.

The Chaplain's quarters were in the far side of the cloisters. Autumn was unsure of the precise staircase, and as he approached, he stepped gingerly out into the rain to look up at the windows. There was a light just above him—that would be it.

He passed through the archway, and slapped up the winding stone stairs, stopping at the second landing. There was a small gold-lettered board above one of the doors, which read: 'The Rev. Bow-Parley.'

Autumn tapped at the door, and waited. Then he tapped again; the door drifted open on a small hallway, with another door at the far end of it. In the room beyond the second door, the light was on.

Smiling to forestall the Chaplain's surprise, the Inspector walked across the carpeted hall, and put his head into the further room.

Bow-Parley knelt in an attitude of grotesque devotion, the back of his head crumpled like the shell of a red-yolked breakfast egg. His chin rested on the edge of the table, and his body was trapped between the table-leg and the chair he had slipped from; he knelt, and his lifeless arms hung down.

One fraction of a millionth of a second too late, Autumn started to turn; his head moved through half a degree before the universe caved in upon it. He felt his knees buckle, but he was unconscious before he reached the floor.

He was out seconds. The room faded into his eyes again like a scene opening on the screen of a cinema.

'*Christ.*'

His eyes were running like an old man's, but it was blood, and the room shimmered as the blood trickled into the lashes. He started to run, but hit the doorpost, not running straight, slipped his footing and spun round automatically as he grabbed the wood. Bow-Parley's flat eye regarded him across the mahogany: a fat dead gentleman peeping over the tabletop.

Then Autumn remembered the desk. The key was in the lock. He turned it. *The Book* was still there.

Autumn ran out on to the landing, and down the stairs, and the stairs came up at him like a catherine wheel. He reached the bottom without falling, slithering the stair-rail under his armpit; when he reached the archway he stood like Samson, with his arms stretched out and his hands pressed against either wall.

Which way.

The rain. Dark.

Has he got back to his room. Too soon. Hiding.

Autumn staggered into the cloister pushing a handkerchief to his bleeding skull. And in the instant a figure detached itself from one of the archways ahead, running, running, running.

'You bastard.'

Autumn was shouting as he ran, keeping upright by running. The darkness of the cloister, of the night, and then the darkness of giddiness and sickness clotted the body of the policeman, stuck round his legs like aspic.

I'll get him.

Rain blew in a gust through the arcade and hit Autumn's face. He keeled giddily backwards, and stopped. The figure ahead had disappeared.

Gone. No. Where?

Behind.

Autumn turned about like a quill-float bobbing on the surface of a pond. With the exaggerated care of a drunken man, he set one foot before the other, and walked slowly back down the cloister.

I passed him.

There was no sound but the roar of the rain, and Autumn knew he was still there, in one of the archways, waiting.

And then the darkness stirred, and they were both running again, Autumn wagging his arms to keep his balance like Charlie Chaplin in a silent film. One of his slippers flew off, curving away into the night.

He cannot get away. He cannot.

In his vertiginous progress, Autumn could see the man ahead of him, not as a shape, but as a movement, a mutation of the darkness. It was the distance between them; in his depleted condition Autumn could not draw closer.

Autumn shouted. His voice rang out. If people would come, help him to stop the man –

The movement in the darkness materialized and became solid. The figure had halted. Autumn toiled on towards it. The figure hesitated, then slid for the third time into one of the stair-case archways. All the pain in the world shouted to get out inside Autumn's head.

Christ.

Autumn slowed up as he reached the archway, and drew close to the wall. His arm dissolved as his elbow struck hard against the stonework, and the sticky handkerchief stuck to his tingling fingers. He shook the handkerchief off his hand, then, leaning against the wall, got a matchbox out.

Trapped. Watch it.

The rain grumbled down in sustained roof-beating tattoos, the dull even frequency of the sound taking the edge off events, so that Autumn had to keep thinking about them.

He felt the cold flagstone strike through the sock on his shoeless foot as he struck the match and held it close to the staircase-board.

Dogg, Flower, Egg, Archangel, he read.

Within five seconds life had become too much for Orson Dogg the psychological Rhodes Scholar. He screamed as maladjustedly as any schizophrene, as a staggering black ghost with blood all over him whipped off the bed-clothes, stared at his pyjama-clad body and departed.

But Autumn got no further than the next landing, and there he sat down on the cold stone, frustrated almost to weeping. He had found himself in a corridor, and the corridor, running round all four sides of the quadrangle, connected with every room in the College.

His man had not been trapped, his man had vanished.

Tantalum scuttled through the rain in company with the Boy from Botley. They had heard Autumn yelling.

'Now then,' shouted the porter.

The face of the Boy from Botley hove into view up the stairs. He saw Autumn, and howled.

''E's 'urt 'imself, Mr Tantalum. 'E's got blood all over 'im, I'm sure 'e 'as, all blood, Mr Tantalum.'

The doors of Archangel, Dogg, Flower, and Egg opened.

'What the bloody hell –'

Stilled, the Inspector thought dreamily as he sat on the stair, the seemly voice, the rich vowels; not ever again would a shaft of sunlight distinguish the sleek head in a still church. Crushed like a juicy red pie-crust.

'Shut up, shut *up*, all of you,' Autumn shouted.

He got up.

'Mrs Bow-Parley' – he spoke to Tantalum, but hardly lifting his head – 'must be kept in the lodge. When she comes.'

'I say –'

Autumn thought how frightened other people could make you. Flower's brashness had crumbled like stale cake. The four undergraduates were huddled under the rusty light, aware that life was rattling on at a thousand miles an hour, absolutely independent of them.

'*No*' – it was a general negative against enquiry, interruption – 'you all stay here except Tantalum, who goes back to the Lodge. He goes back to the Lodge *now*.'

Tantalum backed out of Autumn's presence with his mouth open.

'All blood, Mr Tantalum, all blood all over 'im,' said the Boy from Botley, and fainted on the steps.

Autumn said to the undergraduates: 'Your rooms.' He started with Archangel's, and visited each in turn. Then he said: 'Take off your dressing gowns.' He saw each was wearing pyjamas.

The Inspector swayed slightly and put his hand to his head. He thought, I must go over the College before I cave in.

He said: 'You four wait here.' Then he went out into the cloisters, and one by one, climbed every staircase – occupied and unoccupied – in Warlock.

The dons were all there. Fairlight sitting cross-legged on his carpet in a green velvet smoking jacket, playing with a tape-recorder – 'Banged your head?'; Shipton pulling on his shoes – 'I heard the noise'; Christelow sitting up in bed rather scared – 'Hul – lo –'; Falal blinking as the light was turned on, snuff all down his night shirt – 'Aha, a treasure hunt –'; Undigo writing; McCann wearing a night cap – 'Really!'; Clapp drinking whisky; Rankine in bed; Diamantis in his bath; Lord Pinner snoring, Lord Pinner's teeth submarine.

No good, Autumn thought weakly as he closed Lord Pinner's door; he's done me. He came out into the quadrangle again, sick and very tired. The wound ached maliciously, and the blood on his scalp had gone cold. I do not care who it was, he thought, not now anyway. Outside the Lodge he was sick.

He said to Tantalum: 'Ring the police station. To send policemen and an ambulance.'

Lights were on all over the College, voices rose across the quadrangle. Men were coming out into the cloisters, running towards the Lodge. It might have been ghosts, horror in the air, abstract nastiness. The rain had stopped.

Autumn said to Tantalum: 'You put a call through to me. The Chaplain, five minutes ago.'

'Yes sir –'

'Did you hear him say anything? Before the call was through. Say anything to anyone at his end of the line? Think.'

The eye of the porter, adhering to the wound in Autumn's head like a dry bandage, tore itself painfully away.

'Not like clearly, now. What was it. Something he was saying. I *did* 'ear. Was it "musical" 'e said, now?'

'It was "ethical". Who did he say it to? The name. You heard?'

'No, sir. I didn't –'

'Did you hear him say anything else?'

'No, sir –'

94

There was a knock at the gate.

'Open it,' Autumn said, and leant against the wall.

Julia Bow·Parley stepped briskly through the gate, made to walk straight into the quadrangle, then saw Autumn. She was shocked, seeing the blood on his hair, then her shock gave way to bewilderment as he said nothing but stared back.

He told her.

She said: 'I will sit down. I will go into the Lodge and sit down.'

But she didn't move. Her eyes never left his. It was as if she found in the stare a lifeline, a thin communication with the surface, while her nether self thrashed wildly at incalculable depths.

Tantalum said: 'A cup of tea, madam –'

The dons had arrived, were standing aghast in their dressing gowns.

'What is it? What is it?' cried Lord Pinner, running up. 'I thought I was dreaming –'

Lord Pinner had left his teeth behind. His hair was standing on end, and a corner of his striped pyjama collar stuck out of this plaid dressing gown. It was all unconvincingly domestic, that small group of men in *deshabille*, crowding into the Lodge as if there were some sort of cat to be put out.

An ambulance drew up outside. Two policemen in uniform stepped through the gate. Autumn murmured rapid directions to them, and one of them said: 'That head wants bandaging, sir.'

Then Autumn turned to the dons.

He said: 'It's a bloody sight more than seven years' bad luck to hit a policeman, gentlemen. Perhaps I should have made that clear before. From now on I shall not simply see that justice is done. I shall take a pleasure in doing so. Good night.'

And Autumn walked to the ambulance.

Chapter 11

'No point on this one. Got a penknife?'

Autumn handed Dorcas a pencil from his own pocket.

They were sitting at High Table in the empty Hall. The Hall was dark and cool and very bare, and the cold swathe of oak at which they sat seemed to diminish the two men like clothes that are too big.

'Hurts, doesn't it? Nasty bloody thing – I can just imagine the bastard coming up behind you with that brass poker – yack!' Dorcas made a shivering noise, and jerked his shoulders. Autumn's adventure the night before spoilt, in retrospect, his evening's whist.

'I suppose we'd better get them in,' said Dorcas, for the size of the table and the emptiness of the Hall were making him feel self-conscious.

Autumn leant back in the Master's chair, with his elbows on the arm-rests, bridging his hands gothically before his nose. There was a bandage round his head, and in places it had turned brown.

'Yes, we'll have them in now. I want them all together to kick off with.'

Autumn signalled to Tantalum, who sat at the further end of the Hall, by the door, and beneath the musician's gallery. The porter's footsteps, echoing as they approached High Table, emphasized what had already occurred to Autumn – that there were certain interiors whose proper uses could not be usurped.

'Inspector Autumn will have all the gentlemen in now, please,' Dorcas said, assuming the subordinate role with great haste.

'Very good, sir. They're all outside waitin'.' Tantalum walked away. Dorcas coughed and tapped with Autumn's pencil on the oak, opened a notebook and smoothed the page down, put one arm over the back of his chair, but it slipped off.

'How are you thinking of tackling – ?'

The double doors at the end of the Hall shuddered open and the dons and undergraduates filed in. Even as they entered, the Hall still seemed unpossessed. It needed the smell of food, candlelight, the chink of glass. In the orange haze at dinnertime the eyes of the Georgians in the portraits gazed aslant, immemorially knowing; now, in the morning, they just looked left behind.

'Will you please come closer, gentlemen?'

Autumn's voice threw itself round the walls, into the roofbeams, ricochetted, rebounded. The Collegians ranged themselves rather sheepishly before the dais.

'Good morning, gentlemen. I'm going to see you one by one, but there is a question I want to ask you collectively before I begin. Now then' – Autumn looked down at the people before him – 'which of you visited the Chaplain last evening and left him about midnight?'

The sound of Autumn's voice, echoing round the Hall, finally lost form.

'This is a question I'm not going to ask again. All right. No one? Very well. Will you all wait in your rooms until the porter calls you.'

'They didn't like the way you said that,' Dorcas said, as the last man shut the door. 'What was it again you heard him say – at the end of the phone?'

'Oh – "not strictly ethical." Just that – and he laughed a bit.' Autumn scratched his chin. '"Not strictly ethical."' Autumn screwed up his lips for a despondent little whistle, but merely expelled the air noisily.

'My God, what a risk the other fellow was running – the padre could easily have mentioned his name while he was speaking to you over the phone. He must have bashed his head in the second he put it down – '

The first hint of lunch seeped probatively into the bare Hall from the kitchens beyond the closed doors.

Autumn pulled a list of the inmates of Warlock towards him.

'Let's have Clapp in.'

Clapp, the Bursar, had a way of pulling his mouth down at the corners which made people think he was either very cold or in pain. He walked up to the dais, and sat down in front of the Inspectors, rubbing his hands in the way some people have when they are forced to consider a situation which they would rather ignore.

'I want to find out who saw the Chaplain last.'

'I saw him early on.'

Clapp was plainly torn between relief at being able to say he saw him early, and irritation at having to admit seeing him at all. Implication, accountability, how he hated it.

'Afternoon,' he said, 'early. Two o'clock say.'

'Where?'

'Man's rooms, Shipton's.' Clapp looked as if he were suffering from frostbite.

'Met him there? What did you talk about? Did he – '

'Met him?' Clapp stared at Autumn as if he were a junior officer trying to swing something on him. 'Didn't meet him. Saw him.'

Autumn looked back at the Bursar, and felt his temper beginning to inflate. Clapp noticed it.

'Saw him, you see,' said the Bursar. 'See a man through a window, you don't talk to him. You just see him.'

Autumn brushed away the little piece of graphite that had been the point of his pencil.

'Ah,' said Autumn, 'if Shipton was talking to the Chaplain he may have – '

'Wasn't there,' broke in Clapp, abruptly, 'not when I saw him. Bow-Parley was on his owneyo. Waiting, what?' Clapp felt he had made it very clear. 'Simply saw him, you see. Got a glimpse.'

'What Colonel Clapp means, he saw the Chaplain through the window. Through Mr Shipton's window.' Dorcas revolved his moustache confidently.

Autumn said with testy emphasis: 'What was the Chaplain doing through the window?'

'I don't know that he was doing anything,' Clapp said. 'Standing. Or moving about. Yes. Moving about.' He confirmed his impression with a staccato nod. 'Nosey fellow.'

Autumn drew an aeroplane.

'The last time I saw him. Well,' said Clapp, brisk and shifty. 'I've got a lecture – '

This was strictly true. He had written the notes for it when he came to Oxford from the War Office many years ago. The other thing he had done was to edit a history of the cannon in pictures for the Jubilee of King George V.

'Shipton's rooms. What would you say he wanted in Shipton's rooms, Colonel?'

'Waiting for Shipton, eh? Very likely. Could ask him, Shipton.'

'Perhaps the Chaplain wanted to see what the Vice-Chancellor found so broadening about Shipton's essays,' mused Autumn. 'Did the Vice-Chancellor ever borrow *your* essays, Colonel?'

Clapp seemed to come alive all at once, yet at the same time to suppress his own vitality. He said: 'Manchip was a pacifist.'

Almost without either of the detectives noticing it, there was a pause.

'Yes. Yes. Well, thank you very much, Colonel Clapp,' said Autumn. 'A great help. I wonder if you'd ask Tantalum to call Mr Shipton in?'

The doors opened and closed, and the echo wavered through the Hall.

'What was all that about the essays?' asked Dorcas.

'Oh – Shipton said Manchip borrowed his essays. Nothing much.' Autumn picked his teeth, wondering about Clapp: 'Manchip was a pacifist. . . .'

Shipton sat down in the chair Clapp had vacated. The whole scene now looked rather like a *viva*, with Shipton the harassed candidate who had neither slept nor washed in his eagerness to spend every last moment mugging up the right answers. He looked extremely scruffy.

'I haven't the slightest idea why Bow-Parley was in my rooms. He didn't want *me* – he left no note and he wasn't there when I came back from lunch.'

Autumn found himself thinking about the look that had passed between Bow-Parley and Shipton that other morning on the threshold of Manchip's rooms. He knew he hadn't invented the memory of the thing, but he couldn't be sure he hadn't invented the thing remembered.

There was no doubt about it, Shipton was preoccupied as he sat in front of High Table, even worried. It seemed to Autumn that, though he was perhaps making an attempt to control it, he made none to dissemble it.

The Inspector gazed at the sallow-faced man.

'I'll just ask you one simple question. Mr Shipton – is there anything you can tell me which might throw light?' He paused. 'Anything at all.'

'No,' Shipton shook his head, 'nothing.' He seemed genuinely surprised – surprised, perhaps, that in all the cargo of worry he bore there was nothing he could off-load on to the immediate problem.

'I can tell you nothing at all.'

Autumn turned his pencil over and over between his fingers, and drummed it on the table.

'Well, he was in your rooms, but you don't know why. Thank you, Mr Shipton; that will be all.'

Dorcas watched the dark, dry-haired man walk down the Hall, and nodded significantly.

'Ve-ery interesting – '

'There's Mr Christelow would like to see you right away, sir,' called Tantalum, from by the doors.

Christelow's progress up the Hall was identical in style and pace to that of a man in a walking-race: he tumbled precipitately forward at a great rate, fearfully anxious not to contravene the rules by breaking into a run.

'Forgive me putting myself next without asking – but the *Book* – '

Blimey, thought Autumn, doesn't anything take the edge off their self-concern? They mightn't have thought a lot of the man, but he was a member of their society. You'd think his death –

'It's safe,' said Autumn, 'safe and sound, locked up in my room.'

'Ahhh,' Christelow gave a great sigh of relief and pleasure. 'I felt sure that if anything had happened to it you would certainly have told me last night –'

With a dead man and a cut head on my hands, thought Autumn dryly.

'Yes, it's all right. Either he wasn't after it, or he hadn't time.'

'Poor Bow-Parley. I cannot imagine how he of all people should have provoked a maniacal assault – '

Christelow was speaking more slowly. Now that his own agitation had been stilled he was able to bring the situation into a more humane perspective. Is that the limiting factor in Christelow, the Inspector reflected, or in us all?

Christelow was beginning to feel conscious of his head-long arrival. 'I'm sorry to – to – ' He waved his hand awkwardly. 'Intolerably selfish one is. Somehow these grotesque circumstances bring out one's own grotesqueries. I have no right to impose arbitrary interruptions upon your enquiries.'

'That's all right. Did you see Bow-Parley at any time after the service, yesterday?'

'My last view of him was as he was coming out of the vestry with his wife, and I was on my way to lunch.'

'Shipton looks very worried,' Autumn said suddenly.

'Does he?' Christelow looked surprisedly at the Inspector.

'I dare say I do, too,' said Autumn. 'Thank you, Mr Christelow.'

When Christelow had gone, Autumn slid down into his chair, stretched his long legs out until his feet hung over the edge of the dais, and put his hands behind his head.

'That's how it's going to be,' said Dorcas. 'No one knowing a thing – '

Sudden sound welled up like a spring at the other end of the Hall, and Undigo, short, impetuous and more than usually animated, disregarding the possibility of formalities, approached High Table in quick, jerky strides, like a man learning to skate on very slippery ice.

'I decided not to wait. I have something to say.'

Undigo's address was short, and was more often the expression of his humour when putting the particularities of his colleagues into brief derogatory italics, than of his present extraordinary sternness.

'Bow-Parley would have told you this himself – he asked me whether he should and I said there was no question. His action had been discreditable, but the result left him no option – and now that he is dead it leaves me none. He had been into Shipton's rooms, rifled Shipton's drawers, and found the Vice-Chancellor's diary. In reading through the diary – he had not omitted to do so – he had found an entry in which Manchip recorded his intention of informing *him* that Shipton was carrying on a liaison with Julia Bow-Parley, unless Shipton heeded the warning he had apparently given him.'

'Mr Shipton,' Autumn shouted to Tantalum.

'That is all,' said Undigo coldly. 'That is what Bow-Parley told me.'

Autumn said: 'Why did Bow-Parley suspect Shipton in the first place?'

'I asked him the same thing. He said his suspicion had been aroused one morning after Manchip's demise when he saw Shipton entering the dead man's rooms. When Diamantis spoke of a missing diary he said he felt it his duty to allay or confirm his suspicion. Of course,' said Undigo, 'it wasn't the reason at all. Bow-Parley *wanted* to suspect Shipton, his motive being simple dislike. I dare say he was hoping to find the diary there, but was as surprised as anyone would have been when he actually came across it.'

Autumn said: 'Bow-Parley disliked Shipton.'

'I had always thought it mere chemical antipathy. Possibly Bow-Parley's wife had not been as circumspect as she imagined –'

The diary would be the 'material evidence' Bow-Parley had to show me, thought Autumn.

He said to Dorcas: 'Slip over to Bow-Parley's rooms; see if you can find it –'

Dorcas went, and Undigo and the Inspector sat in silence for a few moments.

Undigo said: 'A domestic interior adds a sinister dimension to investigations.' He glanced round him in the Hall.

'I have observed it in films and my present experience confirms the impression.'

Undigo was perhaps anxious formally to suspend operations until a third party should once more impersonalize any transaction.

'People's front rooms make a policeman in plain clothes somehow monstrous. Would you say so? One would be less likely to be *disturbed* by a questioning at the police-station itself. There would be a harmony between the event and the surroundings – the cups of tea, the uniforms, the questions, all part of a single element. But in places like this' – he looked round him again – 'the thing takes on a mystique quite horrible.'

'Mmmm,' said Autumn.

'But I dare say the attitude is "donnish" – one overlooks the obvious causes for disturbance (the two deaths, after all!) – and devotes oneself by principle to the subtle –'

'Under which category would Shipton's preoccupation with the Chaplain's wife fall?'

'Probably neither. It was not obvious – I mean, overt – and I dare say it was anything but subtle.'

Dorcas scampered up the Hall.

'Not a sign of it,' he said, dismay all over his face. 'Not a sign; looked everywhere.'

Shipton walked in. He looked worried and remote still.

Autumn said: 'Sit down, will you. Tell us again, Dr Undigo, what you have just told us.'

As Undigo spoke, the remoteness faded out of Shipton's expression: it was as if Undigo's story were a rising tide, which set afloat, as it matched in level, the load of worry Shipton had brought with him.

'So it was Bow-Parley,' Shipton said, when Undigo had finished.

'What do you mean?' Autumn asked.

'Bow-Parley who pinched it from *me*. I've been wondering all morning where the damned thing had gone.'

Then he said, irritatedly: 'Oh, yes, what Undigo says is true. I took it from Manchip's rooms.'

Now that his tension had been broached, Shipton

seemed to be regaining his natural truculence. Autumn waited for him to say more.

'*I* knew Manchip had made that memorandum in his blasted diary – he made sure I knew it, the evening after he saw us in what he chose to call a "compromising" situation. "You do not owe *me* more than discretion, sir, but I am determined to protect the Chaplain –" Protect!' Shipton laughed bitterly. 'What did he care about Bow-Parley – about as much as Bow-Parley cared about Julia. He was tapping away at his diary all the time – "I have pledged myself, I have put my warning to you in writing in my diary, and if it is contravened I shall have no choice but to inform Convocation as well as the Chaplain." I gave him my word not to see Julia again without the slightest intention of keeping it. What the devil had it to do with him? But when he died what else could I do but take the diary? It was the first thing I thought of – anyone who went through his papers would certainly find that entry. I had Julia to think of.'

'To the exclusion, of course, of yourself. Don't you realize this gives you the strongest possible motive for having killed Manchip?'

'*I* didn't kill Manchip. I just took his diary. I took it the morning after he was found on the roof. You saw me coming out. I had it under the essays.'

'He had it under the essays,' said Autumn. 'How does anyone know?'

'Christ, man –'

'Now listen to me. You might have killed Manchip because of what he knew about your association with Mrs Bow-Parley, taking the diary at the same time because of what was in it. Then you might have killed Bow-Parley because he had found you in possession of the diary –'

'Killed Bow-Parley –'

'Killed Bow-Parley – if the diary suggests you had a motive for having killed Manchip, then it is in your interests to kill anyone who finds out you have stolen the diary.'

Shipton was silent, looking at Autumn. Then he said: 'I didn't kill –' He broke off, still staring at the policeman.

'All right, then,' he said. 'Since we're exploring the possibilities, riddle me this. If the diary shows I had such a good motive for killing Manchip, and if I actually *did* kill the man, why didn't I afterwards destroy the diary instead of leaving it about to be used in evidence against me?'

Autumn raised his eyebrows pleasantly, as one whose favourite pupil has not only come up to, but exceeded, expectation.

'I'd love to know.'

'Because I didn't kill the bloody man,' Shipton shouted.

'But why didn't you destroy the thing anyway – even if your own explanation of the theft is the true one?'

'Not my property –' Shipton almost pouted.

'Not your –' Autumn looked at him in amazement.

'Look,' said Shipton. 'In the first place my explanation *is* true. I'm not likely to keep something that gives me a motive for having killed a man when I can destroy it. Am I? Unless what I say is true – that I didn't kill him. When I spoke to you that morning coming out of Manchip's rooms I said I'd shifted nothing except my own property. That was true. The information in that diary about Julia and me *is* my property. But that didn't give me the right to chuck the rest of the diary which isn't my property on the fire. You know,' added Shipton rudely, 'the morality of that doesn't seem to me to be very subtle.'

'How determined you are to think well of yourself,' sighed Autumn. The Inspector wondered whether he would get more pleasure out of hanging or out of kicking this young man.

'Perhaps you intended to burn the diary, but put it off, the first time. But you would hardly be likely to procrastinate the second time, after killing Bow-Parley. Once bitten – '

'I didn't even know Bow-Parley had taken the thing till Undigo said so this minute.'

'But you knew it had gone.'

'I knew it had gone. I kept it in the top drawer of my bureau, and I missed it this morning. I'd no idea who'd taken it. Perhaps Julia – Naturally, it was worrying me.'

'It certainly was,' said Autumn.

'But why don't you get the damn' thing –'

'Because it has disappeared for the second time. From Bow-Parley's rooms. Once bitten, twice –'

'You think it was me –'

'I think we should take a look at your rooms. It's too hot for a fire, so you won't have been burning anything. There'll be a nice clean grate.'

Autumn rose, and the three others rose with him. They all filed down the middle of the great Hall, treading on each other's heels. The cooks were whistling in the kitchens, and the odours that had streaked the air earlier in the morning had fattened and were identifiable. They walked down the stone steps into the quadrangle. The sky, plump with cumulus, had a freshly scoured brightness: last night's thunder had cleared the air.

A very short, lugubrious-looking man, with a wide drooping moustache and a camera the size of a hat box, was standing at the bottom of the steps, and took a photograph of Autumn as the four men came out. The party turned right, and walked towards Shipton's staircase. When they reached the geographer's rooms – Undigo with them, for the Inspector had motioned him on – Shipton sat down and put his feet complacently up on the sofa. Autumn walked round the room, glancing at the grate, the waste-paper basket, and the coal scuttle. Dorcas began to move things, and Undigo stared out of the window.

'Aooh!' exclaimed Dorcas

Having bent down to poke under the carpet – a perfectly sensible thing to do, under the circumstances, but an action which nevertheless seemed to reduce the search to the level of a children's game – he had straightened up and banged his head on a low-hanging mirror. His shout of pain made what should have been something of a climax, faintly otherwise. For it was only secondarily that the others noticed, as it lay on the carpet whence it had slithered from behind the mirror, the dark green oblong of Manchip's diary.

Chapter 12

'No, Horace,' said Bum to the short gentleman with the
camera who had photographed Autumn, 'definitely not.
We shouldn't be asked. Specialists, that's different, they're
paid the extra. But not the general reporter. You can call
me fastidious, but I repeat I do not care for bodies. I don't
like 'em, Horace.'

'Lovely,' nodded the short gentleman.

He too was from the *Knell*, for Mr Sharpshoot the News
Editor had decreed that the odd-looking ladies in the non-
smoking carriages were to be beguiled with pictures. Mr
Weed – for that was the short gentleman's name – was to
acquire such pictures as would most pertinently assist in
the creation of one of Mr Sharpshoot's inimitable double-
page spreads.

'Lovely,' nodded Mr Weed again, with sympathetically
cynical emphasis, and his moustache shook. The colossal
spread of this hairy member transformed Mr Weed's own
lack of inches into something close to deformity.

'No,' protested Bum very feelingly, as one whose good
nature had more than once been abused, 'who did they
send for when it was a matter of getting the life-story of
the two-headed Eskimo? Me, old boy – and I got it, armed
with nothing more than *savoir faire* and a cheque for a
thousand quid in my hip pocket. But bodies, Horace, no.
Not at any price. Call me fastidious if you like,' invited
Mr Bum, 'it's no good. I don't like crime, and I wouldn't
do it for another five hundred. And a contract,' he added,
wistfully.

'Wouldn't suit you,' said Mr Weed, understandingly.

Although the temperature was well into the seventies Mr
Weed, like his friend, wore a huge overcoat. It reached to
his heels, or, rather, to the place where his heels had been;
for Mr Weed had the appearance of one who has been
ground down, and his heels had probably borne the brunt
of it. He carried his camera – it must have been the
biggest camera in the world – slung across his right

shoulder on a thick, cruel strap. The terrible weight of the camera had given Mr Weed a permanent list, and the sight of him staggering by with one corner of his overcoat dragging the ground behind him was calculated to make the impressionable burst into tears. Indeed, Mr Weed had once gone to take pictures at a meeting of the Society for the Protection of the Underprivileged and had found himself spirited on to the platform where the speaker continually illustrated his address with gestures in Mr Weed's direction. He had been given sandwiches and Bovril before being sent back to the office in a hired car. All in all, it would have been hardly surprising had Mr Weed carried round his neck a small dog-collar, inscribed with the words 'If found, please encourage.'

'Wouldn't suit me, Horace!' echoed Bum, unbelievingly. 'It'd finish me, boy. Corpses always turned me up – even when I was doing Bereaved Households on the old Maida Vale *Intelligencer*. Dark suit, carnation, the lot, and pleased as punch they were to see you – cups of tea and seed cake. I remember once I was drinking tea in one of these front rooms with a middle-aged lady who'd lost her husband, and she asked me if I'd like to have a look at him. Well – you couldn't really say no, so I said yes what a good idea. Over we went to the coffin and there he was inside in his best suit with a little triangle of white hanky sticking out of his breast pocket. Well, you don't really know what to say, do you, so I said, "He looks well, doesn't he?" and she said, "He ought to. We only came back from Brighton last week." Well, old boy, that rather upset me.'

'Nice the way she remembered the holiday, though,' said Mr Weed.

'Oh, it was a nice thought, Horace, but it didn't sound quite right. It didn't sound quite right to *me*, Horace.'

'It's temperament,' said Mr Weed.

'There was an Irish household I went to round Holloway Road way; they had a wake. Gave me a fright of my life when I went in – they'd tied a piece of string round the neck of the chap in the coffin and looped the other end round the doorknob so that when anyone came in, he sat up.'

'The door opened outwards, of course.'

'The door opened outwards, Horace.'

'Lovely,' said Mr Weed, and jerked his head.

When Mr Weed said 'lovely' he very seldom meant 'lovely'. More often than not his use of the word indicated assent; but it had a variety of applications. Sometimes it was a breathless exhalation, barely audible, as he clicked the shutter upon a pop-breasted chorus girl; on such occasions Mr Weed manoeuvred his subject into ambiguous attitudes with the air of one whose *bona fides* may turn out to be questionable. And sometimes when Mr Weed said 'lovely' – when, for instance, he had been given a three a.m. assignment – it was symptomatic of feelings that had long been rubbed smooth, and was not so much spoken as given off, like exhaust.

'No, it's not on, Horace, not on at all, old boy. I phone two scoops and now they're asking me to do a think piece on "Is it the Work of a Madman?" What's Moira going to feel like when she sees something like that on the front page, and me down here in the thick of it? She goes through torture with that nervous indigestion. No, old boy, if Rind wasn't doing eighteen months I'd resign tomorrow and let 'em get on with it, honestly I would. You've got to draw the line somewhere, and it's not as if it's *my* job. I dunno!'

Mr Bum jerked his head as his habit was when words failed him, an action so instantly and faithfully reproduced by Mr Weed (with the addition of slight labiodental percussion) that the exchange partook of familiar ritual. It was as if deprecatory colloquy of this kind were as inevitable, when one journalist met another, as fire from two sticks. Despite its depressing timbre, the conversation seemed to tone both parties up.

'There he is,' Mr Weed said, as Autumn came out of Shipton's staircase with Undigo and Dorcas. 'He's been in there since before lunch.'

'Get him and me, Horace boy, will you? Jackie may not use it, but Moira'd like one.'

Undigo had hurried away, but Autumn and Dorcas came over the grass towards the lodge where the journalist and the photographer were standing.

'He's a nice fellow,' Bum said to Mr Weed, 'but I don't think he's a got a clue.'

But Autumn was pondering the clue he had got. The trouble with it, he thought, it's such a whacking big clue. Shipton's behaviour more than confirmed his motive; but the confirmation – the secretion of the diary – was too bald not to be a little suspect. *Why* hadn't the man destroyed such incriminating evidence after pinching it? Why admit pinching it at all? It was only Undigo's word against his that Bow-Parley had found the diary in his rooms. Either he was a colossal idiot, or he was telling the truth.

'Take him in, eh?' Dorcas, carrying the diary, spoke absently. His eye was on the photographer, and he pondered publicity.

Autumn didn't answer. The whole lot's got to be sat down and thought about, he reflected. But do I know enough? Can you solve a crossword without recognizing all the clues?

'Take him in?' Dorcas persisted, and knocked a fly from Autumn's shoulder.

'Broken my handcuffs,' grunted Autumn.

Dorcas looked startled: 'We've got plenty – '

Bum approached the Inspectors, linked his arms through each of theirs, and said: 'How's this, Horace?'

'Not too stiff, gentlemen,' whispered the photographer, down on one knee. 'Lovely.'

Not twice, thought Autumn, not even a lunatic would steal it twice and not think to destroy it the second time. And such a daft place to hide it, behind a mirror. . . .

'I'd like a dozen,' said Dorcas.

'How's the head, old boy?' asked Bum.

'Can't send you a dozen, old boy,' the photographer said to Dorcas. 'We'd never have time to print the papers if we started that sort of lark.'

'Finished the old inquisition, I see,' said Bum. 'What's the verdict?'

If he'd been in a hurry there's just a chance he might have stuffed it behind there temporarily, but he had all night to get rid of it. The time has come to sit down and –

'Dunno about the work of a bluddy madman, but the way things happen round here they'll be fetching *me* away in a plain van very soon,' Bum said. 'Eh, Horace?'

Autumn's face suddenly lit up. He stepped forward, grasped Bum's hand and shook it heartily.

'Thank you,' he said. 'Thank you very much indeed.'

Everyone looked surprised. Autumn said to Dorcas: 'Lock the diary up in my rooms. Put it in the safe with the *Book of the Lion*. Here's the key. You'll have to finish questioning the rest on your own. Oh' – he stepped into the street, turning explanatorily as Dorcas opened his mouth – 'know a little place' – he drew out a pair of handcuffs – 'have them ready for me in no time.'

Chapter 13

THAT was it. I should have remembered, thought the Inspector. Not that it'll produce much – an aberration, as like as not. But she *had* spotted the bonfire; and she had a telescope. Mad only north north west perhaps.

The air was balmy in the High. The little bay-windowed tailor's shop on the corner of Alfred Street had replaced its infinitely mutating waistcoats with chaste lengths of *crêpe de Chine*; a sign as certain as the swallows that summer had come to stay. Streams of nice-looking girls in gay dresses and sunglasses sluiced the dusty pavements, as they made their way to the river to watch earnest men rowing boats. For it was Eights' Week, and in addition to the fatal concussions with which this history is more particularly concerned, wholesome 'bumps' were being exchanged upon the Isis. Soon, night would be made hideous by rowing men, raucous after Bump Suppers; Colleges gates would be stormed in a spirit of histrionic revelry, and cries of 'Free beer at Balliol!' would ring out boldly from the throats of men who had read about that sort of thing.

Autumn enjoyed the sunlight as he marched briskly along. The sitting and thinking (he reflected), that would have to wait – until this had been looked into. Another clue revealed as a clue, and the sitting and thinking might be undertaken with greater confidence. Good.

A hand brandishing a long brass cylinder appeared from the attic window of Mrs Spectre's. It had some explanatory significance, for the head of Mrs Spectre's middle-aged daughter appeared beside it, and the telescope was again shaken as if Autumn should thereby understand that the lady was unable to answer the door.

'I can't leave my post,' Miss Spectre cried. 'She said she'd shoot me –'

'Isn't your mother in?'

'Gone to see the boats with Mr Singh. Knock again. She may not have left yet.'

Miss Spectre was embarrassed.

'She takes it all so seriously, you see,' she called down. 'We changed the guard and everything –'

Autumn waited.

'She'll ask me for casualty reports when she comes in,' tittered Miss Spectre unhappily, 'and I'm so unimaginative. I think the people on the television are *nice*, you see. It's hard pretending they're enemies when you feel they're friends. . . .'

Autumn raised his hand to knock a third time, when the door slowly opened, and a voice hissed: 'One false move–'

'It's all right, ma'am. It's only me.'

Mrs Spectre replaced her swordstick in the hallstand.

'I was for leaving by the back entrance, but Mr Singh suggested that as no one would be expecting us to use the front that would be the best way. A most convincing display of Oriental guile.'

'By gum, ma'am, your readiness to distribute the credit to me is hypertypically English,' said Mr Singh, who stood behind her. 'Hanged if it isn't! It was not an altogether unintelligent wheeze, though' – he flashed his bright teeth like a roll of drums – 'I says it myself, as shouldn't.'

Mr Singh was dressed with very great care, and an eye to the season. The dark blue serge of his blazer was relieved at the breast-pocket by the crest of the Worshipful Company of Spectacle Makers, and an I Zingari square snugged into the collar of his expensive shirt. His turban had been replaced by the cheerful striped cap of the Oxford University Ping Pong Sodality. Mr Singh's insurance – as far as idiom went – was comprehensive, and there was of course an outside chance that he was entitled to everything.

He took the arm of Mrs Spectre with great delicacy, and they, with the Inspector, moved off towards the river, pleasure bent.

Mrs Spectre looked at Mr Singh approvingly.

'How many of *us*, Commissioner,' she said, 'would be willing to recline upon a bed of flaming cinders at the drop, so to speak, of a bowl of rice?'

'English rice-pudding is a firm favourite with many

educated Indian gentlemen,' said Mr Singh. 'I myself am partial to that dish when served with strawberry jam. At many of the cultivated English tables at which it has been my good fortune to sit – both Metropolitanly and in the Shires – rice-pudding has been in great demand at the luncheon hour. The westernized stomach has also reacted very favourably to the addition of a little diced rhubarb. We might suggest it to the virgin your daughter as a possible alternative to her mouth-watering prunes-and-custard.'

The sun struck back from the asphalt of St Aldates, fuming like a tar-engine. The party turned into Christ Church, came through the quadrangles, and out into the Meadows.

'Things pretty so-so on the television front?' Autumn asked the old lady as they walked down towards the river bank.

'I have observed,' interjected Mr Singh, who had been humming a Beethoven quartet, 'the television to be popular with the natives in Cawnpore. For ourselves, of course, we prefer a rattling good game of tennis, succeeded by meaty conversation over the odd pink gin.'

'You haven't actually seen anything of the little men since the night of the fire, I take it, Mrs Spectre?' Autumn pursued.

'Not a sign,' boomed the lady.

'I am proud to be considered your ally, ma'am,' said Mr Singh, then lowered his voice so that the lady should not hear, and whispered to Autumn: 'Genuine upper-class eccentricity, biologically attributable to the menopause.'

They had reached the towing-path, and rowing men were crunching moodily past them with great oars slung across their shoulders. Beneath the sunlit poplars old men in faded blazers strolled, while the younger ones sauntered arm-in-arm with pretty girls. Amid the gay scarves, the short sleeves, the sunburnt arms, Autumn in his blue suit felt like a bad case of indecent exposure.

As far as the eye could see, the College barges stretched along the river bank in a concourse of inelegance, sitting down cheerfully in the water like stout parties in the sea-side postcards. The Inspector almost expected to see them filled with happy Cockneys singing 'Knees up Mother Brown', and eating whelks.

'No sight,' yodelled Mr Singh, waving his hand towards the barges, 'could be more agreeably typical.'

The white-jacketed servants stand with their trays, and the women push close to the rail, craning their pretty necks as the long awaited Eights shoot by. 'Rowed, Trinity!' cry the men in blazers, standing on tiptoe, while in the boats little bespectacled Stentors are screaming at their men to 'Give her ten hard,' and the distance between the Eights expands and contracts as if the boats are strung together on elastic. Suddenly it is all over, and the crews are rowing back over the way they have come, great big men looking a little sheepish now that the effort has been made, and affecting not to hear when a gnarled thin old gentleman of about eighty, who looks startlingly like the schoolboy he must once have been, raises his Leander cap and cries out 'Well *done*!' as they paddle by.

And then on the barges there is such a dashing after little pink cakes and dishes of ice-cream and more tea, while Dennis (from the Buttery) takes a stolid inventory of each man's ordering, and Len (from the Bar) makes his way through the tables with the cucumber sandwiches. There is such a taking up of interrupted introductions, and mothers in pink dresses are meeting tutors in tweeds, and it is 'I don't think you've met my –' and 'Do you know my –' and 'Can I introduce my –', while the shyer undergraduates are wondering how their tutors can possibly be interested enough in *them* to want to meet their families, and their tutors are very probably wondering the same thing. And now a fresh cargo of visitors is leaving the further bank in a big black punt the size of a battleship, manned by the College boatman, who wears a blue serge suit and a cap with a shiny peak. He is poling from stem to stern with a very slow reluctant relish, and as he reaches the barge he swings the great punt round and rams it up against the landing stage. And then, as the last passenger steps up on to the barge, a gun goes off, so far away in the distance it sounds like a toy cap-pistol, and once more the ladies crowd to the rails, and another race begins.

'What,' repeated Mr Singh, 'could be more agreeably typical?'

Agreeable it certainly was, but Autumn was feeling a trifle uncomfortable. The random notion of a cracked old lady . . . well, one has only to ask, and if it *is* a delusion . . .

There was a shout, and Autumn looked up to see Orson Dogg leaning over the rail of one of the barges. Mr Dogg had laid aside his transatlantic seersucker in favour of a handsome yellow kilt, dirks and all (for the Doggs, it seemed, were one of the very springiest branches of the clan McClavichord), but was still recognizable by the psychological spectacles of immense thickness that bridged his inquiring nose. It was to Mr Singh that he had specifically addressed himself (for Mr Dogg had once been a lodger himself at Mrs Spectre's, and had enjoyed many a cultivated dispute with Mr Singh over the late-night cocoa) and he was now inviting all three to 'Come aboard'.

Like a highly-bred greyhound with a touch of the tar brush, Mr Singh trotted across the narrow gangplank, and having reached the lower deck of the vessel, stationed himself at the rail and extended a lean hand to his hostess. The Inspector followed close behind the lady, watchful lest her buttoned boots should stray into her cumbrous hem-lines, and pitch her, combs foremost, into the Isis.

Autumn was wondering vaguely what his explanation would sound like if some hard-headed member of the public, anxious to see that the police were doing a sound job, should tap him on the shoulder and ask him what line he was pursuing.

'Well, you see the large old lady with the combs, on the arm of the dark gentleman – she thinks she is being attacked by an army of little men from the television, and when I went to see her I had to give the password –'

No, the public could go and have a bark at itself, sniffed Autumn pettishly.

It was crowded on deck, for it was the practice of other Colleges to overflow on to the Warlock barge when their own vessels became too populous. Nicholas Flower and Balboa Tomlin were seated at a table close to the rail, and Dogg led his visitors towards it.

'I hope Dogg has apologized for the accommodation, Inspector,' said Nicholas Flower. 'I feel as if we are about to weigh anchor for Newcastle and a fresh cargo of Derby Brights.'

The Warlock barge was indeed the most unwholesome of all. It had been acquired by the College in 1895, for though Warlock as a graduate society did not row, it enjoyed watching it. Never a glamorous craft, the barge had in fact burnt on the waters the year following its purchase, when Warden Voggins (that eminent if eccentric High Churchman), having been invited to address the Guild of Non-Conforming Gentlewomen aboard the vessel (it had been selected as neutral territory), arrived smelling strongly of incense and proceeded to ignite a score or so of Roman Candles by way of making his position clear. The barge never recovered the severe charring it sustained on that occasion, and it became in consequence much valued at a later date by the Experimental Theatre Club as a setting for period drama. The years passed, and it sank lower in the water, staggering at its perpetual anchor like a maritime Lady Tippins.

'Oh, *don't*,' said Balboa, as Mr Singh murmured rapt compliments on her becoming attire. 'Whenever anyone says nice things about my clothes I'm always frightened I shall swirl up my dress and say "Knickers to match!" Mama used to do it to me when I was small and there were people staying. It was *awful*.'

Balboa wore a dress of plain black with no sleeves and a curving neckline. On anyone else, it would have suggested a Holloway warderess; but it made Balboa look like a highly seasoned angel.

'Do you think I should offer to undergo treatment, Doggy dear?'

'Why, Balboa, you ask that question more in a fun-loving spirit than out of any real desire for enlightenment. But I am sure if you once studied up a little in psychology you would be as struck as I was at the comprehensive –'

117

'God bless us everyone, what does a whoreson mad-fellow in a kilt know about it?' bellowed Nicholas Flower, chucking lumps of sugar over the rail on to the landing stage below. 'Leave off, you gifted amateur, do. Don't you see the Inspector here? He's the expert, my lad, he's the one who knows a hawk from a handsaw round this neck of the woods.'

I'd like to find out whether Mrs Spectre is capable of making that distinction, Autumn thought. Surrounded by these garrulous youngsters, it's going to be difficult to get a private word with her. Autumn poured Mrs Spectre a cup of tea.

And then, a long way away, in the distance beyond the bend in the river, cheering broke out, sputtering along the line of barges like fire along a fuse, until once more the Eights were sliding energetically past, and the tables were being deserted as everyone crowded to the rails. For a moment, Autumn and Mrs Spectre were alone.

'Mrs Spectre,' Autumn began hurriedly, 'you recollect telling me about the bonfire –'

There was a roar as the Walpurgis Eight came into view. ('Keep your bloody bottoms *down*,' bellowed Pearl Corker through a megaphone on the opposite bank.)

'Careful reconnaissance is always rewarding. I might have been smoked out –'

'Yes, ma'am, I know,' said Autumn desperately. 'And you said they came from the television – and you also said '

People were turning from the rail and sitting down again.

'But of course they *do* get corns there, poor dears,' Balboa was saying, 'and it must be awfully embarrassing deciding whether to go to a doctor or a chiropodist –'

She slumped down into her chair, careless, bored, unconcerned.

'You know,' she said to Autumn, 'I never quite gathered what it was you were asking Dim about notes.' She gazed out across the river. 'A note or something.' When you ran for the bus.' The faint insistence of the words belied the casual tone in which they were uttered.

'You said you wanted to see some note, or something –'

'Bingo!' exploded Nicholas Flower, who had been dropping pieces of sugar on someone down below. He straightened up, his face red from the exertion. 'My last fusillade made a most pleasurable *flat* noise as it bounced off Egg's straw –'

Balboa said: 'Dim isn't here –'

Mr Singh and Mrs Spectre had risen and moved slowly towards the bows of the vessel to place themselves for the next race. Near them, Autumn could see Diamantis, annotating his score card. The ex-secretary had an air of being lost – now that Manchip was dead Diamantis had become a displaced person.

'Poor darling Dim,' said Balboa, searching the deck with her eyes, 'perhaps he's feeling too horribly suspect.' She drummed her fingers on the table.

Nicholas Flower, still leaning over the rail, turned round.

'Nab his passport while you've got the chance, Inspector,' he said. 'Dim had a thumping good motive for killing Bow-Parley – with Manchip dead, Bow-Parley could easily have nipped in between Dim and the election to the Rockinge Chair. Of course,' Flower nibbled a piece of his sugar, 'that leaves Manchip outstanding. We've been assuming Manchip was going to vote for Dim – as indeed Dim told my charming lady companion here – but supposing he wasn't. I wonder' – Flower was leaning against the rail on his folded arms, facing away from them – 'whether Manchip didn't change his mind. At the last moment, say. Decided he was going to give his vote to Bow-Parley on the grounds' – and Flower half turned round, grinning – 'of Fairlight's familiarity with the undergraduettes. And told him so.'

'There's absolutely no reason to suppose for a single instant –' cried Balboa.

'Yes, yes,' Autumn replied absently. 'I think I hear the boats again. I didn't get much of a view of the last one. I think if I just –'

As Autumn rose and edged away from the table through the crowd, he caught sight of Balboa's plump hands. They were laced together as tight as the meshes of a tiger's cage.

Autumn slid past groups of people balancing cups and saucers, pressing his way towards Mrs Spectre. He eased momentarily into a space a few heads away from her, to allow a servant to pass with a tray, and stepping back quickly he collided with Diamantis, who was staring through his fieldglasses at the bend in the river.

'Ah! That diary's turned up,' the Inspector said. 'Looking into it.'

'Oh, good – did you – er – where did you – ?'

'Tell you all about it,' promised Autumn, seizing his opportunity to move up to where Mrs Spectre still leant upon the arm of Mr Singh. As the boats were coming into view round the bend, Autumn was standing directly behind her.

'Madam,' said Autumn, taking the plunge, 'what sort of a van?'

'An ordinary reconnaissance van, one assumes,' said the lady, turning round. 'You refer to the television van?'

'The one you told me the little men come in.'

'They do come in it. I see no other reason for the presence of a van in Radcliffe Square at 0400 hours every other Wednesday. Do you?'

'At 0400 hours?'

'You have a habit of repeating simple statements, Commissioner. The van has turned into Radcliffe Square every other Wednesday for the last six months at that time. It goes in, then it comes out.'

'Do you see what they do, ma'am?'

'There is a church between my house and Radcliffe Square. It is in the way.' The lady said this as if she were breaking the news about cause and effect to a philosophy class. 'They do not make periscopes big enough to see over churches, and even if I had one it would take an octupus to use both it and a telescope at the same time.'

'The last six months, you say?'

'Cor strike me lucky!' exclaimed the lady in an ecstasy of impatience (Lesson 7 from Tring had been 'Exclamatory Colloquialism', and Mr Singh had asked Mrs

Spectre to hear him through them), 'cor strike me lucky, some of you fellows! I *do* say it, Commissioner, and I am constrained to add that when I told Mr Archangel the same thing this morning he appeared to assimilate it at once.'

Autumn's nerves tightened like brake cables.

'Mr Archangel asked you about the van, did he?'

'He seemed to suspect the existence of such a vehicle even before I mentioned anything about it. I was able to confirm it.'

'What did he say?'

'He, too, was sure it was full of the little men, and suggested our best plan would be to lull them into a state of false security by saying nothing to anyone about the van, and pretending we hadn't seen it. He has not, he says, been in contact with the television himself, but informs me that his old nanny in Siberia who can neither read nor write possesses a set, together with an electric toaster and a chromium-plated samovar which says, "Wake up, little Mother" in the morning, and brews the tea, all automatically.'

'O bravo, bravo, well done, first-rate,' sizzled Mr Singh who had been watching the race. 'Never was such sport, I do believe. What a pleasure it is for an Asian wet-bob like myself!'

As Mrs Spectre disentangled her telescope from a large woollen reticule, the Inspector murmured: 'I think Mr Archangel's advice is very sound. We should say nothing, ma'am. We should not even speak about it to Mr Archangel.' He paused. 'It is Wednesday today, Mrs Spectre.'

The lady nodded.

'They are due tonight, and I shall be on watch of course. Circumspect,' she raised a finger restrainingly, 'by all means. But ultimately,' she brought her finger down *crescendo*, 'kill the bastards!'

Chapter 14

THE voice of Falal hung bodilessly in the dimness of the
Hall, and Autumn paused at the threshold, his eye still
full of the bright day outside. Thick shafts of light barred
the interior, dropping down from the high windows, and
behind them, where the dais was lapped in brown
shadow, the thin voice spread like a convolvulus across the
rich, aromatic, dusty air.

'Why, yes, indeed, we were not without our diversions.
Twenty or thirty couple of verses you'd compose after
your breakfast, you would indeed, and a good meal it was
with a chop and some kidneys – fine kidneys they cooked
in my College when I was an undergraduate – and plenty
of marmalade. That was the way to end a good breakfast,
plenty of marmalade. Hnnn, hnnn. Then over Port
Meadow to Godstow and back through Binsey, in the
afternoon – ah, what afternoons they were, all golden and
damp in the autumn time and a smell in the air that
plucked a man's soul out of his body. I remember it all.'

The Inspector walked down the Hall, through the dust
in the sunbeams.

'Then in to dinner. Good dinners they were, I can tell
you. Why, there were three-bottle men in my time, do you
know; yes, I recall them well. There was my acquaintance
Carsonby – a good man he was, he died in Shropshire
many years ago – yes, I have seen my acquaintance
Carsonby take a three-pint sconce full up right to the brim
with old Madeira – old Madeira, indeed it was, I remem-
ber that well – and take it off at a sitting. Not at a draught,
you understand, that wouldn't have done at all, and my
acquaintance Carsonby would not have countenanced it.
Indeed he would not. Well, well, the story of the three-
pint sconce brought him an invitation of the Master to
dine, and dine he did. Hnnn, hnnn. I recall he told me he
made to leave while there was yet one guest remaining,
for my acquaintance Carsonby would not be the last to
leave, Carsonby had a sense of how one went on in society.

But the Master insisted he stay. Insisted, hnnn, hnnn. And very late they sat, I recall it well. Carsonby sent his compliments to the Master at nine o'clock next morning (the Master was his tutor, do you see) and begged to be excused his tutorial hour as he found his head was paining him and he proposed taking a seltzer and remaining in bed. It was Carsonby's way of conceding victory, for his head was as clear as a bell, clear as a bell. He considered it would never do for the Master to be out-done by one of his pupils. Hnnn, hnnn. Excellent, excellent –'

Falal sat in a great wooden armchair – the Master's seat at High Table – with Dorcas at his side. Dorcas roused himself from an attentive torpor as Autumn approached.

'Yes, I remember it all, you see. Everything splendid, and plenty of clever men all working hard and the entire University undistracted by the presence, hnnn, hnnn, of women. Entirely absent, they were, I can tell you. We didn't think much about them, do you know, they stayed away, and we had 'em up to watch us row.'

Dorcas nodded to Autumn.

'Just finishing. Professor Falal's been giving me his movements.'

Over the last sixty years, Autumn thought.

'I was telling this man here about the treasure-hunts we used to have when I was an undergraduate.' Falal turned to Autumn. 'Splendid affairs they were, I congratulate you on your efforts to get them started again. My sole regret last night was that I had already taken my cocoa. Had I not already taken my cocoa, I should have been up and joining you, indeed I should.'

'We need an old hand, Professor.'

'Of course you do, of course you do. Mind you give me good warning of the next. Well, well, I am engaged to sherry with an acquaintance in Balliol so I shall leave you. No women, mind, treasure hunts wouldn't do for them at all, they have no talent for deduction, no talent at all.'

'Well, the Master can no longer dispute that with you, sir.'

'Manchip?' Falal had manoeuvred his way with tolerable dexterity down the steps of the dais. He paused at the bottom. 'No, he cannot, indeed he cannot.' He paused again. 'He thoroughly deserved to be killed,' said Falal, and hobbled away.

'Hard as nails,' Dorcas said, looking after him. He handed Autumn his notes and the key of the safe containing the diary and *The Book of the Lion*.

'Do you have a car?'

'Two or three down at the Station.'

'No, not a police car – one of your own?'

'An old Ford.'

'Good – meet me in it at midnight in Radcliffe Square. Keep well in to the lee of the Bodleian among the others. Got it?'

'Hel-lo! You've been on the job, my boy –'

'We'll see,' said Autumn. 'Midnight. And stay in the car.'

'Right.'

Dorcas, headlong for domestic felicity in the shape of a nice finnan haddock and solicitous enquiry about the day's doings, hurried off to a bus-stop. Autumn walked back across the grass to the SCR.

Dinner in Warlock that evening was a subdued affair, possibly because the current topic – that of Shipton and Manchip's diary – whilst it may have conduced to unlimited silent speculation, offered no openings for conversation; especially since Shipton had elected to dine alone in his rooms. But it was not merely Shipton's absence which had produced the heaviness, it was something more, something which had been accumulating very slowly ever since the night Manchip had been found.

Fairlight broke a roll and ran his finger over the crumb.

'When's it going to stop?' he murmured in a low tone to Rankine. 'I mean the – the –' He broke off, flipping fragments of crust from his napkin. 'I mean, two already. One wonders who –'

The movement of Fairlight's eyes about the Table was brief, furtive, frightened.

Rankine was as much ill at ease as the New Critic.

'The situation has become intolerable, intolerable,' he

said in a high agitated voice. 'Every single one of us could be murdered in our beds and no one any the wiser. I maintain that the College should have been evacuated – no one is safe – the maniac should have been isolated. We sit here not knowing which of us may not be dead by morning, it is sordid, obscene –'

Even Undigo seemed less than himself. Rankine's voice had carried shrilly to the end of the table but Undigo, uncharacteristically, made no riposte.

Falal who had been mumbling a chop said suddenly:

'You are frightened. That is the fact of it. You are all frightened. Which of us will be next is the question you ponder. Well, I for one take the practical view – this afternoon I had large bolts affixed to all my doors. *I* do not intend to be murdered in my bed, indeed I do not, and the murderer - whichever of you he may be – can take that as final!'

Falal peered at each of the other dons in turn and nodded emphatically.

'Really –' muttered Clapp.

But no one seemed disposed to talk. The air of unease which had been mounting since Manchip had been swung down from the roof of the Chapel had jellied, thickened, become specific. It was not unease. It was fear.

Autumn laid down his fork and glanced behind him down the Hall. Orson Dogg and Egg and Nicholas Flower were eating at the undergraduates' table, Dogg speaking emphatically, tapping the table with his finger. Archangel was not to be seen.

Dropping a line to his chromium-plated grandmother, thought the Inspector. *Suspected* the existence of a van! Knew, more likely, and wanted to find out whether the lady, who had spotted the bonfire of books through her telescope, had spotted the van as well. Archangel had told her to say nothing – but telling her to keep quiet could be no more than a temporary expedient. Ladies of that kidney are not reliably shut up for long by mere telling – Autumn had proved it. Which suggested – what? That the function of the van – whatever that function might be – could be expected to be fulfilled in the short time the lady *might* keep quiet. In other words, the van would be disappearing very soon. In other words – in other words, tonight was to be the van's last visit?

This fragment of deductive reasoning pleased the Inspector, not primarily because of its spurious air of extemporaneity (it had taken him the full twenty minutes of a contemplative stroll back from the river) but more because it could be so easily checked. They would find out all about that van tonight. . . .

Autumn's eyes lifted from his plate, and entered instantaneously into the same plane as the eye of Lord Pinner, who was sitting opposite. For a second, the Inspector's fancy yawed. Supposing the Commissioner was going to be right, supposing this Archangel, this Russian, was instigating some abominable flux in behalf of some cause. Suppose they were *all* in it – Lord Pinner, Christelow, Shipton, Fairlight, the lot, all of them True Believers – burning books, dispatching colleagues (a purge? dissension in the Party?)! Everywhere a disordered psychology, each man's actions significant at a secondary level – frenzied attempts to alleviate by subversion some personal inadequacy?

Autumn's eye, and the eye of Lord Pinner, withdrew, each from the plane of the other, and the Inspector wondered whether the business side of birth-control, usury, and the desire to found a College, were only minor aspects of an identity more completely fulfilled in more obscure ways.

When they were drinking their coffee in the S CR after dinner, Undigo came up to Autumn, and said: 'What are you going to do?'

'Nothing yet.'

'Shipton is one of us. I should like to know.'

Autumn looked at Undigo.

'Was he telling the truth?'

Undigo raised his eyebrows, almost as if he had expected this question and had been unable to find an answer.

'I really do not know. I could not say. I wonder how well we ever know anyone.'

'There's one thing – you realized he could have turned your story down flat?'

'My story –'

'The information. No one could have verified it, with Bow-Parley dead. Shipton could have denied setting eyes on the diary.'

'Yes; you are quite right.' Undigo stood with his hands clasped behind him, his legs astride, and levered himself forward from his heels to his toes, and back. 'That would suggest he *was* telling the truth.'

'Yes, it does.' Autumn accepted a cigar. 'I think he is an honest man. Honest on this score, at least. I find it incredible that he should not have destroyed the diary – supposing that he had killed Manchip to suppress information that the diary contained. And doubly incredible that he should not have destroyed it a second time –'

'Unless,' said Undigo, 'he hadn't time. The second time, I mean – in between killing Bow-Parley, hitting you on the head and the general uproar. You visited our rooms immediately afterwards, he could hardly let himself be discovered setting fire –'

'Oh, he had plenty of time. All night, after I'd gone. Plenty of time.' Autumn exhaled, and a blue vein of cigar smoke expanded into indistinguishable capillaries. 'And even if he had decided simply to hide it again, he would have chosen a less footling place than the back of a mirror. No, no. Shipton didn't put it behind that mirror.'

Undigo's large eyebrows rose again.

'Aha,' he said, 'a plant!'

'It seems reasonable. The sort of rough frame-up a killer in a hurry might think of. Bow-Parley may have told the man who killed him about the Shipton entry in the diary. The same thing he told you. After the murder I dare say it occurred to the killer that he could mask himself a bit by implicating Shipton. He probably realized – as we have realized – that planting the diary on Shipton wouldn't incriminate Shipton categorically. But it would do as a temporary diversion – suspicion misdirected, time gained –'

'But how could he be sure you would search Shipton's rooms, and so find –'

'Exactly. He knew *I* didn't know a connexion between Shipton and Manchip's diary existed. *He* would have to have told me. He would have to have told me what *you* told me' – Autumn drained his coffee cup – 'you saved him a job.'

Undigo met the Inspector's gaze, but said nothing.

'Well, well,' said the Inspector, handing his coffee cup to Dimbleby, who was passing with a tray, 'it always turns out to be the butler in the end.'

It was close on midnight when Autumn walked out into the quadrangle. The grass, dark odoriferous velvet, cloyed his feet as he walked over to the Lodge, and when he stepped from it the sound of his heels on the gravel almost startled him.

He walked out into the starlit city where the air hung still, and as he walked, stark, frantic runners sprang up like figures on a darkened stage, thudded past him, and were suddenly gone. 'Harke, Hieronimo, he's mad agayn,' they might have hissed in passing, 'Cover her face, mine eies dazzle, shee died young.' They were undergraduates running to reach their Colleges before midnight, and they deepened Autumn's awareness of the prevenient quality that invests deserted streets at night-time.

Radcliffe Square was a litter of still silent bicycles as Autumn turned into it. The stillness of things always impressed him, the stillness of impressive things (he thought, as the dome of the Radcliffe Camera, the stiff pinnacles of All Souls, the spire of the Church of St Mary, grew in their stillness beneath the moving sky) most of all.

He poked his head through the window of an old Ford, and gazed upon the softly heaving bosom of his colleague.

'Awake, for morning in the bowl of night –'

'Oof!' Dorcas woke up, rubbing his moustache. 'Funny you should quote that. I gave it to my sister for Christmas last year in one of those pocket editions in suède leather. Dear, oh dear, I dozed off. Shocking dreams I get. I thought I was walking into the greengrocer's for three pound of potatoes and I said to the chap behind the counter, "Three pound of King Edwards," and he said, "I can't serve you in that get-up." I was wearing a toreador's outfit –'

'Wish fulfilment,' suggested Autumn, climbing into the seat beside Dorcas.

'I don't think so, old man – I'm an anti-vivisectionist.'

The car was parked very close to the wall of the Bodleian in the middle of a handful of other vehicles. The wall, which was bisected by a gated arch leading into the Old Schools Quadrangle, was to the right of the car, and to the left stood the Radcliffe Camera. In front was the wall of the Fellows' Garden of Exeter, to the left of which was Brasenose Lane, and further left still stood Brasenose itself. Behind the car, at some distance across the cobbles, was Catte Street, which ran along by the wall of the Hawksmoor Quadrangle of All Souls.

Dorcas wedged his little legs more comfortably against the steering wheel.

'Well, come on – let's have it. What are we waiting for?'

Autumn told him.

'A van?'

'A van.'

'So we just wait –'

'We just wait.'

The two detectives spoke together in low voices for a time, falling silent when, once or twice, someone trailed a spidery shadow across the cobbles of the Square, and when, once, a night-foundered reveller pulled himself cursing up the wall of Exeter, sitting astride the top, before slipping uncertainly down on the other side.

A night breeze sprang up, filtering through Bishop Kennicott's fig-tree where it hung bloomily in the darkness over the wall of Exeter, lapping the cobbles and setting the dust adrift. Soon the policemen stopped talking altogether, and the only sound in the Square was the whisper of the wind as it blew softly round the car.

Autumn woke from a doze momentarily convinced that

some dreadful accident had paralysed him from the waist down. His eyes gradually became used to the darkness inside the car again, and he saw that it was Dorcas's head, lying across his thighs like a large pale root. He pushed the head upright without wakening its owner, flexed his legs and shivered in the darkness. It was cold.

From the quadrangles of Merton two flat notes disengaged themselves and broke over the dark town. Wrangling affirmation went up from the other Colleges, prolonged itself, and subsided, the silence racing in again from the meadows and spires and small lanes, with a bell still tolling faintly across the fields towards Binsey. Autumn did not sleep again, although his eyes pricked. He watched, staring through the misty windscreen towards Brasenose and Exeter, turning round to glance into Catte Street, and cocking an ear to listen above the 'Uh-huh-uh-huh —' which came from Dorcas as he slept.

Three o'clock struck, and four o'clock. There had been no movement in the Square for nearly three hours. Autumn rubbed his knee-caps where they had pressed against the dashboard, moving from buttock to buttock to restore the circulation in his bottom. With no sense of climax whatever, a van slipped silently into the Square in front of them, and pulled up in front of Bishop Kennicott's fig-tree.

The approach of the van had not at all violated the stillness of the Square. There was the strange suspension of life which vehicles exude when they come to a halt and no one has stepped out of them, and Autumn wondered for a second whether he had seen anything at all. Then there was a small, distinct, shattering *click*. The door had opened. A figure moved out of the darkness, away from the van, and went towards the gated arch in the wall of the Bodleian.

Dorcas woke up.

'Here! There's someone over there. Where the bloody hell —'

Autumn gripped his arm venomously.

The figure paused at the arch. He stood still in the moonlight, then passed through the gate. They could hear his feet, carefully put down, echoing through the archway. Then there was absolute quiet.

'He picked that bloody lock –'.

'The van, the *van*, he got out of the van,' hissed Autumn. 'For God's sake, shut up –'

For fifteen minutes they sat in silence. Then the figure reappeared through the archway and went back to the van.

'Oh, oh – the *books* –' Dorcas whispered.

The man seemed to be carrying a load both cumbersome and heavy. He carried it in both arms, in front of him, leaning back slightly to take the weight on his chest. The van was only just visible in the deeper pool of darkness beneath the fig-tree, but they saw him pass to the rear of it, fumble with one hand to let down the back, and then pitch whatever he carried inside.

'Nick him?'

As Dorcas spoke, the dark figure was moving back towards the archway.

'Wait,' said Autumn.

They sat and waited. In another fifteen minutes the man was back, laden as before.

'Blimey, he's having a birthday,' muttered Dorcas. 'There must be a couple of dozen there –'

Again they waited, and again the man went back through the arch. He made six journeys. After he had pitched the sixth load into the back of the van, he lifted up and secured the tail-board, then walked round to the front and climbed in.

Dorcas's hand was on the starter.

'Softly,' whispered Autumn. 'Let him turn round first. . . .'

The van moved out of the shadow of the fig-tree, curved round behind the Ford and bumped slowly over the cobbles towards Catte Street. It reached the road, and turned right, disappearing behind the Camera in the direction of the High.

'Right. Keep well over to his near-side where he can't use his mirror.'

The Ford bucked girlishly across the cobbles and slid into Catte Street. As Dorcas swung the wheel right, they saw the van round the corner into the High. Dorcas drove slowly down Catte Street, hovered at the corner, and turned right after the van. The two vehicles proceeded up the High at convoy distance towards Carfax.

At Carfax, the van turned right again, into the Cornmarket, and Dorcas followed suit. They crossed the junction of George Street and the Broad, and entered upon the moonlit asphalt of St Giles. A lorry thundered by in the opposite direction.

'Banbury or Woodstock,' muttered Dorcas, as they approached the fork at the end of the Giler.

'Blast,' said Autumn, as a small sports car shot out from behind the Ford, and fell in about halfway between themselves and the van. 'No, no. Don't pass him. We can still see the thing.'

All three vehicles opted for the Woodstock Road. They passed Somerville, the Radcliffe Infirmary, and the Observatory, and filed at an even thirty between redbrick mansions where family men lay sleeping.

'Woodstock, Witney,' grunted Dorcas. 'Cheltenham. Wales, even. We'll need petrol.'

But at Five Mile Drive the van slewed across the road, and branched off into a side-turning.

'God damn the thing,' said Dorcas as the sports car followed the van. 'What does *he* want?'

Dorcas accelerated slightly, came up to the side turning, and swung across the road after the first two vehicles. They entered the minor road and saw both the van and the sports car stationary about a hundred yards down.

'Pull in here,' said Autumn.

'Blimey – two of them.'

If the driver of the van or the driver of the sports car had noticed the Ford behind them, they gave no sign. Both had climbed out, the van man making to walk round to the rear of his vehicle. He had frozen as he spotted the man from the sports car. The sports car man was sauntering slowly towards him with his hands in his pockets, and when he came face to face with the other he leant nonchalantly against the side of the van. A conference seemed to ensue.

'Is he telling him about us?' whispered Dorcas.

The man from the sports car stepped to a garden gate opposite the van, and swung it invitingly open, turning as he did so to the other man. The van driver hovered uncertainly, then walked through the gate. The driver of the sports car followed him.

'Right,' said Autumn.

The two policemen walked briskly down the road, past the semi-detached houses until they came to the van. It was an old Army 15-cwt.

'Through here,' whispered Dorcas, pointing to a trellis gate, shiny in the moonlight from new paint. 'This was the one.' It had a plaque on it: NO HAWKERS, NO CIRCULARS. 'Doesn't look *criminal*,' Dorcas added uncertainly.

They opened the gate and walked up the garden path. Although the path – paved in concrete and bearing an incised pattern of erratically adjacent lines – was probably no more than five yards long, it wound. There were lumps of white-washed rockery in the garden, and a concrete gnome in a night-cap was fishing in a pool.

'Not criminal at all. Rather nice,' said Dorcas, eyeing the gnome.

Autumn walked into the porch, beneath a small board inscribed 'Dunrovin'.

'We haven't a warrant, you know, old man,' said Dorcas uneasily.

Autumn put his ear to the front door.

'How do we get *in*,' said Dorcas agitatedly.

Autumn knocked at the door.

'Might be perfectly innocent – caretaker or someone just taking a late night look-round in the library –'

'Shut *up*,' said Autumn.

A light went on in the hall, shining through the coloured glass in the front door. The door opened abruptly.

'Hullo,' said the silhouette in the doorway, 'I thought it might be you.'

The silhouette turned slightly, and the hall light caught its face. It was Archangel.

'Come in,' Archangel said.

Chapter 15

ARCHANGEL stood aside to let the policemen enter.

'Do come in.'

Autumn stepped into the hall followed by Dorcas.

'We're in the room on the right,' said Archangel pleasantly, as he shut the front door. 'Let me show you.'

He walked ahead of them down the passage.

'In here.'

The room they entered was lit by electric light which came from plastic candles set in a wooden chandelier. Small white elephants stalked across the mantelpiece beneath a rimless mirror. Across one wall a flight of porcelain snipe were rising. The rest was art-silk cushion covers. 'Oh, my prophetic gnome,' Autumn murmured.

'And this' – Archangel waved towards a half-open door leading into the kitchen – 'is our host.'

Through the doorway walked a fat man with a squint, bearing a large slice of Dundee cake and a glass of fizzy lemonade; the same fat man Autumn had seen the day of his arrival, walking out of Christ Church with his waistcoat undone all the way down.

'Ah,' said Autumn.

'I don't think I've had the pleasure,' sighed the fat man, rather mournfully, sitting down and starting on his Dundee cake.

'I saw *you* the other day. And I'd seen you somewhere before that –'

'Nothing more likely,' said Archangel, smiling.

There was a gasp from Dorcas.

'Look at this!'

Dorcas had picked up a book from the sideboard and was holding it out in front of him as if he were suddenly afflicted with long-sight.

'*Floggo – or the Diary of an English Governess*. Just look at that cover –'

A prim belch escaped the lips of the fat man.

'A spirited work, gentlemen' – he waved the glass of

fizzy lemonade – 'printed at a foreign press in a limited edition and introduced at great, I might almost say, inconvenience' – he managed to level one eye at Archangel – 'great *personal* inconvenience as things turn out, into this country by myself. A collector, I see, sir,' he nodded towards Dorcas, who blushed. 'I shall of course be consulting my legal advisers, but business – business will doubtless be suspended pending umummphphph' – the words were extinguished in the crumb of a mouthful of Dundee cake, and for several seconds the fat man chewed diligently. 'You wouldn't believe it,' he said, swallowing hard, and addressing himself to Dorcas as to an old and valued client, 'the trouble we *avant-gardistes* have. Blimey, I've had classified ads turned down by *The Times*! Dear, oh dear, we might be living in the Middle Ages. Why, you can count all the works of the divine Markee in most of the public libraries on the thumbs of one hand. Progress? Pooh. We're standing still. What we need is a new spirit of literary adventure, a casting off of the old inhibitions, a launching out boldly into the less frequented byways of human behaviour. We need it gentlemen, we need it badly – we need progress – we need – we need – what we really need,' he ended in a burst of confidence, 'is a good homosexual novel for the autumn.'

'The pornographer royal,' said Archangel.

'Let's cut the cackle,' said Autumn.

'Well, you know who I am. And this gent here is Immanuel Kant. The one,' added Archangel, 'that you can't leave lying about –'

'Come on.'

Archangel sat down on the settee, and art silk rose about him like marshmallow.

'The facts? Well, you shall certainly have them, Inspector, but I honestly don't think you'll find they bear very much on *your* problems. Anyway' – Archangel lit a cigarette – 'I suppose you ought to know about me. You could call me a spy – for the Government, of course –'

'MI5?' yelped Dorcas, his voice rising with delight.

'Not exactly, old chap. Customs and Excise. I've been

after him' – he pointed his cigarette at the fat man – 'though I didn't cotton on it was him until a few days ago. But I'd better give you this in the right sequence.'

Autumn had seated himself on a purple-covered pouffe, and Dorcas was taking his ease in a large armchair covered in flowered cretonne. Mr Kant, owlish and sad, sat at his own table, masticating his Dundee cake.

'Dirty books. There's been a real clamp down on the stuff, prosecutions galore, paragraphs in the papers pretty well every day. Well, I'm teaching my grandmother to suck eggs, telling you that,' said Archangel. 'You know it as well as I do. But while the police have been concentrating on cleaning up the retailers, Customs have been more interested in the wholesale end of the business. The stuff comes in bulk from the Continent, they bring it in fishing dinghies, and land it anywhere along the South and South-East coasts – and that's damned difficult to stop. Once it gets here – whoof! It disappears.'

Archangel inhaled.

'Well, of course there's more than one wholesaler in the racket – but not more than two or three really big ones. Customs knew they couldn't stop the books being landed – but if they could winkle out the wholesalers that might be even better.'

'That's our job,' said Autumn.

'Customs would certainly call you in to do the arresting, Inspector,' grinned Archangel, 'but they wanted to do the finding out themselves. After all, it was a question of professional vanity – they were feeling very irritable about the fishing dinghies –'

Autumn grunted.

'Anyway, the problem was – where were the wholesalers? No good asking the known retailers, they just sent their orders to accommodation addresses and got the parcels by post. "Why not get a look at the postmarks on the parcels," one of our chaps suggested, so they tried that. The retailers were anxious to placate the authorities so it wasn't very difficult. Our men examined the wrapping paper and one telling piece of information emerged. Whereas a fair proportion of the stuff simply had a variety of London postmarks, *most* of it had been stamped in Oxford.'

Archangel tapped his ash into an ash-tray shaped like the mouth of a goldfish.

'That looked helpful. Customs sent a man up here straight away – this was about three months ago – with the simple instruction, "Find it." It didn't seem a difficult job – there was enough of the stuff to be taking up a noticeable amount of space somewhere round Oxford, and the chap they sent was an old hand. But he didn't find it. He was here several weeks, and he didn't find it.'

Mr Kant looked sad as he sat at the table but his sadness had developed a faint sly smile.

'If they'd just called us in –' Autumn said.

'With me available!' exclaimed Archangel, with theatrical emphasis. 'I was with Customs before I came up to the University and I'm going back when I've done my degree. Anyway, they recalled Verney – the chap who'd been up here looking for the stuff – and they'd rather given up hope. I ran into Verney and he told me about it and suggested I might keep an eye peeled when he'd gone. Well, that was rather an opportunity for me – if I managed to find this stuff it'd do me a lot of good when I went down.'

Archangel took another pull at his cigarette, and threw it into the ash-tray.

'Needless to say, I had no more luck than Verney – to begin with. And then one bright and sunny afternoon I spotted Immanuel here walking into the post office with a parcel under his arm. Now Immanuel and I are acquaintances from way back. We have had little disputes at more than one of the cross-Channel ports.'

Mr Kant heaved a great sigh, regretful but reminiscent.

'Well, I'll cut it short. I followed Immanuel back here that day, searched his house when he went out, found nothing. I came back in the evening and saw a van outside the house. I sat in my car until the early hours of the morning watching that van and then Immanuel came out and drove away. I followed him again. He went straight to Bodley – and then the whole thing dawned on me. I let him go that night because I wanted to make sure. Bodley – it was an inspiration on Immanuel's part, a bloody inspiration.'

'The scheme,' the fat man murmured, gazing complacently into the fizzy lemonade, 'had a certain simple rationality.'

'The safest place in all England to stow a load of pornography because it's cram-full of it already!' Archangel laughed. 'A copy of every book published goes there under that law of Seventeen-something, you know – every book, whether its Dostoyevsky or de Sade. A thousand or so extra volumes simply wouldn't be noticed – or if they were it would be assumed that they had not yet been catalogued. But,' said Archangel, 'I had to make sure.'

He lit another cigarette.

'I toured the Stack several times next day before I found it. He'd stowed it on some old shelves that looked as if they hadn't been used since Caxton. Rows and rows of the stuff.' Archangel turned and gazed admiringly at Kant. 'You shocking old swine you, you take the bloody biscuit! I pinched one,' turning again to the others, 'just to make sure the stuff *was* Kant's and not part of the normal Bodley receipts – *Fanny Hill* –'

'Jejune,' observed Mr Kant critically, tugging at an oily red hair which hung from his nostril.

'Very aggravating of you to confiscate it,' Archangel grinned at Dorcas. 'I hadn't had a chance of looking at it so I had to get another – and that time,' he turned to Autumn, 'you and McCann nearly copped me. I was up those stairs in no time –'

'You could have saved me a great deal of trouble by telling me all this a lot earlier,' Autumn said.

'Be reasonable, Inspector – I wanted to do this on my own. I have my way to make.'

'Oh, yes, yes, yes.' Autumn rose and paced about the room, picking his way through the furniture, 'I dare say. What about Mrs Spectre?'

'Ah – you've been talking to her. Well, after I let Kant go the first time I came back to Bodley the next night, but of course he didn't turn up. I realized I didn't know how often he visited the cache – for all I knew I might have to sit up every night for a month. Then I remembered Mrs Spectre had seen the bonfire through her telescope so I asked her if she'd ever seen anything else in the Square at night. Van – every other Wednesday, she said. Very helpful indeed, saved me a lot of sleepless nights.'

'And you told her to say nothing?'

'Naturally. I wanted it to myself –'

'Well,' said Dorcas glumly, 'it looks as if *we've* been wasting our time.'

'I'm afraid you have,' said Archangel.

Autumn said nothing, but gazed at the fat man.

'We'll have the pleasure of taking him in, though,' said Dorcas. 'All the dirt, then there's trespass and breaking and entering –'

'Ah, please,' the fat man spoke with some alarm, 'not breaking, no indeed. I have the keys.' He laid a bunch of heavy keys on the table.

Autumn picked them up and swung them round his outstretched little finger.

'McCann's?'

'He pinched them –'

'Borrowed,' put in the fat man fearfully.

'– and took casts. They were hanging up in McCann's little cubbyhole. Sat around with the other inmates, and whipped them when he got the chance. Stuck them back before Bodley closed. I pinched them myself from the same place when I wanted to get into the Stack.'

'I have to admit –' began the fat man.

'McCann,' said Autumn ruminatively, 'McCann. This fellow could have done it a great deal more easily if McCann had helped.'

'God, it isn't likely that *McCann* –'

'Oh, I don't know about likely,' said Autumn moodily. He was remembering the fury of McCann the morning Archangel got into the Stack. But any librarian might have been annoyed. . . .

'I have to admit that I did borrow the keys, gentlemen,' said Kant.

'You borrowed them. And McCann left them on the hook.'

Autumn repeated the words as he pulled out a chair, and sat on the other side of the table with his chin on his hand, staring at the fat man. The lemonade glass clinked as Kant shifted his hand nervously, tapping on the table top. There was silence.

'Now see here, gentlemen,' Kant broke out, 'I hope you'll think I've been cooperative. Nothing's been pinched and no one's a penny the worse. You can call it a – a – a trespass. And my books, my legal adviser will take that matter further, of course, the books –'

'The books. Yes,' said Autumn, still staring hard at Kant, but speaking to Archangel, 'there's a lot of books. There's this lot, and the lot that was burned, and Manchip's diary, and Christelow's Chaucer, and Flower's *Paradise Lost*, and – heigh-ho,' with his chin pivoted on his palm, he opened and closed his jaw so that his head moved up and down.

'Sorry about my end of things,' said Archangel, 'it's just made things more complicated for you without helping at all. But at least you do know where I stand.'

'We'll be checking,' said Dorcas.

'But Kant – well, as far as your inquiries go he must seem a bit like the brick in the joke – just put in to make it more difficult –'

'That's a rather hasty conclusion, I should say,' murmured Autumn, still staring at the fat man. 'Here's this chap wandering into Bodley to hide books and here's someone else wandering in to burn them. Now I call that thick and fast. Don't you call that thick and fast?' he asked Kant.

'Half-time, now, half-time,' said the fat man, winking rapidly at the blackheads which marched like the Himalayas across his nose. 'We can't have that kind of insinuation, you know –'

'We can have,' said Autumn slowly and softly, 'any kind of insinuation we please. But we don't need insinuations when we can have the facts. We're going to get the facts, Kant, and we're going to get them off you. Every fortnight for the last six months you've been in and out of Bodley. You had a key, you had the best chance of destroying *Paradise Lost*, you had the best chance of making the bonfire. I want to know why you burnt those books, Kant, I want to know why, and you're going to tell me, you're going to tell me –' Autumn smacked the flat of his hand on the table top, and his eyes excoriated the face in front of him.

Kant snatched himself back in his chair, knocking over his glass, and the lemonade dripped over his knees.

'Kant,' said Autumn softly, 'you tell me. You tell me.'

Something in an instant had been swung up like a pendulum to the apex of its arc; instantaneously it hovered; instantaneously it fell back. . . .

Indignation began to blaze from the eye of Mr Kant, burnt like a sun in the valleys of his blackheads.

'Now that's the suffering limit. I admit all the other things – and you go and accuse me of something else. Me burn books! Me! Good heavens,' said Mr Kant, laying his hand breathlessly on the binding of *An English Governess*, 'books are my *life*, gentlemen. Those reports in the papers about books being destroyed brought me very near to tears. "England in the twentieth century," I said to myself, "England in the twentieth century." I was upset. I was concerned. I had entrusted one or two little items to Bodley myself. "Where," I asked myself, "are the police? Are they too busy stifling free expression to keep an eye on the nation's heritage?" Forgive me, gentlemen, but I felt it very strongly. I am a sentimental man.' Mr Kant blew his nose.

'Carry me home and bury me decent!' said Archangel.

All the time Autumn had not taken his eyes from the fat man, but he said nothing.

'Did you ever speak to McCann, Immanuel?' Archangel asked.

'Oh, look here, I've told you how it was, I've *told* you. I take it this McCann is the head librarian. I borrowed his keys –'

'You'll tackle McCann?'

'No doubt,' nodded Autumn briefly.

Archangel looked again at Kant.

'You recognized him, didn't you?'

'I saw him the other day,' said Autumn, 'and I think I've seen him before – photograph or something. Been inside, has he?'

'He certainly has. *My Years in a German Girls' School*, by A. Tanner – Lord Justice Tansey took three weeks to read it because he kept letting it fall in horror. Nine months for that, with a dozen other Customs offences taken into consideration. I was in Town the other day looking up his file. Forgery, too – wills and documents and old stuff. He did eighteen months for faking a set of seventeenth-century title deeds for some chap who was after the reversion of an estate in Derbyshire. If the originals hadn't turned up, they'd have got away with it. And he's done time for embezzlement – twice.'

'No murder?'

The fat man's eyes started from his face as if squeezed by invisible thumbs, and in the excess of his agitation he almost managed to straighten his crooked eye.

'Look *here*,' he gasped.

Autumn got up.

'Ah, well, let's lock him up while we've got the chance – his lawyer'll be round in the morning to bail him. Leave your car here, Dorcas, and take that van-load with you. Never mind about the young constables. I'll go back with Archangel.'

'All right you,' said Dorcas to Kant.

'It is hard leaving my little home,' said Mr Kant, as though he were going into solitary confinement for life, 'the atmosphere has been particularly conducive to the creative germ – the creative germ, gentlemen, which has drawn from my pen those various volumes – for I am artist as well as business man – which remain of special appeal to students interested in exploring the often-overlooked recess of the human comedy. Illustrated –'

They passed out into the road, where the night had grown pale with the approach of morning. The moon looked like a half-sucked acid-drop, and the blue stars had turned yellow. The garden gate of 'Dunrovin' clicked to, and a murmurous universal note was heard, as if a mountain of tin-foil were being stirred by a giant hand. It was the dawn song of the birds.

'Like going home after a party,' Archangel said, as he climbed into his car with Autumn. 'Bye-bye,' he called to Dorcas and Kant as they drove off in the van.

Autumn sat hunched up in the bucket seat, his jacket collar turned up against the wind, his long thin thighs buttressing the dashboard, his hands underneath his bottom.

As they turned into the Woodstock Road, Archangel said:

'How did you get it out of the old lady?'

'Oh,' Autumn grunted, 'she told me. She'd mentioned something about a van, something about the little men coming from the television "in their van", when I was asking her about the fire the other day. Didn't register at the time, though I knew afterwards there was something she'd said that I'd forgotten. Then that journalist Bum said something that reminded me of it, and I followed it up on the off-chance. Asked her about the van and she said it came every other Wednesday.'

Archangel laughed.

'She's an odd one, and no mistake.'

The first light of morning struck across the sky as they came into St Giles.

Archangel said: 'I say, do you really think Kant's got anything to do with your business?'

'Possibly.'

'But you know,' Archangel turned down past Balliol, 'Kant wouldn't want to do anything that might call attention to Bodley – not if he was using it as a cache, would he? I mean, if he started burning books out of Bodley surely he must have realized there'd be an investigation? An investigation would make Bodley the centre of attention and very dicey as a storehouse. I'd say he had nothing to do with it –'

'Too simple. What you say would be logical if a man's behaviour were determined at any given moment by a single circumstance. That only happens in detective

143

books. Most of the time behaviour is the result of a complex of circumstances. After all, whether Kant did the burning or not, someone did – yet Kant still went on using the place as a storehouse.'

'Yes, I suppose so, I hadn't thought.'

'We know Kant is a crook, he had all the opportunity in the world to destroy the books, he is utterly suspect. That's one set of circumstances. On the other hand, he wouldn't, as you point out, *want* to call attention to his cache. Another set. But he did go on using the place, even when it came under scrutiny. A third. A complex of circumstances – and there may be others of which we are quite ignorant. Now none of the three sets we know of admits of any conclusion, but in the way each modifies the other we may find a line for further speculation.'

Archangel swung down the Turl.

'Why did he go on using the Bodleian when it was so dangerous? Because he was a fool? Because he took a calculated risk? Because he knew there was going to be no more book-burning, and that the scrutiny would diminish? Well, I don't know which of these may be the reason – but obviously I'm not going to ignore that last one. Now then, why should he want to burn books anyway? Well, maybe he didn't – perhaps someone else wanted him to. Oh, yes, it's a possibility. And it brings us to our line of further speculation.'

'Which is?'

'That he may have been compelled by someone unknown to make use of the opportunity he had to destroy valuable books, that he did so, and that he continued to use Bodley for his own purposes well knowing that the period of book destruction was over.'

'My God, that's ingenious.'

'Sure,' said Autumn dryly, 'but what about the circumstances I *don't* know about? My little bit of theorizing only stands if the evidence I base it on is complete. How do I know it is? No – all I can safely assume is that Kant is suspect. That's all.'

Archangel was silent as they climbed out of the car in front of the College gate.

Then he said: 'Why should anyone want to destroy valuable books?'

Autumn looked evenly at him.

'Ah,' he said.

Archangel knocked at the gate. It was opened by Tantalum, who winked conspiratorially as he let them in. He was more than half convinced they had spent the night with young women.

The thin sunlight was beginning to shine through the gables of Warlock, throwing pale shadows across the quadrangle so that the square looked like the slab-stone of an old green tomb, whose raised patterns have been worn away by time until all relief has gone and only the shapes remain.

They walked across slowly.

'Do you think,' Archangel enquired, 'there's any connexion between the destruction of the books and the murders?'

'Mmmm – yes. I've got a sort of feeling. I don't like "feelings", but I don't disregard them. And there *is* a superficial link between Manchip's death and the books.'

Autumn was thinking of the careful ransacking of Manchip's rooms, and the possibility that the ransacker was after *The Book of the Lion*. But he did not enlarge.

He yawned, standing at the entrance of the Tower.

'Well, bed, I suppose. Are you going to tell them here what you've been up to?'

'Oh, lord, no. They'd think I'd come up in the wrong spirit.'

'A nation is always judged by its Customs, my boy. Why the Russian thing, incidentally?'

Archangel grinned.

'Well, I am by descent. I got in here on the easiest scholarship I could dig up – which was for Russians. I threw in the character work for fun. Undergraduate humour.' Archangel blushed slightly.

Autumn laughed.

'Don't take any wooden roubles.'

'Good night, little father.'

145

When Autumn reached his room it was quite light. He drew the curtains to, pulled off his shoes, hung his jacket on the back of the chair, and flopped down on the bed. Flexing his toes as he stretched himself, he thought about the sitting and thinking – today it should be done. There should be enough pieces of the puzzle now – at least for the gaps to be seen. And with this thought he turned over on his side, and in a second he was asleep.

Chapter 16

WHEN Autumn woke up at ten o'clock that morning he woke with the sensation of having to do that day something which he knew he was well able to do, but which was going to take every ounce of his concentration and effort.

He had come to it at last – he was going to work things out. He was going to take hold of the elements of the case, those that he knew, and – as if they had been the mooring lines of a trawling net – haul them in, hand over hand, until he found out what was on the end.

He turned over and stuck his nose into his pillow balking at the expenditure of effort the process would entail; balking as he had balked since his schooldays at the labour involved in doing well something he knew he was able to do well.

He jerked himself upright, swung his legs round, and sat on the edge of the bed wondering whether he should shave first. He decided to shave. It would be a visible indication that staleness was being shed preparatory to effort. He developed this theme by taking off his crumpled trousers, waistcoat, and shirt, retaining only his underpants and socks. Then he washed.

Someone knocked at his door as he was drying his razor. It was the scout, telling him through the door that breakfast in Hall was over and would he like some in his rooms.

'No, thank you. But tell them to keep some food hot for me if I'm not over by lunch.'

The scout departed, and Autumn opened the door, carefully sported the oak on the outer side, then closed the door and locked it. He opened the curtains, pulled a chair up to the table by the window and sat down in front of a block of writing paper and a Biro. He had put on his shirt again, but not his trousers. He looked out of the window. Right, he said, begin.

He took up the Biro and wrote at the head of the first sheet of paper in capital letters THE THEOREM.

Underneath this, he wrote 'Why was Manchip killed?' and underlined it.

There are two possibilities. He was killed because he found someone trying to pinch *The Book of the Lion*; or he was killed for some other reason.

Autumn wrote down the two hypotheses under (*a*) and (*b*). Then he wrote down, again underlining it, 'Why was Bow-Parley killed?' The same two possibilities – *he* flushed someone in the act of stealing the *The Book of the Lion*; or he was killed for some other reason. Autumn put this down under the (*a*) and (*b*).

Then he thought, is it likely that the some man did both murders? Yes, it is likely. It is very unlikely that there are two killers in a College of thirteen people.

Now take the motives (*a*) and (*b*). Take (*a*).

There are manifold objections to (*a*). Why kill either Manchip or Bow-Parley because they'd caught you in their rooms with *The Book?* You would have a dozen immediate excuses – you were just looking at it, you had dropped in to see if you might borrow it, you were killing time until the occupant of the rooms should return – etc., etc. Any excuse would be simpler, more effective, more apropos, than murder.

And surely anyone wanting to get hold of *The Book* to destroy it *would* have made an excuse and waited another opportunity? Murder would have been a fantastic waste.

(*Memo.*: wouldn't anyone who wanted to lift *The Book* have lifted it from Christelow himself? No. Christelow might be expected to keep a more careful eye on it than anyone else. But note – Christelow mentioned a noise at his window during the night.)

Conclusion: (*a*) is rejected. The idea that the murders were done simply to collar *The Book* is not tenable. The real motive must come under (*b*).

Which can bring us to Shipton – and Manchip's diary.

Autumn had been scribbling hard and fast, digging the pen into the paper until his thumb and forefinger ached. Now he stopped, and swung the Biro like a plumb-line between his fingers.

Then he wrote down: RECENT HISTORY OF MAN-

CHIP'S DIARY, and underneath this heading he made a tabulation.

1. Manchip made a note in his diary of his warning to Shipton in respect of Julia Bow-Parley.

2. Shipton pinched the diary after Manchip's death (he says).

3. Bow-Parley pinched the diary from Shipton and told Undigo about the Shipton entry.

4. *Someone* pinched the diary from Bow-Parley (after Bow-Parley's death).

5. Diary turns up again in Shipton's rooms behind mirror.

What emerges?

A clear motive for the murder of both Manchip and Bow-Parley – killed to suppress information that both held concerning Shipton. The agent? Shipton.

But Shipton doesn't answer, murmured Autumn out loud, for the reasons I gave Undigo yesterday. Autumn took up the pen again, and wrote down as a parenthesis, 'Shipton admitted that what Bow-Parley had told Undigo was true – but he could easily have denied it: if he killed Manchip and Bow-Parley to suppress information, but failed to destroy the diary – which he had, in the first place at least, taken the trouble to steal, and which he knew contained the information he sought to suppress – then he was a candidate for a lunatic asylum'. Conclusion: that what I suggested to Undigo yesterday still stands – that someone who knew about the Shipton/Julia entry in the diary stuck the diary behind Shipton's mirror in a hasty attempt to throw suspicion on Shipton.

This someone would have had to tell me what Undigo told me – that Bow-Parley had confided in him about the entry. Otherwise this someone could not have been sure I would search Shipton's rooms and thus find the diary.

Reasonable to suppose that anyone wanting to divert suspicion thus is the killer.

Undigo?

Clarity, clarity, that's what we need, thought Autumn, biting his thumbs. Now then, do I, at this stage, see any further surface possibilities in the diary? I do not. So I now ask myself two fundamental questions.

Why were these two men murdered *at that time* and *at that place?* Autumn looked up from his writing and sat immobile for many minutes. Then his pen began to move.

Manchip's might have been a planned murder. But I know Bow-Parley's wasn't. Bow-Parley was killed in a hurry, between the time he hung up the phone and my arrival at his rooms. Two minutes. Do you do a murder in two minutes – from choice? Not if you can avoid it – especially when you know there's a copper on his way round. Another thing – I heard Bow-Parley speaking to the murderer, heard him say 'not strictly ethical': how could the murderer be sure that while they conversed and Bow-Parley had the phone to his ear making the connexion, I hadn't heard his *name* spoken? To do a murder after that! And I might have seen him coming away. I did see him (vaguely, anyway).

A conclusion, then. It couldn't be put off. It had to be done in a hurry – there and then.

Why is anyone killed in a hurry? In such unpropitious circumstances a murder is only undertaken for one reason – to shut someone up. Bow-Parley must have known something.

Re-enter the diary. Bow-Parley had the diary: Bow-Parley had found out from it about Shipton's liaison with his wife.

That was why he had to be shut up?

But this brings me back to Shipton – and I have already ditched Shipton (on this count, at least) on good grounds.

Wait a bit. Look at Manchip's murder.

Was Manchip killed in a hurry? Well, he was killed on the roof of the Chapel. Might have gone up there, been followed, and bonk. Might have gone up there *with* someone. Remember he was killed with one of his own dessert knives, which suggests his murderer had been in Manchip's rooms at some time – probably immediately before.

Now it's likely he wasn't lured there – for two reasons: one, I know he liked going up there for the view, and two, why kill a man on a roof anyway? Of course, it was an ingenious way of concealing the body by exposing it as a statue – but it really isn't as reliable as burning it or burying it or chucking it into the river. . . .

So it looks as if the Chapel roof was wished on the murderer? Yes, it does. And therefore Manchip, like Bow-Parley, was killed in a hurry. If the killer could have postponed it, he probably would have done so.

(*Memo.:* on both the occasions of murder the College was impregnable, thus restricting the suspects to the inmates. For this reason alone the murderer would not have chosen to do the murders at those times and those places if he could have avoided it. He must have known he was reducing his own chances. Killers who *choose* to do their killing inside impregnable citadels do not exist outside detective books.)

Manchip, then, was killed for the same reason as Bow-Parley – he had to be silenced.

(*Note:* There is one other explanation of murder done in a hurry under unpropitious circumstances. Rage. But you do not go from light conversation – in which Bow-Parley and his murderer were to my knowledge indulging – to murderous rage in mere seconds. Nor – as in Manchip's case – is it likely that the murderer fell into a maniacal fury and, slipping his hand into his pocket, found one of Manchip's dessert-knives conveniently to hand!)

To silence him then. Oh, god – King Charles's head! Shipton.

It *can't* be Shipton.

Then.

Then Manchip and Bow-Parley shared some other information – beside that about Shipton – which brought them to their deaths?

Think about that.

Neither was expecting to die. Manchip had evidently gone up to the roof of the Chapel with his murderer quite unsuspectingly. And Bow-Parley – as I know – was talking cheerfully to the man who brained him two minutes later.

Inference?

That both had let the murderer know they knew something about him – but neither dreamt that knowledge of this something might be a killing matter.

Good!

Yes, but what was the something?

Consider Bow-Parley on the telephone.

I lifted the receiver and heard him talking to the person with him. What did he sound like? Expansive, cheerful, indulgent, complacent – slightly reproving . . . that 'not strictly ethical', did that refer to the thing he had found out about his guest, his murderer?

(*Note*: I assume the man with Bow-Parley *was* his murderer for two reasons: (1) no one else could have done it in the time, and (2) no one stepped forward when I asked next day whether anyone had been with Bow-Parley at that time.)

Bow-Parley's manner lets Shipton out again. You wouldn't be just pleasantly chiding to a man you'd just discovered had cuckolded you – and there was no sarcasm, no irony about the way he said 'not strictly ethical'.

Aha! The book-destroying? Had they found out about that, found out who it was? No, that won't do. Bow-Parley wouldn't have been cheerfully off-hand with a man who tears up books. 'Not strictly ethical' doesn't cover that.

Question remains: what did both Manchip and Bow-Parley tell this person which made it essential for him to kill them both with all despatch?

Don't know.

But do know it must have seemed of minor importance to them, and of vital importance to him.

(*Memo.*: By this analysis, therefore, the something that Bow-Parley had to tell *me*, the thing that would 'materially assist the investigation', the thing he rang me up about, could not possibly be the something he had found out about the man – the murderer – who was with him in his rooms while he was telephoning to me. 'Material assistance' *is* important: the other thing wasn't. And Bow-Parley would hardly have been chatting cheerfully to a murderer and then, in front of him, make it clear over the telephone that he was about to hand him over to the police!)

Good, thought Autumn.

He scratched his knee absently, still concentrating, rose, and moved to the other window, putting one hand up against the frame, leaning his forehead against the back of it, and staring down into the quadrangle. Two tall American ladies with cameras and sun-glasses were looking at the Pagoda.

Now logically, he thought, what's the next step?

The next step is to consider how these two men might have come by this fatal information, the nature of which is still unknown.

Manchip liked knowing things about people. The entry in his diary about Shi –

Autumn stood suddenly upright, his face slowly turning red. His thoughts had started to race like the screw of a motor-boat when it is lifted clear of the water.

If Manchip put down about Shipton in his diary, did he put down about this?

Autumn stood breathless, biting fiercely at the quick round his thumb-nail. Wait now, wait. Think a bit.

But he did not wait. He stepped quickly to the safe where Dorcas had put the diary with the *Book of the Lion*.

He drew out the diary and sat down. For several minutes his head moved slightly as his eye scanned the close-packed handwriting up and down each page. Then he closed the book, and slipped it on the table in front of him. There was not, at first sight, anything to be seen.

Hope still springs. Think about it again.

Some of the entries are abbreviated. It's just possible that among them – Cryptic, a lot of them, the textual references. Yet –

All right, then, a closer look.

Wait. Not all through, no need to scan all through. *If* the information is there it will be somewhere in the last day's entry. Why? Because the man was killed so that his mouth would be kept shut: you only kill someone for this reason if the information you are afraid he'll impart has only just come into his possession – otherwise he could already have told someone, and your murder would be wasted.

Ergo – if he put it down, he'd only just put it down. Clever!

Autumn smiled faintly.

And then he began to look excited. Bow-Parley. Bow-Parley was murdered for the same reason as Manchip: *he must only just have found out whatever he had found out. And only a few hours before he was killed he had come into the possession of Manchip's diary!*

A closer look, a very much closer look. . .

Autumn felt warm in the pit of his belly; he felt like a traveller set down in a strange countryside who, by careful consideration of the land about him, the lie of cloud, the sun's direction, has at last brought himself to a landmark. He had not felt like that since his arrival in Oxford.

He opened Manchip's diary at the last day's entries. They were complete, for there was a line drawn beneath the last sentence. The date was the day before Manchip had been found propped up on the Chapel roof: that is, the day he was killed. Autumn thought, I should never keep a diary, it is too much numbering one's days.

He pressed the pages back against the stiff green board and read the entries through slowly from beginning to end. The writing was small, and there was a lot of it for one day. Manchip's style ran to words. But the first entry was short enough.

They conceive mischief, and bring forth vanity, and their belly prepareth deceit. Job, 17. An excellent text for the day.

Autumn smiled a little. That was the day Manchip had warned Shipton that he would not tolerate the deception of Bow-Parley. No doubt Manchip had pleased himself with the inwardness of his text: though it turned out to have more inwardness than he had bargained for. Someone was certainly conceiving mischief. . . .

Autumn read on.

My system revolts, having been plagued by an impertinent and excessive quantity of RABBIT FOOD. The chef now knows my mind upon the subject of salads. He must understand that salads are concomitant, subordinate, assistatory; they must not assume THE MAIN ROLE. Consider the human economy of the alimentary canal – the soft palpitating stomach cells, the bloody pulp of the pancreas, the purple wafer of the liver, the veined glaze of the eternally peristaltic intestine. Autumn visualized the chef standing with his head cocked, anxious not to appear to miss a thing. *What barbarism, therefore, to offer the quick lively generous juices this G O L D   V E G E T A B L E   M A T T E R. And baked beans out of a tin! I do not continue.*

There was a space, and then the next entry followed. Autumn read it, then read right through to the end of the day's entries without stopping.

I said a good thing at dinner tonight. I said of Fairlight that he raised his sights so often he seldom had time to aim at anything. Undigo was immoderately amused.

cf. Gynander, 2nd Eclogue, 171. Will amendment repair the sense? The torn piece is not clear. Liddell's note is quite without point.

The brass of the priest with the alb. (Offered a Bishopric and refused.) Keys with the sexton, Great Rollright.

L 122/13. Strike out ending. Nonsense!

The warning to Shipton delivered. I make this note of it as an earnest of my intention to put the matter not only before Bow-Parley but before Convocation itself, unless Shipton abrupts at once this M O N S T R O U S   D E C E I T. An irregular and dishonourable liaison of this kind leaves its taint upon us all. I shall not hesitate if my warning is not heeded to the letter.

Vv 9 to 22, the second fragt. Propt.

The warlike Clapp gives two horses for Sandown – Gollombek's Delight and Charlie Boy. Ten shillings on the nose, I think.

Autumn let out a cackle.

Sherry, Wadham, tomorrow. His sister will be there. I cannot reconcile her harmonious features with her bandy legs.

Argument with Christelow and Undigo and Falal (ridiculous old person), well conducted on my side. I say you do not live WITH a house, you live IN a house. Thus the interior decoration must not be too positive. All must constitute a ground, plain, proportional and authentic, to live against. The life within a house is all the decoration the house requires – fine or poor according to the quality of the living. Consider the Oxford College (I exclude our own!) – neither functional nor excessive, neither an ornament nor a mere instrument, its architecture and its interior appointment is at once midway between, and above, too much and too little – the HUMANE proportion. I do not reproduce their argument.

Par. 2, second line. Cal. Doubtful. Other texts?

Vv 118–133, Sem. Yes.

Ll 89–99. bol. Initially.
Bless my soul.

And there Manchip had drawn his line. 'Bless my soul,' murmured Autumn softly – an eerie benediction. An hour or two later he had died.

Autumn went back and read the entries again. He cast back several pages and studied entries for other days, although by previous deduction he knew the information – if it existed in the diary at all – would be in that last day's entries.

At last he threw down the book. Baffled, is the word, reflected Autumn. I just can't see it. He laced his hands together, put them behind his head and stretched his long body as he sat.

If I am right, and Bow-Parley got what he knew from this diary, what was it that enabled him to see in it what I cannot?

Something in common with Manchip? What did he have in common with Manchip? Bow-Parley was an English scholar, Manchip a classicist. But they were both nosey. They were both nosey. . .

Autumn sat in his shirt-tails, his arms folded, and mused long on what other qualities there had been in these two men which had allowed them – and apparently them alone – to acquire information which a person unknown had found essential to suppress: so essential, that he had seen no disproportion in killing both of them.

In his mind, Autumn heard snatches of previous conversations, fragmentary references.

'His interests are four,' he heard Falal say. 'Gynander, brasses, crosswords, and malice.' 'He's a fool,' chimed in the voice of Rankine. 'If Manchip is unpleasant, he is at least distinguishedly so,' Undigo said. Christelow's story of the golf match: 'The *gush* side of criticism.' And Fairlight saying, 'Manchip does upset people, doesn't he? Poor old Rankine. . .' 'What they call a character,' he heard Nicholas Flower declare, and then McCann, loping up the High Street, speaking of Manchip's 'thorough-pacedness.' The little doctor, too, the night his body was found: 'Such a disagreeable person. An inadequacy complex, promiscuously transferred. . .'

They had spoken, too, of Bow-Parley. But there Autumn had his own observation. Inquisitive, vain, sly. 'That jolly old general practitioner,' young Flower had called him, not a bad description at that. 'The kind of person who always *is* a Baconian,' McCann had said. That kind of snob. And Shipton had said – but then Shipton would have said anything.

Well, there they were. What I do not have, Autumn thought, is a catalyst, something to fuse those traits from either man which might suggest the *kind* of information these two were peculiarly fitted to unearth.

A thought. If the dairy does contain incriminatory information about the killer, then didn't the killer run an enormous risk planting the thing on Shipton?

Yes – but how should he know? No reason to suppose he knew it was there.

Autumn drummed on the writing pad. One thing I can do – show the day's entries to Shipton, see if he can spot anything. I can show him. I know where I am with him.

It was warm in the Tower Room. Outside the sunlight was thick, throwing deep black shadows and striking a bilious glare from the white flagstones round the grass. An undergraduate, a don or two, passed through the Lodge, carrying tennis rackets or towels under their arms. Autumn could smell the blistering paint on the hot wood under the window.

He went through the entries again. Then he sat back and did not move for almost a quarter of an hour. Then he picked up his pen once more.

He pushed aside the sheets he had already covered with his THEOREM, took a fresh one and headed it PERSONAE. For the record, he murmured, I'll list the *a priori* motives that all of them had for killing Manchip.

. Alphabetically, then.

(1) ARCHANGEL

As far as I know, none. As far as I know, Manchip was all for Archangel because Archangel was Russian. All Archangel's activities seem to have been explained. I'm inclined to give him a clear bill.

(2) CLAPP

I remember one thing about Clapp. When I asked him if Manchip ever wanted to look at his essays, he said, 'Manchip was a pacifist'. He said it very quietly. Why do I remember this? I don't know. He also objected to Manchip letting Archangel into the University. I think Clapp is an oddity, and oddities with fascist biases don't like pacifists.

(3) CHRISTELOW

Manchip was rather contemptuous of Christelow's cast of mind ('Oh, you mean the *gush* side of criticism'). Did Christelow feel slighted in not being considered as a candidate for the Rockinge Chair?

(4) DIAMANTIS

I have not seen enough of him. Nervous. Undigo said Manchip bullied him – 'Now he can't drink tea without spilling it.' Such men dangerous? Don't go getting imaginative. Don't forget he was the one who told you the diary had gone. Is that suggestive? Was he personally anxious to get it back? When I saw him down at the Barge he wanted to know where I found it.

(5) DOGG
  ?

(6) EGG
  ?

(7) FAIRLIGHT
    Manchip was to have given Fairlight his casting vote against Bow-Parley in the Rockinge Chair election. Fairlight told me this at Walpurgis. I said. 'Well you'd want to keep him alive, wouldn't you – if what you say is so?' And he said, 'Why should it change?' This was strange reply. Change. Had Manchip changed his mind about the casting vote? If so, Fairlight has vested interest in both deaths. With Manchip alive, Fairlight (in the altered circumstances) loses Chair: with Manchip dead he stands at evens: but with Bow-Parley dead as well he would be certain. . .
    Highly suppositious.
    Anonymous letter: 'Ask Dim about the note.' I did, and got instant reaction.
    Fairlight . . .

(8) FLOWER
    Flower suggested Manchip might have changed his mind about Fairlight. On the grounds of his *affaire* with Miss Tomlin.
    Cocky young man unsuccessful in love.

(9) FALAL
    Collector's item.
    Threatened to 'shoot Manchip with bare hands' because he was filling Oxford with women. Said Manchip 'thoroughly deserved to die'.
    Feel like laughing this off, but know better.

(10) MCCANN
    Formidable.
    Show a connexion between him and Kant and it could lead anywhere. Though there is no overt link between McCann and Manchip.
    McCann . . .

(11) RANKINE

Lord Pinner wants to found College: Rankine has reason to suppose Pinner would bring him in as Master of such College: but Manchip opposes the scheme and is immovable.

Motive like ripe carbuncle.

(12) LORD PINNER

See above.

Lord Pinner's concern to found a College is not disinterested. Vanity – or something else?

(13) TANTALUM

?

(14) SHIPTON

Motive – the entry in Manchip's diary. Rejected on good grounds.

(15) UNDIGO

Without his information about Bow-Parley and the diary I might never have searched Shipton's rooms for it. Nor would Shipton have come under suspicion. Since I assume it was killer who planted diary in Shipton's rooms, and since killer would have had to tell me story Undigo told me, it is reasonable to suspect Undigo.

Motive? Don't know.

Autumn read his list through, and was not impressed. Most of the Collegians had motives for murder, but (on the face of it, and with the possible exception of Fairlight) not for a mouth-stopping murder. And where the collegians could be seen to have a vested interest in Manchip's death, not one of their motives suggested the remotest connexion with the murder of Bow-Parley. But supposing, said Autumn to himself, supposing Bow-Parley had found out who the murderer of Manchip had been. There's your Bow-Parley motive – and you can tie it on to any of the *a priori* motives of any of your suspects.

No I can't, Autumn said gloomily, because it has already been shown that Bow-Parley was conversing in jocular vein with the man who a few seconds later killed him. Is it feasible he would have behaved like that if he'd known his guest was the Vice-Chancellor's murderer?

Autumn bit his thumbs. Of course, if there were two murderers – No, I put that right out of court on grounds of likelihood.

He sat back, his arms stretched out, his hands resting on the table. Well, he thought, as far as I can see the THEOREM – based upon logical supposition, but not suppositious – is sound. Does this mean that I can ignore all the *a priori* motives because they don't square with it?

Bear them in mind.

First, they indicate concretely that most of the Collegians bore an animus toward Manchip. And secondly, although the true motive for the murder must have been of more urgency than any of the *a priori* motives, it – and the reason for Bow-Parley's murder – may well be a modification or extension of any one of them.

Oof! Inspector Autumn let out a great sigh and scratched his navel with what could only have been an air of finality. It was hotter than ever, and he had worked hard; he was not surprised to find himself sweating. He got up, and walked gently round the Tower Room, flapping his shirt ends and creating grateful breezes. Then he sat down and thought: What have I produced?

I have produced this.

I am looking for a man who has done something. This something is wrong, but the degree or quality of the wrongness is not such that either of the two persons who discovered what it was had any reason to suppose they ran a risk in letting him know they knew about it. But the information was so momentous to the man himself that he killed these two men rather than let it get further.

Second – but not so certain – the clue to the information (and thus to the man himself) may be contained in the final set of entries in the diary of the late Vice-Chancellor.

I cannot yet detect it, but I regard its presence there as a probability – not so much because I suspect Manchip habitually recorded such things, as that I know Bow-Parley acquired the information concerning this unknown man at the same time as he acquired Manchip's diary, and was killed immediately afterwards.

And that, murmured Autumn as he wrote these sentences at the bottom of the last sheet of his THEOREM, is my position.

In an exhibition of mild satisfaction he smacked his hands in rapid fire across his belly, then walked to the window and stood looking down. Outside on the green quadrangle three or four people were playing at bowls. Autumn walked to the bed and started pulling on his trousers.

'Soon,' he murmured softly, 'soon. . . .'

Chapter 17

'Too much leg,' shouted the Lord Pinner.

'– much leg,' echoed Rankine.

Fairlight and Rankine and Lord Pinner ladled the woods across the grass while Nicholas Flower and Orson Dogg, who sat with their backs up against the Pagoda, smoked and watched.

It was nearly tea-time. The sun burnt in the sky and the afternoon thickened in the quadrangles. Tarmac stood on the North Oxford roads in toffee-pools, and overhead, aeroplanes from the University Squadron droned boggily through the haze like wasps drowning in syrup: a smell of grass and wall-flowers lifted and shimmered as the College gardens yielded themselves languorously behind stone walls. At Parson's Pleasure the old men sunburnt their dewlappy breasts or hung like molluscs in the slow muddiness of the river.

Autumn buttoned his trousers and pulled on his jacket. Looking at his watch he was startled to see that lunchtime had come and gone a long time ago. He shuffled together the sheets of his THEOREM, slid them between the pages of Manchip's diary and put the book under his arm. Then he went out of the room and walked slowly and meditatively down the twisting stone staircase and out into the hot sunshine.

He stood at the grass verge watching the bowls and doodling mentally. Never know, it might be the chef. Sticking a dessert knife into a despiser of salads. Carnivore sacrificed on altar of chlorophyll. Autumn scuffed his toe against the turf.

'Wotcher!' Nicholas Flower shouted across the grass. Autumn walked over to where the two undergraduates were sitting by the Pagoda.

'Hullo.'

At the other end Fairlight applied a wood to his eye and released it along the grass.

'Too much leg,' cried Lord Pinner.

'– much leg,' cried Rankine.

'Lunatic,' said Nicholas Flower savagely and scrambled aside. The bowl struck the Pagoda wall. 'Deliberately trying to injure me!'

'And why should he want to do that?' smiled Autumn.

'Why, our friend Nicholas has an incipient persecution psychosis in reference to Fairlight,' said Orson Dogg. 'I am hopeful of it developing into a really interesting case –'

Flower kicked the bowl as hard as he could towards Fairlight.

'If only the blighter weren't so confoundedly *smug*. I have a wholesome ambition to shatter his fearful self-esteem, a splendid obsession, my dear Doggtor.'

'Tell him they've offered him the editorship of *John o' London's*,' suggested Autumn.

'He would accept. The man is incapable of discrimination. Look at his subject. *Akenside!*'

'What gave you the idea Manchip might have changed his mind?' asked Autumn, watching Rankine press Lord Pinner to first wood.

'Eh? What? Oh – yes. What do you mean, gave me the idea?' Flower asked with a kind of mock indignation which seemed to be covering a slight embarrassment. 'I get ideas. I am a man of ideas. This was just one of them.'

'I wondered whether your invaluable intuitions were ever backed up by reasons.'

'Reasons?' echoed Flower as if he'd never heard the word before. 'No, I can't go so far as to say there are reasons. You're looking into it.'

'Into what?' Autumn looked at Flower.

'Eee bah gum – is this a cross-talk act or summat?' Flower stared back ingenuously at Autumn. 'Into *that*, into the idea that Fairlight, mature in dullness from his earliest years, might suddenly have lost the patronage of Manchip and knocked him off therefore.'

'Without facts, there's not much to look into.'

'You could ask Fairlight, at least.'

'Ask him what?'

'Really, my old china, you sound as if *I* were under

suspish. Are you trying' – Flower lowered his voice theatrically – '*to trip me up?*'

'Trip *you* up!' Autumn raised his hands and eyes. 'We speak of the impossible.'

Flower laughed, then said: 'Soft you now!' He looked towards the Lodge, where two people had appeared. 'The fair Ophelia – and with a coloured gentleman.'

'Inspector!' There was a shout from the other side of the quadrangle, and McCann was waving from the edge of the green. Autumn rose as Balboa and Mr Singh arrived, and walked over to McCann.

'This thing' – McCann stuttered – 'the policeman, your – what's his name – Dorcas – called. I – why the devil wasn't I –'

Black and hard and glowering.

'This person, this – Kant. Contraband in Bodley. Why was I not told the instant –'

Autumn said nothing.

'Unbelievable. I said it to Dorcas. Un—'

Autumn eyed McCann speculatively. How should I have him?

'One point, of course,' said Autumn easily. 'Kant could have done it all much more comfortably if he could have counted on you.'

How will he –

'Naturally,' said McCann with contempt. 'It is the first thing that would occur to anyone.'

After a pause, McCann said: 'If you believe that you will believe anything.'

Facing McCann and looking over his shoulder, Autumn could see the Pagoda. Balboa and Nicholas, who had walked a little aside, were deep in conversation. Fairlight stood at the other end of the sward, hefting his wood and eyeing the girl and the undergraduate.

Autumn said to McCann: 'We are direct. We profit from our directness.' McCann held his gaze, heavy-lidded, dark. 'There is certainly more to Kant than – Hmmm. Well, it's my problem, my problem.'

'All right, all right,' shouted Lord Pinner from the Pagoda end. 'Bowl away.'

Fairlight took his eyes away from Balboa and Nicholas and laid his wood.

'You connect this man, this – Kant – with the other business, the destruction?' asked McCann.

'I naturally do. The circumstances. But there is an inwardness about him. The murders, even.'

'Yes?'

They began to stroll towards the Pagoda.

'Well up, well up,' cried Lord Pinner.

'– up, well up,' cried Rankine.

Flower was looking sheepish. Balboa had turned her back on him and was standing talking to Mr Singh.

'No, no, Inspector,' said McCann, laying a hand on his arm as they halted together and watched Fairlight lay his second wood. 'It is our problem, our problem more properly.'

For a moment Autumn was tempted to show him the diary. No. Shipton is the only safe bet.

'I suspect we have all of us in the College done far too little. We are too apt to withdraw too promptly.'

As they drew near, Mr Singh raised his straw hat in salutation and said: 'The top of the afternoon to you, Inspector.'

McCann said in a low tone: 'I shall make as thorough and comprehensive an enquiry throughout my staff as I can. If there is the possibility of collusion,' he added dryly, 'it is a possibility that includes others beside myself.'

Autumn said: 'Yes.'

McCann nodded and walked away.

'A cultured Scotsman,' averred Mr Singh. 'He will be feeling the heat more than us, native as he is to a climate of great chilliness. In the way of cooling draughts, however, there is nothing to whack a good hot cup of char – er – tea. We are just on our way to –'

'My dear sir, what a terribly *terribly* lower-middle-class fallacy! Did you not know it was a canard invented and put about by English charladies,' enquired Nicholas Flower, 'uncultured English charladies?'

'Oh, crikey!' exclaimed Mr Singh, horror-struck. 'A

thousand thanks for the tip. We British subjects are gullible to a fault.'

'We certainly are,' said Balboa, looking at Autumn. 'Gullible to a fault – a rule to which I had always imagined the constabulary exempt.'

'Ha, ha, now we are all gaily pulling each other's legs,' chuckled Mr Singh. 'It would be wery hard to think of any thing more agreeably characteristic.'

'Pulling each other's legs,' smiled Autumn. 'How nice!'

The voice of Fairlight came from the other end of the green: 'Change ends now, Lord Pinner? You've got the sun against you there.'

'No, no, doesn't matter, man – we aren't playing a championship.'

'Cynicism in woman,' observed Nicholas Flower, looking at Balboa, 'is the precursor of unsightly wrinkles. Nor is it at all effective, for it is always seen to be entirely *voulu*.'

'Oh, my *God*!' shrieked Balboa. 'Can't you do better than that?'

'Gullible?' mused Autumn. 'I like to think you meant "ingenuous", Miss Tomlin – a lovely Regency word.' He smiled.

'*Honestly!*' exclaimed the exasperated Miss Tomlin. 'Surely you ought to have wrapped things up by *now*. The way you started off in Walpurgis asking all those questions so workmanlike – I thought you'd have the cuffs on us all in *no* time. Though God knows' – she glanced fleetingly to where Fairlight was trotting slowly towards them – 'you haven't had much help.' She looked contemptuously at Nicholas Flower. 'I don't suppose policemen bargain for *silliness* – and –'

'Pray compose yourself, ma'am,' said Autumn solemnly.

Balboa almost stamped her foot.

'You're not even *curious* –'

Fairlight came up panting.

'Indecently hot. Pax, pax, my Lord. Such an exacting game. Mr Dogg will have noted its neurotic insistence upon accuracy. Whoof, the nerves protrude and one sweats. Miss Tomlin, I am reading "A Time for Fretwork" at the Poetry Society this evening – we might run out to Woodstock afterwards and have a bite at the "Bear" –'

Balboa looked at him.

'Mr Singh has kindly invited me to a meat-tea at the Asian Club, and to a flannel-dance afterwards.'

Slipping her arm through that of Mr Singh, she walked primly away.

For a second, Nicholas Flower stared after her: then he did a handstand against the Pagoda wall.

'An echo, as of shot bolts,' murmured Rankine unpleasantly, running one bowl against another in his hands.

'Come along, Rankine, don't stand about. Up to the other end, and you and me'll have a do.'

As Rankine, obedient to his patron's word, trotted away, Tantalum, who had appeared at the grass verge some seconds before, now approached Autumn.

'Mr Dorcas is in the Senior Common Room, sir, and asked me to tell you as soon as you was up.'

'Right.'

The Inspector walked round the quad to the S C R. Hills peep o'er hills, and Alps on Alps arise. He felt he was on the penultimate ridge, not seeing the top, but sensing that if he could just establish the route from here. . . . It raged in him like a toothache, the presentiment, while the behavioural quirks of Balboa Tomlin and Nicholas Flower pressed upon him not at all.

Can't be certain of Manchip's diary, can't be certain. But I've no better place to look.

'Lying in, eh?' Dorcas was eating a biscuit he had dipped into his tea.

'No.'

'*I* got precious little shut-eye. He phoned his lawyer when we got to the nick and the blighter was round at the magistrate's court first thing sharp as you like. Dear – o – dear.' Dorcas clucked his tongue.

'Sprung him then?'

'Yes, sprung him. In and out like a dose of salts. Cheeky so-and-so – wanted the station sergeant to slip out and get him some Rennies – said the breakfast had given him heartburn. When he went he said he was going for a nice swim this afternoon to wash the prison atmosphere off. Said it depended how refreshed he felt after it whether he'd write to *The Times* about the breakfast. Cor!'

'I wouldn't mind a swim myself,' said Autumn. 'It's hot. Yes,' he said to a servant, 'tea.'

He snuffed up the leather and nicotine. The SCR was cooler than many places on a hot afternoon. He looked round him. Falal had *The Times* spread out before him, doing the crossword; he held a pencil in one hand and with the other he spooned blackcurrant jam. Christelow and Undigo were reading, Shipton stood at the other end of the room, drinking tea and looking out of the window into the Master's Garden.

'Now what's our next move, old man?' asked Dorcas, pouring himself some tea.

'Look, when it's hot,' said Autumn, 'I get irritated easily. So don't ask me that again will you?'

'Don't get shirty, old man.'

'This is what I was doing this morning.'

Autumn slipped the THEOREM out of the diary. 'Here. Read it and tell me what you think.'

Fairlight came in and asked for tea. He looked uneasy. Falal turned to Dorcas and asked him one of the clues in his crossword.

'Brain like water for puzzles, Professor Falal.'

'An anagram, I suspect. Yes, definitely an anagram.'

Autumn stood up, Manchip's diary still in his hand, and went across to Shipton. As he passed Fairlight, Fairlight said:

'I'd like a word.'

'Won't be two minutes.'

Shipton was on his own.

'Something you can do for me.'

'A confession?' asked the dry-haired man.

'Not a confession. This' – Autumn tapped the diary – 'the Vice-Chancellor's diary. The last entries. Most of them look explicit enough to me, but I may be missing something. Some of them aren't. I want you to take a look –'

Shipton held out his hand for the diary, after hesitating.

'What's all this?' he said slowly, 'I thought only the entry concerning me interested you –'

'No. Read it through, please. Just the last day. Did you read it through, by the way, when you pinched it?'

'No.'

Autumn stuck his bottom against the window-sill and crossed his legs while Shipton scanned the entry.

'What exactly do you want me to look for?'

'Secondary significances.'

Shipton continued to read.

'I don't think there are any.'

'Yes, yes,' Autumn chewed his lip nodding. 'Look again, though.'

Shipton turned back the page and read the entries through once more.

'No. Not that I can see.'

'Who's the man with the bandy-legged sister?'

'Oh, lord, it might be anyone. You could find out at Wadham, I suppose. Ask the porter.'

'Oh, doesn't matter, doesn't matter.' Autumn stood up abruptly and pushed his hands into his pockets.

'The para-2-second-line stuff is just page refer-ences –'

'Yes, yes, yes.'

'They're the only cryptic entries.'

'Oh, cryptic, cryptic. Tell me, was he always arguing with Christelow and Bow-Parley and Undigo?'

'He was always arguing.'

Autumn clicked his tongue. 'Well,' he said. Then he turned to Shipton. 'I showed it to you because you're the only one who isn't a suspect.'

Shipton's eyebrows went up.

'Thanks –'

For once, his combative tongue was stilled.

'Don't say anything about this.'

Autumn walked over to Fairlight. Dorcas, looking up

from Autumn's notes, saw them move into a remoter corner.

Fairlight was speaking. At first he kept breaking off, rubbing his big smooth chin and looking at the Inspector; then he spoke faster, gathering his nervousness into the momentum of his speaking.

Autumn looked at the carpet while Fairlight spoke. When Fairlight had finished, he said, coolly, like a doctor to a frightened patient:

'What a damn fool you were not telling me.'

'Well –' said Fairlight. He was silent again. 'Well –'

'Give it to me.'

Fairlight handed him a piece of paper. Autumn read what was written on it:

My dear Fairlight,

I feel it only just that you should know my mind has altered as to the most suitable candidate to fill the English Chair. Hitherto, it has been sufficiently obvious where my preference has lain; now, however, I must tell you that my casting vote will go to Bow-Parley.

May I suggest that in your relations with the lady undergraduates you observe, in the future, a greater discretion?

'What about the signature?' asked Autumn.

'What about it?'

'You're sure it's his?'

Fairlight craned his head round to look.

'Why not?'

'When did it come?'

'Mid-morning, the day after. That's when I picked it up.'

'By hand?'

'It was on the ledge at the Lodge.' Fairlight grimaced at the alliteration. 'That's where notes by College messengers are left. Or he might have left it himself the night before.'

'He couldn't. He was dead.'

'No, of course. But it might have been there a couple of days. I don't always look.'

'And so Balboa Tomlin saw it and asked you why you hadn't said anything. Did she think you were scared?'

'What on earth makes you think that?'

'Oh, pooh!' said Autumn, impatiently.

'Dear me, we do take it seriously!' Fairlight plucked up enough courage to be slightly exasperated. 'All he says is he withdraws his support. Are you telling me it's all that important?'

'I don't know. But you seemed to have thought so. Why hide it?'

'Oh, come. One didn't – It was a private situation, a delicate thing. You understand me. It would have been far too *blunt* a – a – To actually have told anyone. Especially the police. And – really' – Fairlight shrugged his shoulders – 'what interest such trifling domestic manoeuvres –'

'You know better than that,' said Autumn, pocketing the note. 'No need for me to tell you to say nothing about *this*, I'm sure.'

'Oh, certainly not, not at all.'

Clapp had come in with Lord Pinner and Rankine.

'Afternoon,' said Clapp generally.

'Most impressive, old man,' said Dorcas as Autumn sat down beside him again, 'most impressive indeed. I couldn't have done it.' He leant forward and brushed a wasp away from the jam. 'I could no more have done it than fly in the air. Action – yes. Theory – no.'

Falal murmured: 'It must be an anagram.' He held a spoonful of jam motionless in the air before him.

'You've wrapped it up nicely, old man,' Dorcas said, 'and now it's a question of where do we go from here –'

Christelow had moved away from where Lord Pinner was apostrophizing fresh air as though it were a proprietary product. Autumn looked up at him.

'Would you have said Bow-Parley and the Vice-Chancellor had anything in common, Mr Christelow?'

'An interesting speculation –'

Undigo, also seeking refuge from Lord Pinner, strolled over to join them, and after speaking to the servant about more tea, stood with his hands in his pockets listening.

Quite suddenly Autumn became oblivious of his surroundings and deaf to the words of Christelow. For something had just gone 'twang' in his mind, something that had made no more noise than a tuning-fork.

'That was in common,' exclaimed Autumn abruptly.

'– little sense of moderation.' Christelow broke off. 'I beg your pardon?'

'Oh – yes,' Autumn nodded, 'of course.'

'I suppose they were snobs. Would you say so, Christelow?' Undigo did not wait for confirmation. 'Yes, certainly. Bow-Parley might have termed it "civilized prejudice", but Manchip would have told the truth and called it snobbery. The Chaplain', Undigo smiled, rattling the money in his pocket, 'was a Baconian. A Baconian and a gentleman.'

Ever so softly, the tuning-fork twanged again. Autumn sat like a man trying to encourage a sneeze.

'How do you mean, Mr Undigo?' Dorcas asked interestedly.

'It depends how you look at it, Inspector.'

'Aha!' Falal exclaimed. 'One, two, three, four – yes, the right number of letters. "Perspicacity." There's a good long word, and a very apt one. An anagram as I suspected. Yes,' he went on, 'Manchip was a snob and his views on women were unbridled, but he wouldn't have taken ten minutes to get "perspicacity", indeed he would not.'

'He would have put you out of countenance, Humphrey, by doing all your anagrams over your shoulder,' smiled Christelow.

Autumn got to his feet.

Lord Pinner shouted across the room: 'I'll tell you in three words what was wrong with Manchip – *out of, touch!*'

'To a degree, certainly,' nodded Rankine.

Autumn felt he had got the sneeze and must balance it, hold it in until he could take it somewhere and tip it out at full force.

Clapp was staring at him.

'Well,' Autumn said cheerfully, 'there are no short-cuts.'

Lord Pinner cried: 'Of course there are. Any successful man's life is a series of short-cuts. That was something our friend Manchip never realized. *Bogged down!*'

Autumn nodded very absently. He picked up the diary and the sheets of paper containing his THEOREM.

Dorcas rose too.

Autumn nodded amiably again, and walked to the door. Dorcas followed him over.

'What do you want me to do next?'

Autumn stood at the threshold of the room, looking past him into the quadrangle.

'You – um –'

'Yes?'

'Oh – just wait at the Station.'

'Rightyo –'

Autumn pushed past him as he spoke.

Miles away, thought Dorcas as he watched his colleague walk off down the cloister. Good job one of us can do without a couple of hours' sleep without losing his grip. . . .

To Autumn it seemed that he must walk carefully. The slightest tremor might dislodge the concentration needed in order to go on hearing the echo of the tuning-signals that had so suddenly sounded. No – not suddenly sounded – suddenly heard. I must hold them steady.

He went into the Tower.

The quadrangle was empty. The mellowness that sets in after tea imparted texture to the shadows so that they looked darker, substantial. Twice, figures came out of the cloisters and passed across the green to the Lodge: once from the Senior Common Room, once from the under-graduates' staircase. Iscariot sounded the quarters, the half, the hour. Tantalum emerged from the shade, marvelling at the heat as it struck up from the ground through the soles of his shoes. The heat persisted, pulsing into the quadrangle as if the sky were being cupped.

Autumn stood again at the door of the Tower. He looked very tired. Success is release, he thought, and its expression is exhaustion. What a pity.

He watched his shadow go before him over the grass. Tantalum stood at the gate, watching him approach, wondering that a policeman should look tired and walk slowly.

'You'd think the stone was alive, the way the 'eat comes back off the walls, sir.'

'It's hot.'

Autumn asked the porter a question, and the porter said: 'No. Parson's Pleasure 'e was off to. About five and twenty minutes ago. Only place, this weather.'

Autumn nodded, and went slowly out into the street.

The man who killed Manchip. The words jogged up and down in Autumn's mind as he walked across the Parks to Parson's Pleasure. *Him.*

Well, he'd be caught with his pants right down.

Chapter 18

Autumn had known they would be undressed – Parson's
Pleasure, a bywater of the Cher, was expressly reserved
for gentlemen who wished to bathe naked – but somehow
he had thought they would not look it.

Such a lot of wrinkled tums. He walked over to the
changing huts as nonchalantly as his clothed status allow-
ed him, and filled his pipe. The grass was covered with
them: young, middle-aged, old: white, brown, mottled.
It was all very well saying the human body was beautiful –
whose human body?

Autumn didn't want to take off his clothes, because he
hoped he wasn't staying that long. He lounged across the
grass with his hands in his pockets, picking his way among
the misshapen limbs.

'Hello, hello, hello –'

Mr Bum and Mr Weed had hailed him. Neither was
entirely naked, for Mr Bum retained his horn-rimmed
spectacles, and Mr Weed his camera.

Mr Bum slapped his chest, and said heartily: 'In the
raw, eh? The stuff to give 'em.'

Autumn sat down.

'Very Greek,' said Mr Bum, waving his arm about him.

'Very painful,' said Mr Weed, shifting his hams.

'Not stripping off, old boy?' said Mr Bum.

'If he's any respect for his bottom, he'll stay the way he is,'
said Mr Weed. 'I feel as if I'm sitting on a bloody hairbrush.'

'Phew – sun's still hot,' said Autumn.

'Sucks all the juice out of you,' said Mr Weed.

'And you haven't much to spare, have you, boy?' Mr
Bum adjusted his spectacles and looked hard at his com-
panion. 'Anyone ever tell you you look like a fakir?'

'I feel like a bloody fakir, old boy.'

Without his clothes, Mr Weed resembled a stick of
locust-root.

Bum turned to the Inspector.

'We came down for a word with Kant. That's a lovely

176

story, now, only we'll have to tone the dirt down. Your oppo gave me the background this morning – quite a night you both had, by all accounts.'

'Oh, sure.'

'There he is – but we'll have to wait till he's dressed, Horace, for the picture.'

Bum pointed and Autumn looked out over the river. Mr Kant was floating on his back beneath the tall elms, kicking his feet up like a baby in his bath. Well, well, wondered Autumn, will he turn out to be the brick after all –

Mr Bum, who was terribly white all over, started to run energetically on the spot.

'Don't know what bad health is, thank God. Touch of catarrh and those piles – fit as a fiddle otherwise.' He chocked his hands beneath his breasts and shook them. 'Good living, Horace. Going in?'

Autumn glanced idly in Kant's direction, daydreaming gently about success. A problem, humane and intellectual –

'No,' said Mr Weed, 'I think the water's dirty.'

– Solved by me. And the evidence available to anyone cognizant of the events, the personalities, and the exhibits. Literally! No going back to the Yard and saying the chap confessed or committed suicide or overreached himself –

'And the Professors,' Mr Weed said sanctimoniously, 'look as if they'd be nicer to know after a spot of chlorination.'

– Nothing fortuitous, nothing haphazard. It was curious the way all the other suspects had melted back into unassailable integrity, so that one found oneself wondering how on earth one could have suspected men so plainly beyond reproach.

A man swam mildly through the thin spiky grass which furred the top of the water near the other side of the river. It was the man who had killed Manchip and Bow-Parley, and Autumn regarded him curiously.

A man who had killed two other men. For the first time, thought Autumn, I am seeing him in that identity.

And then suddenly Autumn's contemplative air was shed as he saw the man who had killed Bow-Parley and Manchip swim right up to Immanuel Kant and begin to talk with him. They were both well over to the other bank, treading water and splashing their arms gently to keep themselves afloat.

Brick in the joke be damned. I knew it, I bloody knew it, that fat phoney's in it somewhere yet –

'Blimey,' Mr Weed ejaculated, 'look at me!' He stared down at the white ribbon which ran across his breast. 'Teach me to wear a camera in the sun.'

Autumn was watching the two men clamber out of the water and on to the bank. They sat with their feet in the water.

Now what, now *what* do I make of that? Autumn stared hard across the river.

'You know, it makes you feel philosophical,' Mr Bum said ruminatively.

'Which?' queried Mr Weed.

'Sitting here with no clothes on among the intellectual cream.'

Autumn had fallen into a reverie, squeezing his lips with his fingers.

'It doesn't make *me* feel philosophical, old boy, it makes me feel uncomfortable.'

'Oh, they're a grand bunch, really –'

'No, no, old boy, I am not referring to the intellectual cream. I am referring to the state of my bottom.'

Birds flew low across the water, screeching away into the trees. Two middle-aged dons with no clothes on strolled together along the sward, smoking their pipes, nodding agreeably.

'I say' – Mr Bum gazed idly about him – 'where's he got to?'

'Who, old boy?'

'Kant.'

Autumn looked up. Both his men had disappeared.

'He's around.'

'Don't want to miss that picture.'

Autumn turned and gazed down the river. Forty yards

away, in the middle of the stream, the man who had killed Bow-Parley and Manchip broke the surface, spluttering amiably. But there was no sign of Kant.

Autumn looked. Then he was on his feet almost before his next thought had become a thought.

'Off?' inquired Mr Bum.

The man who had killed two men had gone under; he reappeared, blowing cheerfully, and started swimming towards the bank, downstream from Autumn and the two journalists.

In that instant Autumn knew where Kant was.

The killer was pulling himself out of the water, brushing the hair out of his eyes, holding his nose as he blew down it. He looked up and saw Autumn and waved. Then his naked arm came down slowly to his side. He had caught the Inspector's eye.

Autumn stood in an agony of what to do first. Get him quick. But Kant –

'Look,' Autumn said to Bum and Weed, who turned round suddenly, startled by the change in his tone, 'there's a man drowning on the bottom of the river – just by the grass – over there, the clump in front of the alders. *Get him out.*'

'What –?'

'*Quick.*'

Bum's jaw dropped, but with commendable resilience he dived straight into the water, followed feet-first by Mr Weed.

Autumn turned round. His man still stood on the bank, his arms at his sides, and Autumn saw the drops of water glitter as they dripped from his fingers.

The Inspector moved forward.

Then the afternoon went mad.

'There was an absolutely splendid turn-out for the first meeting. We had – *ow!*'

With a short sharp scream the man who had been talking leapt to his feet, pointed a shaking finger towards the river, made one fatuous attempt to disguise his private parts with a handful of grass, then ran like the devil.

For round the forbidden bend, approaching at an energetic rate of knots, there rowed the Ladies' Eight.

The whole of Parson's Pleasure was transformed. Men who had been taking their ease – sprawled on their bellies or hugging their knees in the sun – started up like spring-loaded automata and ran for their lives.

Flying figures cannoned into each other, hurled themselves into the hedges, dived six-deep into the bathing huts. One fat don started to climb a tree. The ground shook.

Out in the river the water boiled as the bathers made grimly for the shore. One man crawled out and squeezed himself miserably beneath the spring-board, another crouched in the bullrushes, his bottom sinking deeper into the ooze. Another, despairing of concealment, opened his spectacle case and spread it hopefully before him.

In the instant of total confusion, Autumn's eye had been deflected. His man had disappeared. Autumn ran across the grass.

'I say –'; 'Exposure –'; 'Indecent –'; 'Surely they know –'; 'Well, I put it round my head because I remembered the man who said he was known in Oxford by his features not his –'

The bathers babbled hysterically in the hedges.

The ladies in the boat had begun to scream, and through the falsetto chorale the voice of the coxwain boomed:

'Back your oars and hold your bloody noise,' roared Pearl Corker. 'Some of you're seeing something you'll never see again. Back water, the lot of you!'

Autumn ran to the edge of the river and scanned the long grass. Then he sped across the turf to the hedges, darting amongst the bare crouching men like a sheep dog.

'They'll have to repaint the notice –'; 'I feel quite hysterical –'; 'So insecure –'

Autumn snatched open the doors of the bathing huts one after the other. The bathers, crammed together like sardines and chattering nervously, took no notice of him – a man in a blue suit, dodging among them like a scrum-

half, made no impression after what had already happen-
ed. The afternoon had fragmented.

There was a paling fence with a hedge at the back of
the line of huts, and Autumn climbed over it, glancing
across the field that lay behind.

He scrambled back and walked to the end of the huts,
coming out again on to the open grass by the river. The
Ladies' Eight was slowly reversing round the bend. Across
the water Bum and Weed were supporting a waterlogged
Kant.

Autumn whirled round. A naked figure had darted
swiftly away from one of the hedges. He saw Autumn and
stopped. Then he ran like the wind for the gate.

'STOP!'

Autumn's voice went off like a thunderclap, and the
rooks rose cawing from the tall elms. The twittering voices
of the bathers faded away. The silence was absolute and
sudden.

Autumn began to run. He shouted again.

'THE MAN AT THE GATE – HE MUST BE STOPPED –
STOP HIM –'

The bathers were malleable material; the day had gone
into flux. Giants, magic, gods from machines, they would
accept the lot.

The killer had reached the gate and was through it into
the alley beyond. The bathers had come out of hiding and
stood petrified in the centre of the open turf.

Autumn bore down upon them, yelling.

'AFTER HIM – QUICK –'

The one man with clothes on. Waving his arms in over-
powering, compulsive suggestion. It was a hypnosis that
could only have worked on an afternoon that had already
sheered its moorings.

Wide-eyed and expectant, they stared at him: Autumn
gave them the last shove.

'I AM A POLICE OFFICER. STOP THAT MAN.'

Slowly at first, then faster, the naked men began to
move, swelling across the turf as a cloud swells across the
sky, amorphous, pseudopodial. They squeezed through
the gate like a huge chunk of ectoplasm, tumbling over

each other in the narrow alley, stubbing their toes, scratching their arms against the hedges.

And then they began to run.

Some of them ran upright, their heads set back and their arms tucked well into their sides. Some put their heads forward, stooping along the ground and drawing their legs on after. Some loped along. Some got into their stride and lifted their knees well up. One man swung his elbows like Indian clubs, another shook his heels like an old horse.

There were tall men running and short men, fat men and thin men. Some skipped, some pranced, some lumbered, some waddled. Some went sideways. There were fat men running on thin legs, and thin men running on fat legs. There were dark skins and light skins and mottled skins, some skins were yellow. There were rough men and hairy men and smooth men. Some men were knock-kneed and some men were bandy, and some men were both.

They ran.

Out of Parson's Pleasure, out into the little alley, out on to the river bank and along the river path; past the may bushes and the pollarded alders and the yellow gorse; each man with his eyes before his feet, naked under the sun and with the smell of the hunt in his nostrils.

And far out beyond the leaders, the man who had killed Manchip and Bow-Parley; the man for whom all was already all up; to be caught with his pants right down.

Chapter 19

So many eyewitnesses were there that it became the one Oxford story that no one ever got wrong. Given one man who could say he was just passing Keble, there were always two or three others who would chip in: 'Oh, I was in Blackwell's –' or 'I was down by the Parks –'

The Broad had the biggest concentration, for as well as the people in the street there were any amount looking out of windows in Exeter and Balliol. There were quite a few in the neighbourhood of Wadham and down by the laboratories, but if any one lot had the edge over the others it was the people in the region of the Martyr's Memorial. They saw the end of it all.

Nobody ever got it wrong, but an extensive and somewhat variable apocrypha sprang up, centred largely on the alleged reactions of the various onlookers. Much of this was no more than commonplace, rather uninventive exaggeration – yet one or two of the tales survive in Junior and Senior Common Rooms. The two High Churchmen, for instance, who strolled out of Keble and ran right into it: 'Baptists,' murmured one, 'and they accused Pusey of excess!' And there was supposed to be one of Oxford's most famous scientists standing outside the Pitt Rivers Museum who instantly ascribed the whole thing to 'some trick of the dying sun' . . .

To be calling it an 'Oxford story' is perhaps a little to domesticate the affair. The decision to print or not to print a story about men with no clothes on running wild through the streets of a University town had Mr Sharpshoot of the *Knell* twining his hands in his hair and bending a Brittania-metal tea-spoon into the figure of eight. Bum on the telephone, a Bum heroic, a Bum beside himself, a Bum possessed, had managed to convince him that he was perfectly sober. At five-thirty Mr Sharpshoot – who was now standing over his sub-editors with all his waistcoat buttons done up into the wrong holes – decided to desert the odd-looking ladies in non-smoking carriages, and damn the consequences. The *Evening Knell* put on 10,000 copies and Mr Bum underwent a shattering metamorphosis as a profile on the front page.

With Bum not only on, but in, the story – Bum's rescue of the pornographer was recorded in bold type beneath his picture – the rest of the papers fell back on their opinion-columns, 'With the Queen Mother barely returned from her triumphal tour,' thundered Cackhandidus, 'I ask these men: WAS IT THE RIGHT TIME?'

For human interest, of course, there was Mrs Spectre, heroine of the hour: television as well as the papers took her up. 'Tell me, Mrs Spectre, love, what is your greatest ambition?' asked a smiling Wilfred Pickles. Mrs Spectre's answer spoke more loudly than words, and the programme was faded out as the charge from her twelve-bore was lodging itself in the posteriors of her questioner.

But we go beyond our story.

A cricket match was in progress in the Parks, and the bowler was running slowly up to the wicket. At the very instant of delivery he saw them, swung right round on one heel, and discharged the ball at square-leg umpire. Square-leg umpire had seen them too, and when the ball struck him sharply on the elbow he shook his arm softly as though a leaf had descended upon it.

They were running steadily, keeping to the grass because of the stones. They were strung out like men on a cross-country race, but their nakedness gave them more the appearance of a Greek frieze executed by a pocket-cartoonist. Some of them were getting their second wind.

The cricketers were turned to stone, standing like waxworks in the hot sun; cover-point, catching sight of them as he bent down with his hands on his knees, had lost his balance, toppled over, and now crouched on all-fours immobile as a dog pointing. In the longer grass, in the outfield, and under trees, couples sat bolt upright, hair still rumpled, shoulder straps still loose, hands still in plackets. Had the bees ceased to buzz? Were the skylarks falling? Had eternity begun? The line of bare men moved in the summer light as if summoned in their nakedness to the end of the world.

'Pimple,' said a chemist over his shoulder to another as he looked out of the window of the laboratory, 'lay down your retort-spoon carefully and come and look out of the window.

'There are several men running down the road with no clothes on.'

'What a thing to do.'

'I wonder why?'

'It's against the law.'

'Mmmmm.'

'There they go.'

'I've never seen anyone with no clothes on in the street before.'

'Neither have I.'

'I suppose it could only happen in Oxford.'

'Uh?'

'Happen in Oxford.'

'How do you mean?'

'Oh... well...'

Never shall I hear the last of this, groaned the Inspector as he ran. Never, never, never. Those blasted girls, sending everyone raving mad. I wish I'd let him go – he couldn't have got fat. I could have phoned Dorcas. I could have just gone after him myself. Instead of this terrible, awful... Oh, dear, dear, dear. I wish I could have the last few minutes to live over again, I wish a great big lorry would run us all over, I wish we could all wake up, I wish --

'What the bloody hell are *you* staring at?' he roared at a thunder-struck policeman who was clawing at his collar at the side of the road. 'D'you think we're doing this for bloody fun?' The policeman shook himself galvanically and contrived to set himself in motion. He caught the Inspector up.

'This here's a turn-up for the book. I've never seen so many together all at one time before. We might be able to

185

head 'em off into Wadham if we could turn the leaders. Like they do with maddened steers.'

A motorist trundling along in front of the chase caught sight of them in his back mirror and swerved violently, bumping up the kerb and driving straight into the Pitt Rivers Museum. Two ladies with shopping baskets burst into tears.

'It's this sort of thing gets a town a bad name,' vouchsafed the constable.

Reality was already reasserting itself among some of the runners. 'But what can you do when you have no clothes on and are running,' gasped a very thin, middle-aged don who was still wearing a pair of pince-nez, 'except continue to run?'

'There is only one thing to do,' breathed another, 'and that is catch him.'

'Yes – it is our only hope.'

'If we catch him I may still get that living –'

'If we catch him I may yet have my Professorship –'

'If we don't catch him,' growled a hairy-chested don, 'we shall go to gaol.'

Almost as if he had heard them, their quarry dug his elbows in hard and spurted further ahead.

What the hell does he do it for, wondered Autumn, who was slowly working his way to the head of the column. He must know he can't get away. Instinct, I suppose. To remain untouched as long as possible even though there's no way out.

The killer turned into the Broad, running right down the centre of the road. Not a single spectator offered the slightest interference. Not a soul shouted. The whole street had petrified. An errand-boy fell off his bike and sat motionless on the pavement as the wheels of the machine slowly revolved. The only sound was the thump-thump of bare feet on asphalt.

Two Heads of Houses tottered out of Blackwell's with Penguins under their arms. One glanced rheumily towards the road and saw the runners.

'Yes,' nodded the other, as his companion drew his

attention to the spectacle, 'it is an advertising campaign, depend upon it.'

A philosophy don and his pupil stood at a window in Balliol, watching.

'Let us take this as a hypothetical case,' said the don, waving in the direction of the naked men. 'If we set empiricism aside, what shall we require?'

'We shall require glasses,' said his pupil.

All traffic was at a standstill, each vehicle having run into the back of the one before it. A window in Exeter shot up and a large trumpet appeared, shattering the appalling silence with the opening bars of 'Colonel Bogie':

Whaa–whaaa wha–wha wha–wha wha wha wha–wha–

'Ohhhhhh,' breathed Orson Dogg, clasping his hands in ecstasy, 'exhibitionists. Lots and lots and lots.' He darted out into the road and fell in with the runners, producing a notebook and engaging the rearmost man in earnest conversation.

Wha–wha wha–wha–wha wha–wha–wha wha–whaaaaa

Autumn, gritting his teeth, was running hard and lay third, with the constable fifth or sixth. But the killer still held a twenty-yard lead and was going well. Autumn put his head down and passed the two men ahead of him, drawing level with a little fat bandy-legged man who was fizzing along like an electric hare. The killer shot directly across the Corn market into George Street and pelted toward the Ritz Cinema. He veered right into Gloucester Green, ran straight across by the car-park, then out along by the side of the Playhouse and into Beaumont Street. It was there, as he turned right again, that Mrs Spectre saw him.

Whaaa–whaaaa–

Mrs Spectre walked down the steps of the Ashmolean, her telescope under her arm. She came out into the street opposite the Randolph Hotel and halted abruptly. Approaching her at a feverish canter was a naked man, followed at a distance of ten yards by a man in a blue suit, who was himself followed at varying intervals by more naked men and a police constable. In an instant, Mrs Spectre had the whole thing in hand.

Whaa–whaaaaa–

Taking a firm grasp on her already extended telescope, she swung it round her head and, with a heave and a twist, hurled it through the air. The long brass tube flashed in the sunlight, twirling like a *bolas*, and with unerring accuracy passed between the shins of the killer. There was an explosive *smack* as he hit the ground face downwards. His jaw cracked against the stone steps of the Memorial, and he lay still.

Mrs Spectre walked imperiously over the road to where Autumn knelt panting beside his quarry.

'Who,' she demanded, 'is this person?'

Whaaaaaaaaaaaaa –

Autumn looked up.

'His name is Christelow,' he said.

Chapter 20

'My trouble,' said Christelow, 'has always been my ability to recognize what is worthwhile – and what just falls short of it.'

He nodded wryly.

'I have a good mind. I fancy it is a better mind than, say, Undigo's. But Undigo – well, for one thing, Undigo's pupils have more Firsts than mine do, I am *interesting*, I stimulate, but – well, amiable and individual intellectuality is not enough. I know it, you see, I know it.'

He raised his eyes to Autumn's.

'And what is worse, I find myself quite unable to put up with what falls ever so slightly short. I *wanted* the kind of success that a string of learned and painstaking commentaries would have brought me with the slogging scholarly people. I could never do as Fairlight does – effect to despise that side. But I just don't seem to have the strength of purpose to set about it myself.'

Christelow laughed almost shyly.

'I suppose all this simply means that as a person I like to stand well with everyone. Dear me, that sounds shockingly feeble. But I think it is true. I have a tolerably high opinion of my powers but it is a fact that I am never able to think thoroughly well of myself unless I have been able to persuade everyone else to think the same.'

This time he laughed out loud to cover his embarrassment.

'It was just never enough for me to know that my mind was a good mind, that it was one of the best (and I may say this without too great immodesty for there are many who would say it for me) in the University, and to be admitted something of a front-ranker with the progressive critical and creative people. I wanted the scholars as well. But' – and Christelow's eye was sheepish – 'I just couldn't get down to it. The slog, I mean. *Do* the books. There would always have been such a lot of leeway, you see – why, Undigo has one standard work and several editions, quite apart from his little collection of essays. *My* essays are considered more significant than Undigo's – as Undigo would tell you – but that standard work . . .'

Christelow shook his head.

'And indolence, I'm afraid, wasn't all. There was vanity. All the time it works against my inclination to have everyone think well of me. "Why should I care," I ask myself, "if the pedants withhold their accolade? I am well received amongst my own kind. Why should a fine mind put itself about to please others?"'

Christelow broke off.

'I have a wretched vanity.' He was silent again. 'Yes,' he went on softly, 'I suppose that really is it.'

He stopped again. Then he said:

'Like many people who pretend they could do a thing if they put their minds to it, I made this an excuse for not doing it. The standard works were not forthcoming, and I pretended I didn't really mind. But neither vanity nor indolence allowed me any satisfaction. Without works, they seldom do. I really did consider – as I really do consider still – the creative aesthetic mind with the active critical approach superior to the simply scholastic. But' – he raised his hands – 'it wasn't enough. A mixture of both is better than either. I could not deceive myself.'

Christelow savoured his words.

'All this will sound somewhat obsessive, but you must bear in mind the context – a sequestered society where the pedants out-number the Rest. The sense of competition is sharpened, and the problem is how to compete most tellingly. Well, one cannot go on and on demonstrating the superiority of one's own attitude if the other side refuses to accept the demonstration – especially when one does not believe, anyway, that one's own attitude though superior is comprehensively so. No.'

The look that Christelow now directed at the Inspector was half-questioning.

'One has to beat them at their own game. You see that?'

He leaned back in the wooden chair.

'This – all this that I am telling you now – this is the

background, this so to speak is *me*. This is how I fit in, am congruous with the things I have done. You see that?'

He paused.

'Beat them at their own game. Beating them quite irrefutably and – for sheer luxurious good measure – confirming in the most eloquent way possible the superiority of the creative critical approach. Well, that was my' – he chose his word – 'my ambition. I adduced a method and set about it. Did I succeed?' Christelow gazed levelly at Autumn. 'To appropriate Undigo's phrase, Would you say so?'

Autumn glanced round the circle of faces in the Senior Common Room.

'My answer to that question was "Yes". *The Book of the Lion*,' the Inspector pitched it on to the table, 'is Christelow's own creation from beginning to end.'

There was not a movement. No one spoke. The silence lasted several seconds, for the dons were not absolutely sure that the Inspector had in fact said what they supposed they had heard. Then Undigo leaned forward and picked up *The Book*.

'Christelow –' He opened *The Book* but continued to stare at Autumn. Then: 'He *did* it?'

'It was all my unwritten works,' said Christelow simply. 'It was all my mind, all my liberality – such as that may be. It took a long, long time. When I had done it I knew it meant a great deal to me – it, and the enterprise of which it was the keystone. But I had not known how much until I stood behind Manchip with a knife in my hand . . .'

'He did this,' said Undigo, still staring at Autumn. 'And to authenticate it into the bargain!' Undigo looked down at *The Book*. 'What incredible quality of mind –'

'But perverse,' said Autumn mildly.

Undigo did not hear him.

'If the thing were a simple fake one might begin to be able to comprehend – but he had to re-create the entire idiom of an age – vocabulary, grammar, usage. Why, it's fantastic. A vast scholarly apparatus – and the unimaginable skill to apply it in such an act of creation. The thing is so – so *genuine*. Chaucer –'

Undigo stopped speaking as though his incredulity could find no further expression. Then he said:

'Who *has* seen through it?' He turned sharply to Autumn. 'Who? Manchip, Bow-Parley? *You?*'

'In a special sense,' said Autumn, 'all three of us. But I'll come to that in due course. A very special sense – '

'Incredible,' breathed Undigo, staring at *The Book*.

'But look here,' interjected Fairlight, 'how did you come to it at all –'

'You're not a Chaucerian, are you?' enquired Shipton curiously.

Autumn laughed.

'No, no. You – at least, the English scholars among you – could have seen through *The Book* far more easily than I – as a Chaucer poem, that is.'

'But we didn't.' Undigo tapped his finger on the arm of his chair. 'Christelow succeeded.'

'And I must add that you could all' – and Autumn's eye roved, perceptibly shining, from face to face – 'have seen through it in the sense that *I* saw through it. You could have seen through the problem. It was all there, precisely there, as much under the nose of each and every one of you as it was under mine. . . .'

'You will have realized,' Christelow said, 'that the essence of my success would have remained a secret. There was to have been no ultimate revelation. I was not, you must understand, trying to make anyone look silly. It wasn't a *joke*, you know, a taking down of academic trousers. No such thing.

'But' – Christelow rubbed his hands – 'what a commentary I should have been able to write – on my own work!' He enjoyed his laugh. 'That was what was going to give me the strict academic standing which I lacked, and enable me to take up my favourite position of being thought well of by all.

'But my supreme achievement would have to be something only I . . .'

Christelow broke off.

'Which is why I took the risk of – '

Autumn nodded.

'You might have been a free man now if you'd resisted that particular temptation.'

'Oh, who could have resisted? I spoke of my vanity.' Christelow shook his head. 'No, Inspector, I had to do it.'

'And what *was* the mysterious risk?' enquired Fairlight.

'All in good time,' Autumn said.

'Bow-Parley and Manchip knew that Christelow had faked *The Book*?' asked Rankine.

'It is why they were killed.'

'I do not envy them their perception,' murmured Falal.

'I am exceedingly surprised that *they* should have discovered the fraud,' persisted Rankine. 'Bow-Parley was no scholar, and Manchip's subject was Greek. Evidently there were aspects of their characters of which we were ignorant –'

Autumn smiled slightly.

'No, no – as I shall show you.'

'Look, the thing that interests me is how the Inspector did it,' put in Fairlight. 'Tell us that. You haven't given any hint how you came to it yourself –'

'And the books, what about the burning of the books? And the man Kant, and why Christelow tried to drown him?' McCann asked.

'You'll be told everything, but let's have the story in sequence,' said Autumn.

'Could have sworn it was suicide,' grumbled Lord Pinner.

'I was extremely exercised over the physical expression of my – of my plan,' Christelow went on. 'I supposed myself competent to produce the poem – but there was the question of preparing the manuscript.'

'The penny dropped when I saw you and Kant to-

gether in Parson's Pleasure,' Autumn said softly. 'I re-
membered Archangel had told me Kant had done time
for forgery –'

'Yes – Mr Kant was my solution. I had to find an
expert penman – an expert penman whose – ah – *forte*
would be antique documents. You may wonder – as I did
– how a respectable don puts himself into touch with
such a person. Well, I recalled that newspapers maintain
large libraries of cuttings to do with notable crimes and it
occurred to me that a diligent inquiry in such a library
might uncover something to my purpose. It uncovered
Mr Kant. I found his name in a report concerning the
forgery of some ancient title deeds –'

'Archangel mentioned that one.'

'Yes; it put me on to him, as they say. He had served his
term of imprisonment and I got into touch with him
easily enough. He has a curious little *boutique* in the
Charing Cross Road –'

Autumn nodded.

'You know it? Ah – officially. Well, I found him willing
to come to terms with me – indeed, the scheme appealed to
his imagination. In many ways he *is* an imaginative
person – his plan to use Bodley as a warehouse for porno-
graphy makes that very clear! I should say that it was I
who obtained for him a copy of McCann's key – it was
part of our agreement. I was very ready to do it, for it
made me as privy to his own dealings as he had been made
to mine. The possibility of blackmail – Mr Kant is an
enterprising person – was thus averted. And' – Christelow
broke off, hesitating slightly – 'Kant's idea of gaining
access to Bodley suggested a further dimension to my own
deception.'

'The next,' Autumn measured the words as he glanced
from face to face in the Senior Common Room, 'was
masterly.'

Christelow was silent for a few moments, staring at the
floor, his hands clasped between his knees. Then he said:
'What were the considerations, Inspector, governing

the acceptance or rejection of my poem? It is a rhetorical question and I will answer it. The Chaucerian quality of the thing itself, and the skill with which the manuscript had been prepared – these were two of the considerations, and I liked to think it was qualified to succeed on both. But it depended also upon a third.'

Christelow's glance was quizzical.

'The frame of mind of those who would be examining it.'

He smiled slightly and the Inspector waited.

'The first obvious precaution was to let someone else do the actual "discovering". Well, my friend was selling his library and it was an easy thing to slip the poem on one of his shelves and wait for him to come upon it. That got me off to a safe start – suspicion could hardly slip in at *that* door. But I felt it was not yet enough, that the foundations had to be further reinforced.'

Again Christelow stopped speaking and considered the floor between his feet. He went on:

'If you are in a frame of mind to expect a fraud and a fraud comes under your eye you will detect it. That is so? But if you are in a frame of mind to expect something genuine and a fraud comes under your eye you are less likely to detect it. As I say, I supposed the quality of the thing would see me through – as it did – but I felt it would help if I disarmed suspicion from the *outside*.

'I, too, had seen the newspaper reports of the destruction of books in libraries in various parts of the world, destruction which your Commissioner – as I recollect you told us on the first agreeable evening we spent together in College – supposed had now begun in Oxford. I recall his hypothesis was that this world-wide vandalism was part of an organized revolutionary assault upon tradition? Indeed, I remember supposing something of the sort myself. It seems feasible.'

Christelow nodded.

'But in Oxford, no. In Oxford it was I. And I need hardly add – at least, I trust I need hardly add – that I am no revolutionary.'

Autumn plucked at the hair of his sideboards.

'It was with great reluctance that Mr Kant allowed himself to be persuaded to destroy the books for me. His objections were less moral than expedient: he had no wish to draw attention to Bodley, which he had by this time been using for some months. But of course he had no choice. As soon as *The Book* was completed, the destruction began.'

Christelow paused.

'You will begin to see my drift. Apprehension over the burning of ancient and highly prized books became part of the Oxford consciousness. The whole thing developed an ambience, an aura, spread a cloud of anxiety. The feeling became sufficiently acute to warrant the dispatch of a distinguished officer from Scotland Yard itself.'

Christelow inclined courteously towards the Inspector.

'Now then. In such an atmosphere concern over any given book – any given book of value – is not going to be for that book's authenticity. It is going to be for that book's *safety*.'

Christelow left him with it for a few moments. It was staggeringly simple.

'Especially will this be so where the book is a particularly celebrated book – a book, say, that has been *discovered*. What would be the thought of anyone examining such a "discovery" in a context of destruction? Would it not be something in the nature of "Here I am with just such a precious volume as was burned the other day in Radcliffe Square. How fortunate I am to be able to handle it. Now that it has been salvaged from oblivion I trust every precaution will be taken for its safety"?

'Would it not be so?'

Christelow spread his hands, offering the notion.

'It is a question of emphasis. I do not say – it would be absurd to suppose – that the atmosphere I took pains to promote turned discerning scholars into undiscerning scholars. I merely contend it started them off in the right frame of mind – a frame of mind to expect something quite genuine. . . .'

'God, how terribly terribly clever,' breathed Fairlight.

'Oh, clever. We all knew Christelow was clever,' said Undigo.

'Emphasis,' Christelow said again, 'I believe it helped me enormously.'

A thought struck him.

'It was never, by the by, my original intention to resort to the cruder possibilities of the psychology I was preparing. *Tone* was what I was after. I rejected as fit only for fiction the idea that I might invent evidence to show that *The Book* was in specific danger – but circumstances forced a little of that on to me.

'After Manchip had – had died – it seemed prudent to provide some kind of rough motive. I contrived that it should appear as though his rooms had been carefully ransacked – the implication of course being that someone had been after something and that the something might have been *The Book*. Yes, a *very* rough device. And I could not leave his rooms in obvious disorder since that would have raised an immediate hue and cry thus denying me the day's cooling of the trail that I in fact obtained.

'And that tapping I said I'd heard at my window during the night – dear me, *very* crude. They were *ad hoc* extensions of my arrangements, these, and had I gone further in that direction I might well have rubbed the bloom from the idea altogether. Suggestion is never so ineffective as when it is over-specific.'

Christelow brought his hands together at the finger-tips.

'Climate, climate – that is the word.' He tapped his finger-tips. 'I was not offering evidence, I was creating a climate. A climate of acceptance.'

'Wonder how far it did help him,' said Clapp abruptly.

'I do not think it can have failed of helping him,' Undigo said slowly, 'in the circumstances. I suppose we are all used to handling rare manuscripts. I know I do not give much thought to their safety. But – I don't say I can recall my precise state of mind, but I do quite clearly remember thinking on one occasion as I examined *The*

Book of the Lion that I hoped Christelow would not be careless with it. The circumstances –'

McCann said: 'I had the same thought, though ordinarily I imagine it would not have occurred to me –'

'And I –' nodded Shipton.

Fairlight was rapidly recovering from the access of admiration induced in him by the revelation of Christelow's ingenuity.

'Well, no, honestly I cannot say the same, Christelow's was a clever idea but I seem to have remained immune. Possibly because my concern was and always is for the text –'

'What?' roared Undigo. 'Concerned for the *text*! Fairlight, in that complacent assertion you commit scholastic suicide. Concerned for the *text* and you didn't spot the fraud –'

'Really, Undigo, it may not please you to remember that *I* was the only one of us who had not officially approved *The Book* –'

'Sheer ill-nature,' said Falal.

A babble of voices arose and the SCR was thick with recrimination.

'Now geography,' Shipton grinned at the Inspector, 'never lets you down. . . .'

Christelow got up and paced once round his narrow cell. Then he sat down again.

'Did Kant know you'd killed these two men?'

Christelow shook his head.

'No, he did not. Kant had no inkling that I was the agent. I could not have relied on his complicity to that extent. Indeed, after the police had arrested him it was the fear that he might inform on me in respect of *The Book* and the burnings which made me decide to do away with him –'

'At one point when I was interviewing him at his house that night I thought he was going to give the game away –'

'I couldn't risk it. I heard your colleague Inspector Dorcas telling you Kant had gone for a swim, and I made

up my mind to do it at once. I set off for Parson's
Pleasure —'

Christelow broke off, staring at the further wall.

'Killing,' he said in a low shocked tone, 'becomes the
least of one's worries.'

Autumn stood up and walked over to the window,
where he gazed through the bars.

'Manchip – did Manchip invite you to go up to the
roof with him?' he asked.

'I certainly did not choose the place myself. It was a
habit of his, as I think you know. He had telephoned me
that evening. I knew he knew as soon as I saw his face. He
just said, "How very clever." I knew beyond all possibility
of doubt that I should kill him, I felt that knowledge rise
in me from the very instant that I set eyes on his face. I
realized then how much the thing meant to me.'

Christelow went on speaking, and Autumn noted the
curious change in his manner and his voice. The urbanity
was gone.

'I kept him talking. He was slicing a pear. He hadn't
the slightest idea of the thing's importance. He kept talk-
ing, chaffing me, and I let him believe it was simply an
academic joke. Then he said he would take a turn. I went
with him, picking the knife up as I went out of the room.
We walked in the quadrangle and the sky was terribly
dark. He said I was very clever, and kept on saying it.
Then he said we should go up on the roof. We went up. I
just stuck it in him.'

Autumn watched the bicycles passing in the road out-
side, between the two bars.

'The circumstances were utterly unpropitious – but I
had to do it – there and then. He would have told, you see.
I had to kill him. I couldn't put it off. There and then. I
propped him up – another statue. What else could I have
done? If I'd left him lying in a heap he would have been
seen immediately.'

Christelow stopped speaking. In a few moments he
said: 'I killed him. I know exactly what that means. It was
the *ultima thule* of my selfishness. I had not known I could
be so selfish.

Christelow raised his head and looked half-embarrassedly at Autumn.

'In the circumstances it sounds quite ridiculous, but I *do* apologize for hitting you –'

Autumn said: 'What was that "not strictly ethical" I heard Bow-Parley say?'

'Ah, he was in high good humour, having detected it. "Not strictly ethical but entahly ingenious – " Bow-Parley, poor fellow, always saw himself as a dangerous liberal –'

'He had no notion of the risk he ran letting you know he'd spotted it?'

'No more than Manchip. He was immensely pleased with himself for having worked out the –'

'No, he had not worked that out. He had seen it – but only because he had been guided to it. At least,' added Autumn, 'I am morally certain that was how it was. You see, the clue was in Manchip's diary and it is most likely that Bow-Parley, having come into possession of the diary, got it from there.'

Christelow's face had fallen somewhat.

'The diary I hid behind Shipton's mirror –' His voice died away. Then he smiled palely. 'So that was how *you* first got on the scent.'

'Not how I *first* got on the scent –'

'Dear, dear, if only I had bothered to look in the diary myself –'

'Oh, it was by no means explicit in the diary.' Autumn paused. 'It was not explicit at all. There were a number of items without which I should not have been able to take advantage of the information in Manchip's diary at all.'

Christelow said: 'Putting the diary behind Shipton's mirror was just so much red herring to complicate the trail – I am happy to say that I never imagined for one moment that it would ever seriously incriminate Shipton. Undigo was rather helpful to me in this matter – I had thought I would have myself to tell you about Bow-Parley stealing the diary away from Shipton (Bow-Parley had told me about that), but Undigo saved me the trouble –'

Christelow broke off and thought for some seconds.

'If Bow-Parley did get the clue from Manchip's diary, why did he not tell me as much?'

'No doubt he wanted you to think that the detection had been all his own work.'

'Mmmm, yes. It is in character.'

'I'm certain he did get it from the diary. He was so perfectly fitted to do so. . . .'

'Was he really? Was he?'

Rankine had been studying the last entries in Manchip's diary as Autumn had been speaking.

'Was he? I see nothing, nothing at all. How was Bow-Parley fitted to see what I cannot?'

'No, no,' interjected Fairlight in an ecstasy of impatience, 'how were *you* fitted, Inspector. How did *you* do it? Out with it at last.'

Autumn looked at them.

'I found out what Manchip and Bow-Parley had in common.'

Chapter 21

AUTUMN produced his THEOREM.

'You'll have to hear this first.'

He read it over. Then he said:

'There were four conclusions. The man I was after had done something wrong. It wasn't so wrong that the two people who found out about it dreamed they ran any risk when they let him know they knew. But it was so important to the man himself that he killed them both to shut them up. Less certainly, the information might be found in some form in Manchip's diary.'

'That was my foundation.'

Shipton said: 'Very sound as it turned out.'

'I'd no idea what kind of information it was I was after. I thought I might find it by sorting out what it was in Manchip and Bow-Parley that had enabled *them* to unearth it – what they had in common.'

'Noseyness?' suggested Fairlight.

'Yes – I wrote down all the things all of you had said about them – but I lacked a catalyst. A catalyst to bring together the particular aspects in either of them which helped them to do what *I* was trying to do –'

'I must say I'd be hard put to it even now,' McCann said, 'to say what it might have been in Manchip and Bow-Parley which let them see through *The Book*.'

Autumn turned to McCann.

'They didn't see through *The Book*. Not *The Book* itself.'

'Well, what – ?'

'I'll tell you.'

Autumn gathered his papers together.

'I was turning over all I knew about them as I came over here for tea yesterday, and wondering at the same time about the diary. I was chatting to Christelow when it occurred to me quite unapropos that one of the things they had in common was *The Book*. Having discarded the possibility that they'd been killed by someone who was *after The Book*, I had paid it no further attention. But now it struck me that the fact that they'd both been in possession of the thing might have some significance.'

Autumn glanced at Shipton, from Shipton to Undigo, and from Undigo to Falal.

'After that the catalyst began to form – from things you three said that tea-time. And from something Christelow said himself.'

Autumn had been holding the sheaf of papers which contained his THEOREM and now he slipped them back in his file.

'Dr Undigo, do you remember saying Bow-Parley was a Baconian and a gentleman?'

'He ought to – he's said it more than once.' Fairlight grinned maliciously.

'True, true.' Undigo was good-humoured. 'Yes, I do remember saying it.'

Autumn leant forward, his elbows on his knees, his hands clasped.

'And Shipton – when I gave you the diary to look at you said the page-references were "cryptic". That word suddenly sounded interesting – '

'And now, sir, what did I say, eh? Tell me that. Something witty, I'll be bound.' Falal cupped one hand behind his ear.

'Well, Professor, you were doing a crossword and you were having a bit of a tussle with one of the clues. When you got it you cried out, "Yes, it *was* an anagram." And just after that Christelow said something like "Oh, Manchip would have done all your anagrams over your shoulder."'

Autumn bit his lower lip.

'Those are the things you said and although I still didn't know exactly what it was I was looking for your words congealed in my mind round the idea of *The Book* – crosswords and Manchip and cryptic page references and Bow-Parley being a Baconian and anagrams . . .'

Autumn set his hands on his knees.

'I went back to my room and took down the diary and *The Book*. I stared at them rather idiotically for a bit. Then

I had another look at the last page of the diary. Then I riffled through *The Book*. And then I thought about page references. With no set idea at all, I began to go through the page references in the diary as if they referred to *The Book*. And the last one –'

Autumn reached out and took hold of *The Book* and the diary.

'The last one told me just why Manchip the crossword man and Bow-Parley the Baconian had been so perfectly equipped for discovering what they did discover.'

He held out the diary open at the final page.

'The last one – the one just before "Bless my soul".'

'"Bless my soul." Why that, I wonder?' Rankine was puzzled.

'I imagine it was Manchip's concession to his own surprise.'

'Well, well,' said Undigo staring at the last entry. 'I dare say these line references could mean anything.'

'Refer it to *The Book*.'

Autumn thumbed through the manuscript.

'What does it say? "Ll. 89–99, bol. Initially." Cryptic indeed. Well, let's see. Let us take lines 89–99 in *The Book* and see what there is.'

Autumn held *The Book* on his knees and the dons crowded round. They read:

> *Caste now your royal eie on everich hond,*
> *How pleyn disordinaunce is in your lond;*
> *Rancour and Ryot now are sovereyn,*
> *In oon accord to wierken aller peyn;*
> *Swich traytours mote be shent and that anon –*
> *To-hanged on a galwes, everich-on.*
> *Els is the king namore a king, I rede –*
> *Lost is his croun, his pouer and his drede.*
>
> *Oft lurketh Deeth wythyn the greene shawe,*
> *Whan foul rebelling trampleth on the lawe . . .*

'Well, gentleman,' Autumn said, 'there you are!'

Lord Pinner stared at him.

'What do you mean, there we are?'

Fairlight said: 'I don't see –'

'*Is* there something we should be seeking?' asked Shipton.

There was a cackle of laughter from Falal, who was still studying the passage.

'Oh, bless my soul, indeed there is. Capital, capital. Yes, yes, plain as the nose on my face. Splendid, splendid!'

'I am being slow –' said Undigo.

'You are, my dear fellow, indeed you are. Look again, look again,' Falal urged. 'Why, what a first-class deviser of treasure-hunts our colleague Christelow would have been!'

'Oh,' exclaimed Undigo, still looking at *The Book*, 'oh.'

'Got it?' asked Autumn.

'Yes. "Initially."'

Autumn took a pencil from his pocket and did something to the passage indicated.

'No need to wring the climax dry.'

He held it up.

> Caste now your royal eie on everich hond,
> How pleyn disordinaunce is in your lond;
> Rancour and Ryot now are sovereyn,
> In oon accord to wierken aller peyn;
> Swich traytours mote be shent and that anon –
> To-hanged on a galwes, everich-on.
> Els is the king namore a king, I rede –
> Lost is his croun, his pouer and his drede.
>
> 'Oft lurketh Deeth wythyn the greene shawe,
> Whan foul rebelling trampleth on the lawe. . .

'Manchip's anagrammatic skill got him there unaided. There *are* people to whom such things are visible almost as a reflex. And Bow-Parley – how well the Baconian taste fitted him to scrutinize, decipher, and then apply the information in the diary! Cryptograms and rumours of cryptograms – isn't that the Baconian heaven?'

'This little bit here,' asked Fairlight, '"bol"?'

'*Book of the Lion*, I suppose. I dare say "bol" gave Bow-Parley his first hint. I went the long way round.'

'Well, I'm damned,' said Shipton.

'But a cryptogram – what an asinine risk to run,' Rankine exclaimed.

'Oh, no, no, no, no.' Falal turned to the scientist. 'How painfully uninformed of men and things you must be to have delivered yourself of such a sentiment. Could any vain man have resisted such a gesture? Consider – here is a work that we understand to be fraudulent. But no one – not even the Inspector who has shamed us all with his perspicacity – has *seen through it*. As far as the internal evidence takes us it is by Chaucer. Yes, internally we have found no flaw. Well, then, Christelow had to have *some* means of identification – even though he had no intention of putting it to use. He had to hug to himself the *possibility* of demonstration. He had done his work too well. There was no flaw. He had to introduce one. Oh yes, my dear man, it is what we should all have done – had we the wit.'

'Manuscript could have been proved a fake chemically,' barked Clapp.

'Oh, tut tut, short-sighted, my dear chap, I do not recall your name, short-sighted in the extreme, you disappoint me. To show a fraudulent manuscript is not to show a fraudulent poem. Oh come, of course it is not. There are many fraudulent First Folios – but the plays in them, however corrupt, are by Shakespeare. Indeed they are.'

'But after Manchip had spotted the cryptogram, wasn't Christelow tempted to tear the page out?' asked McCann.

'He told me he decided to leave it in,' answered Autumn, 'partly because he thought it might be tricky explaining the missing page away, but mainly because he was convinced that Manchip's spotting it had been sheer bad luck. He said he would certainly have torn it out after Bow-Parley's death – but I was there so quickly he only had time to wallop me and run.'

'Oh, what a man!' cackled Falal. 'What a man our colleague Christelow was!'

'Mmmm,' agreed the Inspector, 'Christelow was a person. A real person.'

Autumn walked swiftly across the quadrangle carrying his grip. From one of the staircases Nicholas Flower appeared. He started across the grass toward the Inspector, and they met in the middle.

'Inspector Autumn, I have a confession and an apology to make.'

'So my guess was correct.'

Flower raised his eyebrows.

'What do you mean?'

'The letter to Dim, allegedly signed by Manchip.'

Flower turned deep crimson.

'Ah, hrrrm.' He cleared his throat. 'You guessed.'

'I'm afraid it was very plain. You were so anxious to tell me that Manchip might have changed his mind.'

'Ah.'

Flower looked sheepish and stuck his hands in his pocket. Then he said: 'I – er – wanted to shake him a bit, you see. Stir his confounded complacency. A note like that from Manchip gave him such a jolly good motive for the murder. The blighter was scared stiff – as I knew he would be – and he didn't let on. So I sent you that other note to tip you off. Made his behaviour look terribly suspicious.'

They walked towards the Lodge.

'Wanted to show Balboa what a coward the man is.'

Flower trailed his toes over the turf.

'Trouble is after she found out about it she took it out of me as well as him. By the Pagoda when they were playing bowls. Said it proved I was too young for her.'

Flower heaved a great sigh.

'Hot-bottomed little mare,' he said tenderly.

They walked into the Lodge.

'What happened to the naked lads?' Flower asked, cheering up a bit as he remembered the chase.

'We sent them home in bobbies' capes.'

They paused together at the gate.

'Well,' said Autumn, 'I'll say cheerio.'

'I'm having a party next term. Will you come?'

'Thanks.'

'Goodbye.'

'Goodbye.'

As the Inspector walked away he caught sight of Balboa Tomlin on the arm of Mr Singh. They had not seen him, but Mr Singh had seen Nicholas Flower. As he turned the corner, Autumn saw Mr Singh raise his hand to Nicholas. But if it was meant to be Mr Churchill's V-sign, Mr Singh had got it wrong.

Autumn came into Radcliffe Square and stood a moment in the sunlight. Bodley was before him and he saw through the windows the brown books and the heads of men reading.

'Sa–a–ave him,' he heard again the voice of Bow-Parley, 'sa–a–ave him from the horn of the unicorn –'

Autumn turned away.

'And from the mouth of the lion,' he added out loud.